SIBLING RIVALRY

Impulsively, Fiona stood on tiptoe and brushed a kiss over Grayson's cheek. She was suddenly aware that he'd gone very still. Alarmed at her own boldness, she took a quick step back. "Goodnight, Gray. Thanks to you, this has been a truly wonderful Christmas."

With a swirl of petticoats she danced away, leaving him to stare after her. For the longest time he merely stood watching, until she disappeared inside the house. When at last he picked up the lantern and started home, a figure stepped from the darkness and watched his departure through narrowed eyes.

Overcome with black jealousy, Flem's hands curled into fists at his side. He'd come here hoping to finish the argument Gray had started before—but now he had yet another score to settle with him . . .

PARADISE FALLS

RUTH RYAN LANGAN

BERKLEY SENSATION, NEW YORK

PARADISE FALLS

A Berkley Sensation Book / published by arrangement with the author

PRINTING HISTORY
Berkley Sensation edition / March 2004

For information address: The Berkley Publishing Group,
a division of Penguin Group (USA) Inc.,
375 Hudson Street, New York, New York 10014.

ISBN: 0-425-19484-1

BERKLEY SENSATION™
Berkley Sensation Books are published by The Berkley Publishing Group,
a division of Penguin Group (USA) Inc.,
375 Hudson Street, New York, New York 10014.
BERKLEY SENSATION and the "B" design
are trademarks belonging to Penguin Group (USA) Inc.

PRINTED IN THE UNITED STATES OF AMERICA

10 9 8 7 6 5 4 3 2 1

For Nora,
the sister of my heart

And for Tom,
my heart and soul

PROLOGUE

◆━◆❈◆━◆

The Atlantic Ocean—1879

"AM I DEAD then?" Bridget Downey opened her eyes and struggled to make out the figure of her husband, Daniel, kneeling beside her.

"You're alive, love."

"Fiona?"

Daniel looked down at the little girl beside him, the mirror image of her mother. Hair dark and curly, and skin so fair she could have been made of spun glass. Laughing eyes as blue as the sky over Galway. She was the love of his life. "Fiona's fine."

The little girl snuggled closer to her father. Throughout the long voyage from their home in Ireland she had clung to him, watching as he'd lovingly tended her mother.

"The storm?" Bridget's eyes widened in fear.

"It's gone now. We made it through, love." Such simple words to describe the terror he'd felt during the storm that had raged for three days and nights, tossing the ship about like a child's toy, leaving almost everyone aboard the *Molly B* out of Dublin desperately ill.

While other passengers had fled the stench of sickness and death to seek the fresh air topside, Daniel had remained beside his Bridget, cleaning her, spooning what little food he could manage to beg, barter, or steal to keep her alive. When he wasn't tending his wife, he was seeing to the needs of his beloved Fiona.

To pass the long, desperate hours he'd regaled the child with tales of his own childhood in Galway, and of his hopes and dreams for the future. Of his determination to leave the only life he and Bridget had ever known, in order to carve out a better life for their daughter in this strange new world.

"Your mother fears this new land, thinking they're barbarians because of their long Civil War. But they've put that behind them now. President Rutherford B. Hayes has brought dignity and honesty to the government." Daniel grew somber. "You must remember his name, lass. To be a good citizen, you must know about the ones who lead your country. Education is the soul's food, Fiona. In Ireland, all we could ever hope for would be scraps. But in America, it will be a banquet. And I intend that we will eat our fill of it. Here in this great land, instead of marrying to secure your future, you can do whatever you choose with your life."

"Shouldn't I ever marry, Da?"

His eyes crinkled with humor. "I hope you will one day. But only if it's for the right reason."

"What's the right reason, Da?"

"Love. That's the only reason to bind yourself to another for a lifetime, Fiona." He glanced over at his wife, and his eyes softened.

"But how will I know, Da?"

He took her hands in his. "You'll know, though it won't be easy. It isn't just the way a man looks, although that may be what first attracts you. Nor will it matter what he does. Whether a man works with his hands, or has the greatest mind in the universe, it's what's in his heart that matters. Never waste your love. Remember that, child. Give your heart to someone whose own heart is worthy."

Fiona knew, from her father's solemn demeanor, that he was telling her something of great importance. And because it mattered so much to please him, she listened intently and nodded in agreement. "I'll remember, Da."

From the upper deck a great roar went up that seemed to send a shudder rippling through the entire ship.

Bridget cringed. "What's happened now?"

"We'll see." Daniel removed his damp coat and wrapped it around his shivering wife before lifting her into his arms. "Take hold of my belt, Fiona, so we don't get separated."

The little girl did as he commanded, and the three of them struggled up the slippery steps, making their way cautiously to the ship's rail. After the fetid air below, the cold, bracing wind was a shock to the system. The sun had already set, leaving the sky an inky canvas above their heads.

The ship slowed, then stopped, and the anchor was lowered as they entered the harbor.

They stared in fascination at the strange sights that assaulted their senses. Lights, so many of them—from ships at anchor, from lanterns in carriages and pony carts racing along the docks, fetching passengers and cargo in a frenzy of activity. People shouting in a dozen different languages. Men cursing. Dock workers milling about, all with a purpose.

"Look, Bridget, Fiona." Daniel's voice was hushed, as though they were in a great cathedral. "We've reached New York harbor."

The little girl looked up at her father, tugging on his leg. "Is this America, Da?"

"It is. And so much more, Fiona. This is why we left home and family and risked everything. I knew the crossing would cause us suffering, and for that I'm truly sorry. But this . . ." He lifted his little daughter up, so that both his women were in his arms, staring at the dizzying blur before them. "This was worth every painful moment. For that is all behind us now. What you see here is our future."

ONE

"I MADE IT. I made it." A freckled youth of eighteen jostled his way through the crush of eager young students gathered around the list that had been nailed to the door of Bennett College. Each summer, after rigorous examinations in history, geometry, and mathematics, the list of students accepted for entrance to the small New England college was posted on the door of the chapel.

Fiona Downey took an elbow to her ribs and was shoved to one side. Though she was as eager as the others to learn her fate, she resisted the urge to push her way to the front. It wouldn't do for the daughter of a respected Bennett professor to behave in an unruly fashion.

A respected Bennett professor. How grand that sounded. Her father had begun life in America as a gardener to a wealthy family in Boston. Fiona and her mother had lived with him in a shed on the grounds of a fine, big home with rolling lawns and an army of servants. Bridget had helped the cook in the big house until her health had begun to fail her. When Daniel found work on the grounds of Bennett College, he knew he was one step closer to his goal. He'd studied early in the morning and late into the night and had taken every test required, until at last he'd been accepted as a teacher.

For Daniel, it had been the culmination of a lifetime dream. At last, he and his family would live the good life he'd envisioned when he'd left his childhood home to seek a better life.

And now, hopefully, it would be Fiona's turn. She stood, feeling more than a little breathless, and waited for the crowd to thin.

"What about me?" The freckled youth's friend struggled to make it to the front of the crowd but was quickly shoved aside by a taller student.

"I didn't see your name." A moment later, he was greeted with a dazzling smile. "You're in, Ethan."

"You're sure?" The two ignored the jostling as they studied their names on the precious list. With matching grins they raced off to share the news with family and friends.

When at last the others drifted away Fiona hurried up to scan each name until she came to her own.

She closed her eyes a moment, and fought the sting of tears. "I did it." She hugged her arms about her chest and took in several deep breaths. "Oh, Da, you'll be so proud."

With a laugh of pure delight she turned and began racing across the campus, her mind awhirl. Within a few weeks she would be living her dream, preparing herself for a life as a college student.

Not many women achieved such a goal, but Fiona had never doubted she would do it. She'd had a rare opportunity that few girls her age ever experienced. With her father a history professor at Bennett, and her mother devoted to reading aloud from the classics, it was inevitable that Fiona's mind had been filled with knowledge beyond her tender age.

Perhaps it had been the crushing poverty her parents had experienced in their homeland, or perhaps they were simply driven to succeed. Whatever the reason, they had instilled in Fiona a need to excel in everything she pursued.

She glanced skyward. Had the sun always been this bright? Or was it because of her happy news? That had her looking around, as though to store up as much of this special day as possible, so that she would never forget it. The sky was palest blue, with just a few high, puffy clouds on the horizon. The hollyhocks that climbed to the roof of the Johnson cottage seemed even more colorful as they danced on the slight breeze. Up ahead a horse and cart slowed while the driver tipped his hat to a lady with a basket on her arm. Their voices drifted toward her, and Fiona recognized the trill of Mrs. O'Connell's laughter.

Fiona's heart was nearly filled to bursting as she moved along the tree-shaded street lined with neat little houses owned by the college. The smallest ones were offered to the newer professors, with the larger, grander houses given to those who had been teaching the longest. The one Fiona shared with her parents was a tiny white cottage with shutters painted soft butter-yellow. A picket fence groaned under the weight of climbing roses, which her mother lovingly tended each summer. Fiona inhaled their perfume as she sailed up the steps of the porch.

"Mum. Da." The door slammed at her back. "Oh, you're going to be so happy when I tell you . . ." Her voice trailed off when she caught sight of her mother's tear-stained face. "What is it, Mum? What's happened?"

Instead of a reply, her mother collapsed into a chair and buried her face in her handkerchief. A bearded man stepped from her parents' bedroom, unrolling his sleeves. Fiona recognized Dr. Hadly. His grave manner had her heart skipping several beats. "What's happened to Da? Has he been hurt?"

The doctor shook his head and placed a hand on her arm. "I'm sorry, Fiona. Your father's gone."

"Gone?" She shrank from his touch. "What are you saying?"

The old man sighed. Of all the things he was called upon to do, this was always the hardest. Especially when the loved ones were given no warning. "It was his heart, Fiona." He glanced at Bridget Downey, who sat quietly weeping. "You're going to have to be strong now for your mother."

"No!" Fiona started past him, determined to see for herself. "You're wrong, Doctor. Da isn't dead. He can't be. He can't."

"Child." The doctor was about to stop her until he saw her eyes—a little too bright. And the way she was holding herself, so rigid and straight, as though afraid to bend even an inch, for fear of snapping. He stepped away from the closed door and watched in quiet resignation as Fiona shoved it open and stepped inside.

"Da." She stared at the figure on the bed. He was dressed, as always, in a proper dark suit. Despite the expense, he owned two of them, so that one would always be clean and perfectly pressed. His tie had been loosened, the neck of his crisp white shirt unbuttoned, the only sign of anything out of the ordinary.

Fiona had always loved the way her father looked. A bit stern, perhaps, to his students, but the twinkle in his blue eyes always gave away his sense of humor. Beneath his professor's demeanor lurked the heart of a sweet, gentle tease.

She loved the way his slightly graying hair was always perfectly combed. Seeing it mussed, she reached out and smoothed it away from his forehead. Her hand paused in midair. Had his eyelids flickered just a bit?

Of course. The doctor was wrong, as she'd suspected.

She dropped down onto the edge of the bed and caught her father's hands in hers. There was still some warmth there, though they seemed heavy to the touch. She'd always loved Da's hands. So big and yet so gentle. The way they squeezed her shoulder when he was pleased with something she'd done. The way he tugged on a lock of her hair when he was teasing her about something silly.

"I made it, Da." She stared hungrily at his face, desperate to see him open his eyes and give her that smile that never failed to lighten her burden and touch her heart. "I've been accepted to Bennett College."

Had he squeezed her hand? She looked down, but could see no movement.

Releasing his hands she leaned over him, pressing her ear to his chest, desperate to hear his calm, steady heartbeat. "I couldn't wait to tell you, Da. I know how proud this makes you. We'll be together now in the classroom. You'll lecture and I'll take notes. And afterward, we'll walk home together and talk and talk. Oh, the things we'll be able to share now."

In the other room she could hear soft weeping, but here in the bedroom, there was only an eerie silence. It frightened her more than her mother's cries.

"Don't leave me, Da." She shook him slightly and waited to hear him say something. Anything. "Please, Da. I can't bear it."

She could hear the high, sharp edge of hysteria in her voice and bit her lip to stop the trembling. To keep from screaming, she turned her face into his shirt and breathed him in, filling her lungs, her heart, her very soul with the smell of him, needing to store it up for all the long, lonely years to come.

Even while she struggled to deny the truth, it slipped through her defenses. The tears she'd been fighting now spilled over, adding to her pain. Through the mist, through the numbness that settled over her like a shroud, came the awful realization that her father was gone. Truly gone.

This day that had begun as her greatest triumph was now a day of bleak, unrelieved pain. Somewhere in a small, dark corner of her mind was the knowledge that her world of books and letters, her life on this cozy, comfortable campus, all her sweet dreams for the future, had just died along with her beloved Da.

"IT'S TIME, MUM."

Fiona drew an arm around her mother's shoulders and led her toward the waiting horse and wagon, where their trunks were already stowed.

A long, drawn-out sigh seemed to well up from deep within as Bridget trailed a hand along the porch railing and plucked a rose from the vine, before burying her face in it. The look of her, so frail and beaten, twisted a knife in Fiona's heart.

Mother and daughter spoke not a word as they rode to the train station. Once there they watched in silence as the driver unloaded their meager belongings.

So little, Fiona thought, *to show for a lifetime*. A life filled with love and laughter, a life of struggle and happiness they'd shared together.

Together. How was it possible that now, just two weeks after losing her father, she must lose her mother as well?

The days since her father's death were still a blur. Everything seemed to move in slow motion. The simple box in the parlor, flanked by vases filled with Bridget's precious flowers and Daniel's beloved books. Students and faculty forming a steady stream as they stopped by the house to offer condolences. The funeral, a solemn affair held in the chapel of the college, and afterward, the storm-tossed skies opening up to drench the mourners who stood in a small cluster around the open grave.

The day after Daniel Downey was put in the ground, an official from the college had arrived to announce that Bridget and Fiona would have to vacate the house, to make room for the professor who would take Daniel's place on the faculty. A family friend, Professor Norton, aware of their dire circumstances, had offered Fiona an opportunity to teach in a school in northern Michigan, and live with a host family.

"Paradise Falls is nothing like Bennett, my dear. It's a farming community, and the work will be hard. Because it's so late in the summer, most positions have already been filled, and there are few choices left."

"I don't mind hard work, Professor."

"I know." He patted her arm. "Fortunately, you'll have very few expenses, since your lodging includes meals. But you'll be far from home, living among strangers."

She'd felt a moment of absolute terror, before seeing the questioning look on her mother's face. She owed it to Bridget to be brave and strong. Owed it, as well, to her father's memory. "I'll take the position, Professor. I'm grateful for the opportunity to earn my keep."

"And you, Bridget?" Philip Norton turned to the woman who seemed to have aged years since losing her beloved Daniel. She was like a flower cut from the vine, wilted and fading a bit more each day. "Where will you go?"

"I've written my sister, Nola, in Chicago. She has agreed to take me in until I can find some means of supporting myself."

The professor turned away, but not before Fiona caught his look of utter disbelief. The thought of Bridget Downey supporting herself seemed ludicrous. It only reinforced Fiona's realization that her mother's situation was desperate. Daniel had always been his wife's fierce champion, treating her with such great care. Fiona had followed his example, shouldering more and more of the responsibilities as she'd watched her mother's strength ebb through the years.

Now mother and daughter stood in the train station, stiff and awkward, as they struggled to hold back a torrent of conflicting emotions.

"The days will go quickly. You'll see, Mum."

Bridget twisted her handkerchief around and around her hand.

Such a soft hand, Fiona thought. Guilt and fear lay like a stone in her chest at the realization that she was abandoning her responsibility. It didn't matter that she had no choice. It was just one more layer of pain to endure. "It's only for a year, Mum. I'll save my money and as soon as I have enough to send for you, we'll be together."

At a call from the conductor, the two women fell into each other's arms and choked back sobs.

"I'll be fine, Fiona." Bridget's voice was little more than a strained whisper. "We'll both be fine. You'll write often?"

"Every day, Mum."

"Hush now. Don't make idle promises." Bridget pressed a finger to Fiona's lips. "You'll be busy with your new responsibilities. Just write when you can."

The conductor gave a final call and the two women peeled apart, step by painful step. Fiona stood watching as her mother climbed aboard the train that would take her to Chicago, and her sister's tiny row house, where Bridget would share a bed with several little nieces.

As the train slowly slipped from the station, Fiona caught sight of her mother's tear-streaked face in the window. She waved until the train dipped out of sight, then sank down on a wooden bench, drained beyond belief.

When the boarding call sounded for the train that would take her to Michigan, she refused to think about what she was doing as she put one foot in front of the other, forcing herself to climb aboard and find a seat.

The cars overflowed with businessmen in stiff, dark suits and women carrying squalling babies, calling sharply to older children who giggled and fidgeted. In the oppressive summer air the cars reeked of sweat and humanity, of rotting meat and overripe fruit carried in baskets or wrapped in linen. A childhood memory, of a ship's fetid hold crowded with moaning passengers, crept into Fiona's mind, leaving her momentarily stunned.

As the train pulled from the station, Fiona closed her eyes and fought the weariness that seemed to have drained her of all her strength. At first she was annoyed by the clatter of wheels, and had to fight a feeling of nausea at the awkward swaying motion of the car. What had she been thinking, to accept a position so far from home? She began to entertain thoughts of getting off at the next stop and making her way back to Bennett. At least there she would be surrounded by people and places that were comfortable and familiar. What did it matter if she had no home, no means of supporting herself? Even if she couldn't use her education, she could always take a job as a housemaid.

Though it was more than a little tempting, she knew she wasn't ready to give up the dream. She had a fine mind. Hadn't Da said as much? She owed it to herself, to Da, to her mum, to teach. Still, the thought of giving up, of returning to Bennett, was so tempting.

As the train gradually ate up the miles of track, she was lulled into a troubled sleep. It was the first rest she'd experienced in days.

Dear Mum

I hope your train ride was of much shorter duration than mine, and more pleasing to the eye and ear. I was recently jolted from sleep by a series of ear-splitting whistles as our train came to a sudden, shuddering

*halt. I watched as the conductor stepped down and
shouted to a farmer and his dog herding cows across
the tracks.*

*I suspect, from the flat fields stretching as far as
the eye can see, that we must be in Ohio.*

Fiona paused in her letter to her mother to stare out
the window. From the map she'd prepared before leaving
Massachusetts, she was able to keep track of her journey.
The first rush of passengers had disembarked in New
York, with more following in Pennsylvania. Now the train
car was nearly empty, except for an old man and a little
boy. *Grandfather and grandson?* she wondered.

She couldn't recall her own grandparents, or the life
she'd known in Ireland. Her mother had come from Cork,
her father from Galway. Both her parents had carried the
lilt of home in their brogues, as did their daughter, despite
her many years in this land.

Fiona glanced at the wee lad, asleep on the old man's
lap, and felt a sudden rush of pain at her loss. It was still
so fresh and new, this idea that her father was truly gone,
and it hit her at the oddest times, leaving her struggling
not to weep aloud.

The herd of cows cleared the tracks and the conductor
climbed aboard. After a series of toots and whistles, the
train began inching forward. Mile after mile of flat fields
followed, and though Fiona tried to absorb as much as
she could of the countryside, the monotony of it had her
closing her eyes once more. The pencil slipped from
nerveless fingers; the letter to her mother forgotten.

After several hours Fiona again awoke. Someone had
opened a window, and she breathed in fresh clean air that
carried the hint of evergreen. There were clear sparkling
lakes and apple orchards, the fruit heavy on the branches.
As the hills became steeper, she could see, off in the distance, a farmhouse looking lost in the fields of wheat and

corn and tomatoes stretching as far as the eye could see.

Despite her weariness Fiona sat up straighter, wondering again at the strange fate that had brought her so far from all that was comfortable and familiar. She couldn't deny the little ripple of excitement at the thought of the town that held her future. Paradise Falls. She'd seen pictures of Niagara. Would this be as impressive? Did people come from all over to see this natural phenomenon? And what of the children she would be teaching? She imagined herself opening all those eager young minds to history and mathematics and literature, could see in her mind's eye a lovely ivy-covered schoolhouse, and perhaps a chapel nearby, much like the one at Bennett.

Oh, it was such a lovely dream. One that had her smiling as she bent to her letter.

> *I anticipate the end of my journey, Mum, and the beginning of my new life. I tried to find Paradise Falls on my map, but to no avail. No matter. Soon enough I shall be there, to see and experience it firsthand.*
>
> *With love and prayers that you are resting comfortably,*
>
> *Your loving daughter*

The train moved through a forest of pine trees tall enough to blot out all trace of the sun. By the time they came out on the other side, the air had grown cold, forcing Fiona to reach for her shawl. With her face to the window she watched a spectacular sunset reflected in the water of the lake that seemed to stretch all the way to the horizon.

Seeing the conductor passing through, she lifted a hand to stop him. "How long before we reach Paradise Falls?"

The old man tugged on his beard. "Not until morning, miss. That's the end of the line, just after Little Bavaria."

"Little Bavaria?" She liked the sound of it. "Will we cross the ocean, then?"

He chuckled. "It's right here in Michigan. These are German settlements, miss. As you'd expect, most of the folks living in Little Bavaria are from the Alpine regions of Germany and Switzerland. I guess the rocky hillsides of northern Michigan remind them of the land they left. They brought their language and crafts with them, and Little Bavaria is known around these parts for its fine woodworking and leather goods." He chuckled and touched a hand to his stomach. "But most of all they're known for their food. There's none better."

As he moved on she found herself thinking about food. Reaching into her satchel, she removed a precious apple. Before she could take a bite she felt a movement beside her and looked over to see the little boy standing in the aisle watching her.

Up close, his face was streaked with dirt. Mud was caked beneath his fingernails. His ill-fitting clothes were threadbare, but his smile was angelic.

Fiona gave him a gentle smile. "Are you hungry?"

He nodded and stared at the apple as though it were gold.

She'd carefully rationed her food, packing most in her mother's bag so that Bridget would have enough to last until she reached Chicago. Still, the look of the lad, all big hungry eyes and solemn little mouth, touched Fiona's tender heart.

Without a word she reached into her satchel and removed a small knife, cutting the apple into quarters. She handed the lad two, so that he could share with the old man.

He gave a quick smile and danced away. Minutes later his grandfather turned and smiled at her, showing a gap where his teeth had once been. Fiona returned the smile. As darkness settled over the land, she nibbled her fruit and caught occasional glimpses of light far out on the water.

There had been fishermen in Massachusetts. That fact brought her comfort. She wasn't going to a foreign land, after all. How different could Paradise Falls be from the home she'd left behind?

All through the night, as she drifted in and out of sleep, she thought about what lay at the end of her journey. She snuggled under her shawl, fighting a sense of over-whelming excitement laced with moments of pure terror.

Da's beloved voice washed over her. *"Remember, Fiona, that all of life is a blank slate, on which we can write whatever we choose."*

Soothed, Fiona swallowed back her fear, and vowed to write the grandest adventure of them all.

TWO

THIN MORNING SUNLIGHT filtered through the leaves of trees lining the railroad tracks, creating a kaleidoscope against Fiona's lids. She opened her eyes, fighting a feeling of complete disorientation, before she realized where she was. The train was slowing. She peered out the window but could see nothing except forest.

"Paradise Falls," came the conductor's voice.

Knowing first impressions were important, Fiona reached into her valise and withdrew stiff new boots and a bonnet. It wouldn't do to meet her hosts looking weary from her travels. She set aside her everyday boots and slipped her feet into the shiny new ones. After stuffing her old boots into her valise, she pulled on the bonnet, tucking little wisps of hair up under her brim. She smoothed down her skirts before picking up her valise.

As soon as the train came to a shuddering halt she followed the old man and his grandson down the length of the car and accepted the conductor's hand as she stepped from the train.

The station was little more than a crude shed. Inside a bearded man was seated at a wooden desk, marking in a ledger. When the conductor, assisted by one of the coal-stokers, dropped Fiona's trunk with a thud, the station-master looked up in surprise.

"Sorry, Edwin. You should've told me. I'd have given you a hand with that. Looks heavy." He glanced toward Fiona. "Don't get many visitors to Paradise Falls." His words were delivered in clipped tones, with a thick accent Fiona didn't recognize. He carefully set down his pencil and stepped around the desk.

Fiona extended her hand. "My name is Fiona Downey."

"The schoolmistress?" The man couldn't hide his surprise as he looked her over. "Didn't know you'd be coming in today. Neither did the Haydn family, I'll wager."

Her heart sank. That would mean there was no one here to greet her.

"Fine people, the Haydns. You won't find anyone better in Paradise Falls." The stationmaster looked pointedly at her trunk. "Don't think you'd care to haul that all the way to the Haydn farm. Just leave it here until someone's heading that way. I'll see they deliver it."

"Thank you. How will I find the Haydn farm?"

He stepped to the door and pointed. "Just follow that road up the hill and around a couple of bends. It'll be the sixth farm you come to. No more'n a half-dozen miles, I figure."

Six miles. She saw the conductor step aboard the train, and gave serious consideration to following him. Then her sanity returned and she managed to smile at the station manager. "Thank you. I don't know your name."

"Gerhardt Shultz."

"Mr. Shultz, do you think I might leave my valise here with my trunk?"

"Yes, indeed." He took it from her hand.

"Thank you." She turned away and walked out of the little shed into blinding sunlight.

Squaring her shoulders, she started up the dirt path, wondering what had happened to the old man and little boy who had shared her train ride. In the excitement of retrieving her trunk and getting directions to her destination, she had lost track of them. Seeing no one on the trail ahead of her, she decided they must have been picked up by family.

Family.

The very word brought a heaviness to her heart, and she had to fight the tears that threatened. She'd once been part of a family. Now she felt like the loneliest person in the world.

"Oh, Da." Her words came tumbling out in a cry of anguish. "How I wish you could be here with me."

She shivered as a breeze whispered across her cheek, tugging at the ribbons of her bonnet, just the way her father often had.

Though her doubts remained, a little of her fears seemed to subside.

As she passed the first squalid farm, and studied the leaning outbuildings and meager crops in the fields, the thought of her grand adventure mocked her. Grand indeed. This seemed to be the sort of grinding poverty her parents had endured, before coming to America. It would seem that she'd traded one set of problems for another. Perhaps she should have gone to Chicago with her mother. Even if the only work she found would be cleaning other people's homes, at least she and her mother could be together.

Here she was, nothing more than a fool, trapped in a web of her own making. Now there was nothing to do

but endure it as best she could, and hope that by year's
end she had enough money saved to leave this dreary
place and make a home with her mother any place but
Paradise Falls.

"Was this what drove you from Ireland, Da?"

The sound of her own voice startled her and she
walked faster. The sun was now high overhead, sending
little rivers of sweat down her back. Her boots were stiff
and she thought about sitting on a boulder and removing
them. But what would her hosts think if the schoolteacher
should arrive barefoot?

Her hair beneath the bonnet grew damp. After half an
hour she'd tossed her hat back from her head, leaving it
bouncing against her back, secured by the ribbons at her
throat. She was so grateful for the breeze she gave not a
thought to the havoc it might be playing with her hair,
which tended to curl into little corkscrews in the heat.

The second farm she passed was no better than the first,
though the house seemed pretty enough, with sunflowers
growing by the porch. By the time she'd passed the third
farm the road grew steep, climbing through heavily
wooded forest. Her gown was damp with sweat and her
boots weighed her down with every step. The fields here
seemed larger, each farm farther away from its neighbor,
but, she reasoned, it might only seem that way because
she was so desperately weary.

After passing yet another farm she paused under a tree
and removed her boots, carrying one in each hand. The
hem of her gown swept the dust of the trail, though she
no longer cared how dirty it got. All she wanted was to
reach her destination and enjoy a sip of water.

As she moved doggedly forward, she was too tired to
appreciate the symmetry of the fields she was passing. The
soil here seemed richer, darker, but that might mean it
had recently rained. When she spotted the name *Haydn*

on the side of the barn up ahead, she thought she might weep with relief.

She sat down in the grass by the side of the road, determined to slip into her boots and smooth her hair before meeting her hosts. But before she could even begin to repair the damage of her long walk, she caught sight of a horse and wagon coming up over a rise.

When the driver spotted her he pulled back on the reins and sat staring at her with a look of complete surprise.

"Hello." She got to her feet, unaware that she was still holding a boot in each hand.

"Hello, yourself." With sunlight streaming over him, he looked like a drawing from one of her da's books on mythology. His hair glinted with gold highlights. His skin, too, was bronzed by the sun, while his eyes were palest blue, like the sky in early morning, before the sunlight warmed it. "Are you lost?"

She was so dazzled by the look of him, it took her a moment to answer. She shook her head. "It seems I've found what I was looking for. The Haydn farm."

"Why are you looking for the Haydn farm?"

"I'll be living there while I teach school."

"You're the new teacher?" He laughed then, a loud, joyous sound that had her smiling in spite of her weariness. "Oh, this is going to be great fun."

"Fun?"

He nodded and jumped down. "The fun will begin when Ma sees you." He offered his hand. "I'm Fleming Haydn. My friends call me Flem."

"Flem." She stuck out her hand, then seeing the boot dangling from her fingers, laughed and dropped it before accepting his handshake. "My name is Fiona Downey."

He lifted her boot out of the dirt and handed it back to her. "Are you going to wear these, Fiona Downey, or carry them?"

She blushed slightly before plopping down in the grass.

"I think I'd better wear them. I don't want to meet your family looking like this."

"I don't see why not." He knelt beside her, his smile widening. "I think you look positively delightful. Not at all like a schoolmarm."

She ducked her head and finished lacing her boots before getting to her feet and brushing off her skirts.

"Come on. I'll take you up to the house." Flem climbed up to the wagon seat and reached down to help her up beside him.

It seemed to Fiona that he kept her hand tucked in his a bit longer than was necessary before releasing her and flicking the reins. But his boyish smile put her at ease.

As the horse started forward he glanced over to see her furiously shoving her hair beneath her bonnet. "It won't help, you know."

"What won't?" She looked over at him.

"Trying to make yourself presentable."

"Why not?"

He gave a deep chuckle. "My ma expected you to be like our last teacher. Her name was Hilda Hornby. She taught in Paradise Falls for more than twenty years before going to her eternal reward. That was three years ago."

Fiona clapped a hand to her mouth. "You mean the children haven't been to school in three years?"

He nodded. "But that's not the problem."

"What is?"

"Miss Hornby was a spinster, with crooked teeth, thick spectacles, and a face that would have stopped a plow-horse at twenty paces. What's more, she never bought a new dress in all the years she lived here. Ma claimed that she used to sew her dresses from feed sacks, but I swear she was born in that shapeless gray rag she wore every day of her life." He gave Fiona a long, appraising look that brought a rush of heat to her cheeks. "When my ma offered to put up the town teacher, she was expecting someone like Miss Hornby to keep her company."

"I didn't mean to deceive her . . ."

He threw back his head and roared. "I didn't say you did. Besides, if you had two heads and breathed fire, Ma would still have offered you board."

"She must be a very kind—"

"Kindness has nothing to do with it. The school board pays ten dollars a month to anyone willing to provide room and board to a teacher. If there's one thing my mother knows, it's how to squeeze a dollar from a lump of sand." He reined in the horse and helped Fiona down, then led the way to the backdoor.

Inside a woman looked up from the table where she was rolling dough. Despite the heat of the day, gray hair was slicked back from her face and secured in a perfect knot at her nape. She wore a faded blue gown, and over it an apron of bleached muslin that was dusted with flour.

"Ma." Flem was grinning as though enjoying himself immensely. "Look who just arrived. It's the new schoolteacher, Fiona Downey."

The woman's smile faded. She took considerable time studying Fiona through narrowed eyes as she crossed the room.

Positioning himself so that his mother couldn't see, Flem winked at Fiona. "This is my mother, Ulrica Rose Haydn."

"You know I hate the name Ulrica, Fleming. I had an aunt by that name, and she was my least favorite." Rose ignored Fiona's outstretched hand while she meticulously dried her hands on her apron. "We weren't expecting you until next week, when school starts, Miss Downey."

"I'm sorry, Mrs. Haydn. I thought you would have received my letter of introduction by now."

"There's been no letter." Rose's tone was accusing.

Fiona flushed. "I mailed it almost two weeks ago."

"There is no regular mail delivery in Paradise Falls. If

someone wants to contact us, they usually send a message with the conductor of the train."

"I see." Fiona glanced at the table, set for four, and wondered how much longer she could stand without keeling over. Whether from hunger or exhaustion, her legs were threatening to betray her. The kitchen smelled of yeast and baking bread and all manner of wonderful spices that had her mouth watering. "If I could trouble you for a glass of water."

Rose turned away and pointed to a bucket in the corner of the kitchen. "There's a dipper. Help yourself."

Fiona crossed the room and lifted the dipper to her lips, drinking deeply. When she looked up, Rose had returned her attention to the dough, rolling, kneading, pounding, then flipping it over to roll and knead again. She seemed to be taking great pleasure in pounding the lump of dough.

Without missing a beat she called, "Fleming, show the teacher where she'll be staying."

"This way." He led Fiona through the parlor to what appeared to be an enclosed sunporch across the front end of the house. It had been made into a bedroom with the addition of a daybed, a scarred wooden chest, a desk and chair. Over the windows, sheets had been strung along wooden poles and tied back on either side. When untied, they would afford privacy.

"I'll fetch you a basin of water." Flem was still grinning when he walked away, as though enjoying a private joke.

Minutes later he returned with a basin and pitcher, which he set on top of the wooden chest. "Ma says to clean up for supper. As soon as Gray gets here, we'll eat."

"Gray . . . ?"

"My brother." He nodded toward the approaching horse and wagon that could be seen through the windows. "That's him now. I think I'll go wash up, before he sees me. Otherwise, he's bound to find some work he wants done."

Flem ambled away, leaving Fiona to stare at the man who leaped down from the wagon and wrestled her trunk from the back and up the steps. Behind him raced the biggest hound she'd ever seen. It was nearly as tall as a colt, its shaggy coat the color of caramel.

She hurried to open the door to the sunporch.

The man was so tall, Fiona had to tilt her head back to see his face. Unlike Flem, his hair was black as coal and his eyes, though blue, more nearly resembled the sky at midnight. The sleeves of his shirt were rolled to his elbows. His pants and shirt were streaked with dirt and damp with sweat.

He paused on the threshold and simply stared at her. "You'd be the teacher."

She stepped aside. "You'll want to put that down. I know it's heavy."

"Not so heavy." He set it in a corner, then turned to see the hound sniffing at her feet. "You know better than to come in here, Chester."

Fiona knelt down and touched a hand to the hound's head. "Hello, Chester." She looked up. "Why can't he come in here?"

"Because Ma would hit him with her broom if she caught him inside. She has no use for him."

He walked outside, with the dog at his heels, and retrieved her satchel before setting it down on top of the trunk. This time the hound remained on the step while his master went inside.

As he crossed the room Fiona couldn't help staring at the way his damp shirt stuck to his skin, revealing a ripple of corded muscle across his back and shoulders. Such wide shoulders. Though the conductor had been a big man, it had taken the help of a second man straining beneath the weight of her trunk, yet this man had carried it with seemingly little effort.

He carefully wiped his hand on his pants before extending it to her. "I'm Grayson Haydn. Everyone calls me Gray."

"Hello, Gray. I'm Fiona Downey." She was aware of his big, calloused fingers wrapped around hers ever-so-gently, as though taking great care not to hurt her. "Thank you for fetching my things."

"You're welcome. Gerhardt Shultz told me you walked here. Too bad he didn't know I was heading into town. If you'd waited at the station, I'd have saved you the long walk."

She nearly groaned at the thought that she'd taken that long, miserable walk in vain. Aloud she merely smiled. "It's all right. I'm here now."

Under her scrutiny he suddenly colored and turned away. "Sorry. I've tracked mud into your room. I'd better wash and fetch my father."

It was on the tip of Fiona's tongue to ask where his father was, but he was already out the door and climbing up to the seat of the wagon, with the hound close on his heels. He snapped the reins and the horse headed toward the barn.

She turned her attention to her trunk, grateful that she would have time to change into something clean and fresh before facing the Haydn family for supper.

Because there was nowhere to hang her clothes, she laid them out on the bed and sifted through them until she found a simple dark skirt and crisp white shirtwaist with a high, modest neckline and narrow, fitted sleeves. She ran a brush through her dark curls and tied them off her face with a ribbon. Since she couldn't bear the thought of forcing her feet into her new boots, she slipped into her old ones, gratefully wiggling her toes.

Hearing voices in the other room, she took a deep breath and opened the door of her room.

The parlor was empty, as was the dining room. She followed the sound of voices to the kitchen, where the Haydn family had already gathered. Their conversation ceased abruptly, and everyone turned to stare at her as she stood in the doorway.

Rose turned from the stove, where she was stirring something in a pot. Seeing Fiona's clean clothes, she gave a huff of disdain. "No need to dress for supper here. We're simple farm people. Live simple. Eat simple." She pointed with her spoon. "Broderick, our new teacher, Fiona Downey."

Fiona walked to the head of the table where a handsome, white-haired man sat, with Grayson close beside him. "Hello, Mr. Haydn. It's very nice meeting you. I'm grateful that you and your wife are willing to share your home with me."

With Grayson's help the older man extended his hand and she shook it. One side of his face curved upward in a smile, while the other side remained immobile, giving him a bizarre, lopsided appearance.

She recognized the symptoms of stroke. Her father's best friend, Professor Ian Goodenough, had suffered such a misfortune. She and Da and visited him weekly until he'd left Bennett to live with his married daughter in Boston.

"Are you a good teacher?" His words were oddly slurred, since only one side of his mouth worked properly.

"Oh, I do hope so. Only time will tell. This is my first teaching assignment."

That brought another sniff of displeasure from Rose, who set a pot of stew in the middle of the table before taking her seat at the opposite end. She pointed to the chair that had been added beside Fleming's. "You sit there."

Fleming shot her a grin, putting her at ease as she sat.

Rose filled her own bowl first, then passed the stew to Fleming, who ladled some into his bowl before passing it to Fiona, who took only a little before passing it to Grayson. She watched as he filled first his father's bowl and then his own.

They followed the same ritual with the freshly baked bread, and then the butter, followed by the jug of milk.

When the plates were filled, Rose stared pointedly at Fiona while saying, "We thank Thee for this food."

In the next breath she added, "We are a God-fearing, churchgoing family. I expect anyone who lives under our roof to do the same."

Before Fiona could even respond Rose bent to her meal.

While Rose and Flem ate, Grayson cut his father's meat and vegetables into small bites, then closed his father's hand around a spoon. With each bite, the son dutifully wiped his father's chin before taking a quick bite of his own meal.

Because she was seated directly across from him, Fiona was acutely aware of the care Grayson was taking to see to his father's comfort. She thought of her own father and how she would have loved to care for him. If only she could.

Oh, Da, please don't let me embarrass myself by weeping in front of these strangers.

She closed her eyes, fighting the sting of tears. When she opened them, she realized that both Grayson and Broderick were watching her. She felt the warmth of a blush on her cheeks and ducked her head quickly.

She was grateful that the food was tasty. At least she wouldn't have to lie. "This is grand, Mrs. Haydn."

"No need to flatter. As I said, we eat simple food here."

"To someone who hasn't eaten in two days, it tastes heavenly."

"Two days?" Gray's head came up sharply.

Fiona's cheeks reddened. She hadn't meant to let that slip. "The train ride was . . . longer than I'd anticipated."

"Where is your home?" Broderick Haydn seemed unaware that his spoon was halfway to his mouth, and dripping on the tablecloth. But his wife noticed and gave a hiss of displeasure.

"Massachusetts. A pretty little town called Bennett."

"You miss it." Without glancing at his wife the old man carefully set his spoon back in the bowl.

"I do. Yes. This is the first time I've ever been away."

"Do you have family there?"

She shook her head. Her voice lowered, softened, her brogue deepening, and she could feel the tears close at hand. "Not anymore."

"Have some more stew." Grayson shoved the pot toward her.

"Thank you. I will." Fiona was grateful for the interruption. After filling her bowl she glanced over at the big, shy man, wondering if he had any idea what a favor he'd done, or if it had been entirely accidental.

"Rain's coming." Gray wiped his father's mouth. "I'm going to move up the haying." He glanced at his brother. "I could use a hand."

Rose's head came up. "I need Flem to help with the canning."

"You've never needed his help before."

"The tomatoes are rotting on the vines. I can't keep ahead of them."

Her husband dropped his spoon with a clatter, causing everyone to look over. He strained to pick it up, but his fingers refused to open. "I could pick the tomatoes."

Rose fixed him with a look. "By the time you got them up to the house, canning season would be over."

Fiona couldn't even imagine her own mother speaking in such a manner to her father, especially in front of a stranger. But they seemed unaware that she was even there until she spoke. "I could pick tomatoes and help with the canning, Mrs. Haydn."

Rose set down her fork with a snap. "You are paid to teach. I am paid to feed and shelter you."

Fiona stared hard at her plate, knowing her face was flaming. Silence settled over the table as the others finished their meal without a word.

"I see you made strudel." Flem turned to Fiona with a wide smile. "Ma knows it's my favorite."

Rose carried a platter to the table and began passing around the dessert, still warm from the oven.

After one bite Fiona's smile returned. "I thought you said the food was plain. I've never tasted anything quite like this before."

Rose looked aghast. "Never tasted strudel? What kind of place is this Massachusetts?"

"They're mostly Irish." Fleming grinned at the others. "I think that would explain the accent."

Fiona seemed startled. "I have an accent?"

"So thick you could cut it with a knife. You didn't know?"

She could feel her cheeks burning. It had never occurred to her that others would hear the lilt of Ireland in her voice. "Is it offensive?"

Flem gave a low chuckle. "That depends. If you're Irish, I suppose it's pleasant enough."

In the awkward silence that followed, Grayson shoved back his chair. "If you've had enough, Papa, I'll help you out to the back porch now. You'll want to smoke your pipe before bedtime."

The old man nodded his agreement, and the two men moved slowly away from the table.

Fiona got to her feet. "I'll help you with the dishes, Mrs. Haydn."

"The kitchen is mine." Rose's words left no room for

argument. "I'll have a lunch prepared each morning, which you can take to school. If you're awake early enough tomorrow, Grayson can drop you at the school-house on his way to the fields. The building's been empty for several years now, and will require some work. If you're not up in time, you'll have to walk."

"Is the school far from here?"

"Not far." Rose cut a second slice of strudel for Flem-ing, who'd lingered at the table. "No more than a couple of miles."

Flem made a great show of kissing his mother's hand as she set down the strudel.

"Stop that foolishness." Though she spoke the words sternly enough, there was the faintest flicker of humor in her eyes.

"Only if you promise me a third piece when I finish this."

"We'll see." She turned away and met Fiona's eyes. The spark of humor vanished as quickly as it had come. "We use the parlor in winter time. In summer we sit on the back porch until bedtime. You can sit with Grayson and Broderick, or go to your room." She turned away and began stacking the dishes.

Rose's sharp dismissal brought a grin to Flem's face, as though he found his mother's temper amusing.

It took Fiona only a moment to decide that, as pleasant as the night air might be, what she needed was escape.

Once in her room she thought about dealing with all the things from her trunk. But the sight of the bed was too great a temptation. Not even the unfinished letter to her mother could dissuade her.

Piling all her clothes on the desk, she drew the curtains and undressed quickly, before crawling into bed.

From somewhere beyond her door she could hear the quiet hum of voices in the kitchen. Rose's voice, low, angry, and Flem's, warm with laughter. Once or twice she thought she heard her name, but it seemed too much effort to make out the words.

It doesn't matter, she thought wearily. Let them say what they would about her. They could criticize her accent, or speculate on how she'd lived so long without ever tasting strudel. Flem could relate how foolish she'd looked when he'd come upon her, boots in hand, or the fact that she was far too young to be taken seriously as a teacher.

The sweet, rich scent of pipe smoke drifted past the window, and she was reminded of how much her da had loved to sit and smoke on the pretty little porch, with his wife on one side of him and his daughter on the other.

She swallowed back the tears that threatened. For now, for this night, she had a roof over her head, and enough to eat. For at least the next year, she had no choice but to make her home with the Haydn family in Paradise Falls. And then she would do whatever it took to get as far away from this place as possible.

It was her last coherent thought before sleep claimed her.

THREE

❖◆❖

Dearest Mum

  *I have time for only a few lines this morning. I'll
be seeing the school where I'll be teaching. I can't
wait to tell you all about it later.*

Love
Fiona

FIONA DRESSED QUICKLY, then blew out the
lantern and drew open the curtains, revealing a sky barely
tinged with pale ribbons of dawn. Quiet as a whisper she
slipped from her room and hurried through the house to
the kitchen, hoping Gray hadn't yet left for the fields.

She stepped into the kitchen and closed the door softly
behind her. When she turned, she spotted Broderick seated
at the table, sipping coffee. With each sip he drooled, and
it ran in little rivers down his chin, soaking the front of a
dishtowel that had been tied around his neck.

"Good morning."

He gave her his lopsided smile. "An early bird, are you?"

"I'm eager to see the school. Have I missed Gray?"

Just then the door was shoved open with the toe of a boot and Gray entered, carrying two enormous jugs of milk. For a moment he merely stared at her, as though surprised to see her up and dressed at such an hour. With a scowl he set the jugs on a clean towel by the backdoor before wiping his hands on his pants.

Feeling a need to be useful Fiona motioned toward the stove. "I'll bet you're both hungry. I could make some breakfast."

Gray's scowl deepened. "No one but Ma cooks in here. It's her way." He turned to his father while pouring coffee into a cup. "Milking's done. I'd best get to the fields. You sure you want to go to the barn?"

The older man set aside his coffee. "Always been more at home there than here."

"But there, no one'll hear you if you should fall."

"Either way, no one'll care."

Gray paused with the cup halfway to his mouth. "I'll care."

His father tugged on the makeshift bib and blotted his mouth. "I know, son. Give me a hand up."

Gray wrapped a big arm around Broderick's waist and easily lifted him to his feet. As the two shuffled toward the back door, Gray called over his shoulder, "Maybe you could fetch the lunch Ma made for us. It's there on the table."

Fiona picked up two linen-wrapped parcels and two jugs of water before following the men to the barn.

Once there Gray eased his father down onto a hard bench and handed him a sturdy stick. "This should help you get around some. You can probably feed the chickens, but I don't think you should bother with the pigs. Let Flem handle them."

Broderick gave a grunt of scorn.

"He'll do it if you tell him to. And ask his help to get up to the house for a midday meal."

"Shouldn't have to ask my own son for help."

"It's just Flem's way. He's careless."

Gray hitched the team to a wagon. After setting the food and water in the back he helped Fiona up, and climbed up beside her. At once the hound, that had appeared to be asleep at Broderick's feet, jumped up to the hard wooden seat and settled himself between Gray and Fiona, with his head resting on Gray's knees.

Gray ran a hand over the dog's ruff. "If Flem needs to find me, I'll be cutting the north field today."

His father nodded.

"Don't try to do too much."

Another nod and a quick wave of hand in dismissal before the older man visibly slumped on the bench.

Gray flicked the reins and the team leaned into the harness. With a creak of leather and wheels, the wagon rolled out of the barn and across the backyard toward the distant meadow.

Fiona saw Gray turn once to glance at the figure still seated on the bench where he'd left him. Then he gave his full attention to the team as they started up an incline.

"Did your father's stroke happen recently?"

"I guess it's been a month or more now." He glanced over. "It doesn't sicken you to see him . . . that way?"

She grasped the edge of the seat as the wagon lurched. "Sicken me? What a thing to say. You're lucky he's still alive."

"That's the way I see it, too. I told him as much. But he thinks he's become a burden now that he can't do all the things he used to."

Fiona glanced up at the thin, pale light struggling to break through the clouds. "I guess it's hard for a man to see his wife and sons doing what he once did." Her voice lowered. "I'd give anything if I could take care of my father. I wouldn't mind if he couldn't do anything more than lie in his bed the whole day. I'd gladly feed him, shave him, as long as I could hear his voice."

Recognizing her pain Gray stroked the dog's head to keep from staring at her. "How long has he been gone?"

She looked away, hoping she could speak over the lump in her throat. "Two weeks."

They rode for nearly a mile in silence, and Fiona found herself grateful for Gray's quiet presence. The last thing she wanted was to answer questions, or talk about things that could still bring her to tears. As if sensing that, he didn't press, but left her alone with her thoughts.

She studied his big hands, holding the reins between his knees.

He gave one of his rare smiles. It seemed to transform his entire face, lighting those midnight eyes, revealing a dimple in his cheek. "I like this time of day best."

"Why?"

He shrugged. "I like knowing the day is fresh before me. Like a field that hasn't been harvested yet."

"You like cutting crops?"

Again that shrug. "Harvesting. Plowing. It's hard work, but it satisfies me. I like the rhythm of it. And the look of it when it's done. All those perfect rows, and knowing I shaped them."

She looked out over the fields of wheat and corn, seeing for the first time how precisely they'd been laid out. "They're perfect. And so pretty."

Gray flushed with pleasure, wondering why her words should please him so.

"Why isn't Flem with you? Doesn't he help with the farm chores?"

His smile faded. He seemed to consider his words carefully before saying softly, "Flem likes to sleep late. How do you like your room?"

She blinked at the abrupt change of subject. "It's fine. I'm afraid I left it cluttered. I hope your mother won't take offense. I didn't have anywhere to put my clothes, so I set them on the bed after I straightened it."

His eyes narrowed in thought. "What you need is a line for hanging your clothes. I'll string one tonight after supper."

"There's no need. You have enough to do."

"It's no trouble."

"Then I thank you, Gray. A line would be grand."

As the wagon rolled along a dirt path, Gray slowed the team. "Would you like to see my favorite spot?"

"I'd like that."

With careful maneuvering, the wagon veered off the path and followed a narrow trail. Up ahead Fiona could hear the sound of rushing water.

As they rounded a bend, Gray brought the team to a halt and stepped down before reaching a hand to help her.

A short walk later he paused and pointed across a chasm to water tumbling down rocks. "This is Paradise Falls."

Hearing the pride in his voice, she tried not to show the disappointment that washed through her. She'd been expecting a vista sweeping for hundreds of yards, with water rushing over steep cliffs into swiftly moving water below. Instead there was just a narrow river tumbling over rock ledges into a stream.

"Is this all there is?"

He nodded. "In the spring, when the snow melts, the Paradise River roars through this area on its way to the mighty Superior. Sometimes, when it overflows its banks, it floods the fields. When it recedes, it leaves rich silt behind. That's why my father chose this place for his farm when he was no older than I am now. Thanks to his choice, we have the richest soil around."

It was, Fiona thought, the most she'd ever heard Gray

say at one time. When he realized how much he'd revealed, his cheeks flushed and he coughed to cover his embarrassment.

He shifted to watch the flight of a hawk, then returned his attention to the falls. "It's pretty, isn't it?"

"It is. Yes." And it was, she realized. If it lacked the magnificence of Niagara, there was still a pristine beauty about it. Here in the middle of a wilderness, the foaming water, tumbling over rocks, then spilling down, down until it met the rushing stream below was an amazing sight.

"It would be nice to come here one day and just sit listening to the thundering of the water."

He nodded. "I do that sometimes. When my chores are finished. There's a peace here." He glanced at her, then away. "It seems I always come here whenever there's anything important happening in my life."

"That's lovely. I suppose, then, it's only right that I should come here today, before seeing the school where I'll be teaching."

"I thought so." Gray led the way back to the wagon and helped her up to the hard seat before flicking the reins. After following the trail for several miles the team left the dirt path and started across a recently plowed field.

Gray pointed to the distant woods. "There's your school."

Your school.

The words shivered through her, giving her an unexpected thrill.

She could see, standing in a clearing, a log cabin. Though she sat perfectly still, there was a little voice in her head that was shouting for joy. She clasped her hands together tightly.

"My school." Her voice wavered, and she hoped he hadn't noticed.

"It's been vacant for three years now. Don't expect too much."

"I won't." But she couldn't help herself. She sat up straighter as they drew near.

It was little more than a log shack. The wooden steps leading to the porch had been warped by the elements, and tilted precariously in the middle. The hinges of the door had given way and it hung half open, swaying slightly in the breeze.

Off to one side of the school an outhouse lay toppled on its side, the wood so rotten the walls had caved in.

Gray climbed from the wagon and offered his hand to help Fiona down. As before, she felt the strength in him, and beneath the strength, the gentleness, as though he were taking great care with her.

The hound bounded off, sniffing the ground.

"Going to need some cleaning." Gray climbed the steps and forced the door open. As he did, the second hinge gave way and the door fell to the porch with such force it broke through the rotten timbers, leaving a gaping hole in the porch.

"Watch your step now," he called when he saw Fiona coming up behind him.

She paused in the doorway and looked around with a growing sense of dread. There was a hole in the roof that had allowed the leaves of trees to blow inside. The floor was littered with branches and leaves, as well as the remains of several dead animals. There were chinks between some of the logs big enough to allow forest creatures to crawl through.

Gray sighed, the only sign of his displeasure. "I didn't bring nearly enough tools. Just a broom and dustpan, and a shovel. I'll get someone in town to come out and seal those walls with pitch, and mend that hole in the roof."

He walked to the wagon and retrieved the things he'd brought, then handed her a water jug and her lunch. "I'm sorry to leave you with all this."

"As your mother pointed out last night, it isn't your

responsibility." Fiona set aside the food and water and managed a weak smile. "You have your chores to see to, and I have mine. We'd best get to them."

He climbed up to the seat of the wagon. Before he could flick the reins the hound came racing from the nearby woods and jumped up, settling himself beside his master.

"I'll come by at the end of the day. If you're still here, I'll drive you home. If you want to head home before I get here, I'll understand."

Fiona nodded, and lifted a hand to shield the rising sun from her eyes as he tugged on the reins, turning the team toward the distant fields of wheat.

Straightening her shoulders she picked up the broom and dustpan and started up the rotting steps of the school. Maybe it wasn't the ivy-covered place of her dreams, but it was hers now. And she intended to make it a welcoming place for the students.

FIONA SET ASIDE the broom and surveyed the inside of the schoolhouse. It had been swept clean of all debris. She had polished the little stove with sand until it gleamed, and decided she would now tackle the scarred wooden teacher's desk, and then the crude tables and chairs that served as student desks.

Her gown was filthy. Her hair hung down in damp strings. But she was satisfied that she was making progress.

She looked up at the sound of a wagon. As soon as Gray brought his team to a halt, a boy jumped out of the back carrying an array of tools and supplies.

"What's this?" Fiona hurried over.

"You need help if you're to get your school ready." He turned to the boy. "This is Will VanderSleet. Will, this is Miss Downey."

"Miss Downey." The boy's cheeks bore bright spots

of color, and he avoided looking directly at her, staring instead at the toe of his shabby boots.

"Hello, Will." She glanced over the boy's head to Gray. "Do you think one lad is enough to see to all the repairs needed here?"

"Will's been doing odd jobs around Paradise Falls since he was old enough to carry his pa's tools. He'll do just fine."

At his words, the boy stood a little straighter.

"Well, then." She smiled at Will, who flushed and looked away. "I'll be grateful for your help, Will."

Gray was already climbing up to the seat of the wagon.

She took a step toward him. "You can't stay?"

He shook his head. "Sorry. No time." He flicked the reins and as the wagon lurched ahead, his hound raced alongside, tail wagging with excitement.

Fiona watched as the boy took his time walking around the outside of the building before climbing the rotting steps to inspect the inside. A short time later, while she scrubbed years of dirt from the wooden desk, she heard the sound of hammer and saw. By the time she'd turned her attention to the tables and chairs, she realized that the roof no longer showed any daylight. She glanced up in surprise to see that the hole had been patched. Will was busy attaching new hinges to the door.

When that was finished he cleared his throat. "Ma'am?"

Fiona looked over.

"I'll be tearing out the old porch and steps, before I replace them. You might want to step outside now before I start. Otherwise, you'll have to stay in here until the new porch and steps are in place."

"Thank you, Will." She got to her feet, pressing a hand to the small of her back. How long had she been bent over these tables? Long enough to have her muscles protesting.

Once outside, it felt good to be in the sunlight. She walked a short distance to a stream and knelt on the banks, plunging her hands up to her elbows, before splashing water over her face and drinking deeply. With a sigh of pure pleasure she remained there, enjoying the cool water and the whisper of breeze that ruffled her hair. It would be so easy to stay here just this way for the rest of the day. Instead she found a shady spot beneath a tall oak and unwrapped the linen towel Rose had prepared the night before. Inside were several hard-boiled eggs, thick slabs of bread slathered with blackberry preserves, and an apple. Just looking at all that food, Fiona realized she was ravenous.

She walked around to the front of the schoolhouse, where Will was prying the last of the steps away. "It's time for some lunch, Will."

He shook his head. "I didn't think to bring any, Miss Downey."

"That's all right. Mrs. Haydn made enough for both of us. Come along."

She led him to the shady spot and divided the food. For a moment the boy looked at it as though he couldn't believe his eyes. Then, with a shy smile, he tucked into his food, and Fiona did the same.

"How old are you, Will?" Fiona watched as he bit into an egg.

"Fourteen, come winter."

"So young to know so much about fixing things."

He flushed. "My pa could fix anything. He let me work alongside him and taught me all he could."

"Is your father busy today?"

"My pa's dead. And my ma. I live with my uncle." He said the words so matter-of-factly, she caught her breath.

"I'm sorry, Will." She looked away, wondering if she would ever be able to speak of her father's passing with an equal lack of passion.

When at last Fiona sat back, she gave a sigh of pure contentment. "I can't remember when such simple food tasted so grand." She drank from the jug, then passed it to Will.

"It was good." The boy wiped his mouth with his sleeve and took a long drink of water. "Thank you, Ma'am."

He returned to his work while Fiona folded the linen towel and carried the jug to the stream to fill it.

Hearing the sound of a horse she turned, expecting to see Gray. Instead she saw Flem just climbing down from the seat of a wagon.

"What's this?" He flashed her a brilliant smile. "I came here expecting to see the new teacher, Miss Downey. Instead I find some poor, filthy creature who looks like she's been mucking stalls."

His smile was so infectious Fiona couldn't resist returning his with one of her own. "Oh, Flem, it's just been the grandest day. Will here has repaired the roof and door and is now replacing the steps and porch. Look at the fine work he's done."

The boy beamed at her words of praise.

"And what of that?" With a look of derision Flem pointed to the toppled outhouse. "Anyone with half a brain would've made that the first order of business."

Stung by his words, Will hung his head.

"Well, it is important, of course." Fiona knew her cheeks were bright pink, but it couldn't be helped. After all, an outhouse was an indelicate subject. Besides, he'd made it sound as if Will had made a terrible error in judgment. She could see that the boy felt ashamed. "There's still time to have it in order before the students start school next week. I think Will made a wise choice to start on the schoolhouse before dealing with that."

Flem's easy smile returned with a quick shrug of his

shoulders. "Whatever you say, teacher. Isn't that right, Will?"

The boy flushed and returned his attention to the wood he was nailing to the porch.

Flem caught her elbow. "Come on."

She tried to pull back, but he had a firm grasp on her. "Where are we going?"

"Just through the woods a bit. There's something there I think you'll like."

"But the work—"

"Will still be here when you get back. Besides, you can't get inside your precious schoolhouse until Will finishes that porch. And I doubt he needs you to hand him the wood. Come on." With a laugh he looped his arm through hers and led her toward the woods, leaving the boy to stare after them.

Since he'd made it impossible to resist, she decided to relax and enjoy this charmer's company. "All right. But only for a few minutes. I really do have work to do."

It was lovely and refreshingly cool as they stepped beneath the canopy of trees shading them from the sunlight. In the silence of the forest they could hear the ripple of water where the stream meandered through the woods. Low-hanging branches of trees snagged Fiona's hair, tossing them wildly about her face.

After a short walk she dug in her heels, determined to go no further. "What did you want to show me?"

"It's just up here." Flem drew her deeper into the woods before pausing to point to the wild roses lining the banks of the stream.

"Oh. Aren't they lovely?" Fiona bent to inhale their fragrance.

Flem stood back watching her with a smile of pure male appreciation. She might not be aware of the way her sweaty clothes clung to her, but he was. "I knew you'd like them."

When he broke off a long stem heavy with flowers she
caught his arm. "Oh, no. You mustn't pick them."

He seemed surprised by her outburst. "Why not?"

"They're wildflowers. They'll only live a little while
in water before dying. But if you leave them on the vine,
they'll live for weeks."

"So what?" Ignoring her protest he continued picking
until he had a huge bouquet which he thrust into her arms.
"If I hadn't brought you here, nobody would have ever
even seen them. Then what good would they be?" When
she could think of nothing to say in reply, he gave a smug
smile. "Why shouldn't you enjoy them, even if it is only
for a few hours?"

How could she argue with such logic? Besides, now
that she was holding them, she couldn't help but bury her
face in them and breathe in their perfume. For a moment
she was swept back to the lovely little house in Bennett,
and her mother's roses.

"Oh, Flem, they're really lovely. I'd forgotten how
much I love the smell of roses."

"You see?" He caught her arm and made a great show
of helping her over a fallen log. After they'd crossed it,
he kept his arm looped through hers.

"But I still say you should have left them as you'd
found them."

"And I say that the pleasure in your eyes is reason
enough to disagree."

She laughed and gave a toss of her head. "You're in-
corrigible."

"I'll admit to that, as long as you admit that I'm right."

"I don't know about being right, but you're certainly
determined to have your way."

"I always do. You may as well get used to it."

"And what do you do when you don't get your way?"

"I'll tell you if it ever happens."

They were both laughing as they stepped out of the

woods and rounded the corner of the schoolhouse, where Gray was standing beside Will.

Heat flared briefly in Gray's eyes as he looked at the two of them all flushed and disheveled.

Just seeing Gray had Fiona's cheeks turning several shades of red.

Flem looked from one to the other, clearly enjoying Fiona's embarrassment as much as his brother's annoyance. He crossed his arms over his chest and casually leaned a hip against the wall of the school. "Well, well, big brother. What are you doing here?"

"I've come to take Will and Fiona home."

"A pity you came all this way after cutting hay all day. If you'd asked, I could have saved you the time." Flem's smile grew in direct proportion to Gray's frown. As if to add to his brother's misery he said slyly, "Fiona and I were walking in the woods."

Fiona looked from one brother to the other, wondering at the simmering anger she could sense. What was there between them that they should be so prickly with one another? "Flem wanted to show me some wild roses." She held them out. "Aren't they pretty?"

Gray gave them a dismissive glance. "They'll be dead in a day."

Flem chuckled. "Well now, that's exactly what our practical little teacher said. But what does it matter, if they bring her pleasure today? Isn't her smile worth the death of a few wildflowers?"

When Gray didn't respond, Flem turned to Fiona. "I'm heading home now. Would you like to ride along?"

She shook her head. "I'd like to take some time to walk around the schoolhouse and admire Will's work."

"Suit yourself. But you'd have a lot more fun with me." With a little swagger Flem climbed up to the seat of the wagon and took off with a jingle of harness. As if to mock them, the happy tune he was whistling drifted back to them on the breeze.

When he was gone Fiona walked up the steps and paused on the porch. "This is just grand, Will."

The boy glowed at her praise.

She opened the door, noting the smooth motion of the hinges. Once inside she studied the gleaming wood of the desk, the freshly swept floor, the seamless expanse of roof overhead.

Will and Gray stood behind her.

"I'll seal the walls tomorrow with pitch," the boy said softly. "And then I'll rebuild the outhouse."

Gray turned away. "We'd better get home."

Outside Gray helped Fiona up to the wagon seat, then gave Will a hand with his tools. When the boy climbed into the back, the hound followed. With a delighted laugh Will gathered the dog into his arms and ruffled his fur.

As they started off across the field Fiona swiveled her head for another glimpse of the schoolhouse.

When she turned back she saw Gray watching her. "Are you sorry it's so small?"

"It isn't small." Her lips curved into an embarrassed smile. "Well, maybe it is. But I think it's just fine. I was afraid, after all the hard work Will and I did, it might not really be there."

"It's there. And it'll be there tomorrow. And the day after."

"But will I?"

"What's that supposed to mean?"

She looked down at her hands. "I've been thinking about what Flem said last night. I wasn't aware of my brogue, but it could cause the students and their families to decide I'm not fit to teach."

He shrugged. "I wouldn't know anything about that."

They rode in silence until she sighed and looked over her shoulder at the boy who was seated in the back of the wagon, still clutching the hound to his chest. "Thank you for bringing me Will today. I never could have managed alone."

They pulled up to a tired-looking farmhouse where a man waited in the doorway. His boots were caked with mud, his pants dirt-stained and torn at one knee. His thinning hair was combed straight back from a face that looked pinched and stern.

There was no welcoming call from the man, nor did his eyes reflect any friendliness.

Gray helped Will unload his tools, then reached into his pocket and placed some coins in his hand. "You be ready at dawn."

"I will." The lad waved to Fiona, before racing up the steps and disappearing inside.

When Gray returned to the wagon Fiona said softly, "Is that his uncle?"

Gray nodded. "Dolph VanderSleet."

The hound climbed over the seat and settled himself between Gray and Fiona, with his big front paws and head resting on Fiona's lap.

Gray looked surprised. "Chester doesn't much like females. Probably because Ma took the broom to him so much as a pup. You can shove him away if he bothers you."

"I don't mind a bit." Fiona reached down and began scratching behind the hound's ears, earning a few loving licks from his tongue for her effort. "I always wanted a dog of my own, but Mum said they eat too much. Besides, our little yard had no place for a dog to run."

"You lived in a town?"

She nodded. "It was a pretty place."

Gray shook his head. "Don't think I'd ever like living in a town."

"Why?"

He shrugged. "I'd be like Chester there, wanting room to run."

As they crossed the meadow and drew near the barn they could see Flem's horse already turned into a stall.

Gray cleared his throat. "I'm sorry I came along and spoiled your chance to ride home with Flem. You could have been inside and washed up for supper by now."

"I don't mind. I enjoyed riding with you and Will and Chester." She gave the dog an affectionate pat.

They rolled into the barn, and Gray jumped down before helping Fiona from the wagon.

He reached up to the wagon seat and retrieved the bouquet of wild roses. "You forgot these."

Their fragrance had already begun to fade, and the petals had wilted. It should have given him some sense of satisfaction to know he'd been right, but as he handed them to her, the only thing he could see was the sadness in her eyes.

As she started away he stopped her with a hand to her arm. "I can't say one way or the other about the people of Paradise Falls, but as for me, I like the sound of your brogue. In fact, I could just sit and listen to you talk all day."

His unexpected kindness caught her off-guard. To hide the tears that sprang to her eyes she fled the barn, her face flaming.

Behind her, an embarrassed Grayson Haydn muttered every rich, ripe oath he could think of as he unhitched the team.

What had possessed him to say such a bold thing to someone as shy and sweet as Fiona Downey?

He'd never seen anyone quite like her. So slim and tiny, with all those lovely dark curls. Her eyes rivaled the sky on a summer day.

He loved hearing her talk. Not just the lilt of her brogue, though that was quite a contrast to the clipped tones of his neighbors, but also the words themselves. Big words rolled right off her tongue, making it plain that she was an educated lady.

He must have sounded like a complete fool, admitting how much he liked hearing her speak.

With every minute that passed he worked up a head of steam, cursing himself for his clumsiness. With the harness set aside and the horses fed and watered, he searched out new chores that would delay the moment when he would have to go inside and face the new teacher across the table at supper.

FOUR

"YOU'RE LATE." ROSE looked up from the table and glowered at her older son.

Gray took his time plunging his hands into the bucket of water and scrubbing with soap, then carefully drying, before taking his seat beside his father. Across the table he could see that Fiona had changed her clothes and brushed her hair into a neat knot. Despite her efforts little wisps had already pried loose to curl around her cheeks. Cheeks that turned as red as autumn apples when he looked at her.

He ducked his head and busied himself cutting the pork into tiny bites on his father's plate before placing a fork in Broderick's hand.

Rose's voice took on an accusing note. "I could have used your help with the canning, Grayson."

"You had Flem." Gray broke a roll, taking his time buttering it.

"He can't do everything. I had to send him to town for

salt, since you didn't bother to bring me any."

Gray mopped at his father's chin. "I gave your list to Mrs. Schneider at the store, last time I was there."

"The salt wasn't with the supplies." Rose set down her fork with a clatter. "I'll wager she charged us for it, though."

"If she did, she'll make it right." Gray wrapped his father's fingers around a steaming cup of tea and guided it to his lips. "The Schneiders are honest people."

"So you say." Rose pushed back her chair and crossed to the stove. "But that doesn't excuse the fact that poor Flem had to drive the team all the way to town and back just for a sack of salt, getting back too late to help me with the picking and canning."

Fiona darted a glance at Flem's face, waiting for him to admit that he'd managed to find time to stop by the schoolhouse. He merely winked and smiled, before returning his attention to his food. When Rose retrieved a platter of pork, he was the first to help himself to seconds.

Broderick set down his cup, taking great care not to splash. "Now you've had a chance to see your school, Miss Downey, what do you think?"

Fiona's smile bloomed. "It's grand, though it's in need of much repair. But Gray brought young Will VanderSleet to help me. That boy's a wonder."

The old man nodded. "His father could do anything. A shame he didn't live long enough to teach the boy all he knew."

"He seems to have learned enough. I don't know what I'd have done without Will today."

Rose wasn't about to let go of her righteous anger yet. Her eyes flashed as she turned on Gray. "You had time to fetch young VanderSleet, but you couldn't help your mother pick tomatoes?"

"I told you I'd be cutting today. And will be, for the rest of the week. Maybe, if Flem doesn't have to go to town again tomorrow, he could lend a hand. If not with the cutting, then at least with your tomatoes." Gray deliberately turned his back on his mother to dab at his father's chin. He kept his tone deceptively soft. "Are you ready for a smoke on the porch, Papa?"

"I am." With Gray's help, Broderick got slowly to his feet.

"We haven't finished supper yet." Rose's voice grew shrill. "I made linzer torte."

"I've had enough." Broderick turned to his oldest son. "How about you, Grayson?"

Gray nodded, and the two men walked away, letting the back door slam behind them.

In the silence that followed, Flem chuckled, causing both women to glance at him.

"I guess that leaves more dessert for me." He patted his mother's shoulder as he pushed away from the table and helped himself to the torte cooling on a sideboard.

"I'll do that." Rose walked up beside him and began slicing while Flem dipped his spoon in the sweet berry filling and tasted with the eagerness of a little boy. Then he leaned over and kissed his mother's cheek. "Young VanderSleet might be our new teacher's hero, but you're mine."

"Oh, you." Rose was blushing as she turned away.

When she placed a plate of torte in front of Fiona, the young woman shook her head.

"No, thank you, Mrs. Haydn. I've had enough." Fiona got to her feet. But tonight, instead of taking to her bedroom, she decided to join Gray and his father on the back porch. She was too excited about the thought of the coming school year to settle down just yet.

Broderick was seated in a wooden rocking chair. Gray sat on the top step of the porch, with his back to the rail, whittling on a block of wood. Seeing Fiona he started to get up, but before he could she brushed past him and quickly settled herself on the bottom step, taking care to tuck the hem of her long skirt around her ankles for modesty.

Broderick took the pipe from his mouth. "Does the smell of my tobacco offend you, Miss Downey?"

Fiona gave a firm toss of her head. "I love the smell of it. My da used to smoke a pipe." She wrapped her arms around her knees. "You've a lovely farm, Mr. Haydn. The sight of all those fields is grand, indeed."

The old man nodded thoughtfully while a cloud of smoke drifted around his head. "There was a time I could plow from sunup to sundown, without a thought to resting. I was always proud of the fact that I could do the work of three men."

"It seems you've taught your son to do the same."

"One of them." He drew smoke, exhaled. "Do you have any family? Cousins, aunts, uncles?"

She shook her head. "I don't know if there are any distant relatives left in Ireland, but here in America, there were just the three of us. My da, my mum, and me."

"Gray tells me your father passed recently. What of your mother?"

"She's staying with a sister in Chicago until I earn enough to send for her." Fiona rested her chin on her knees and closed her eyes against the pain.

Would it ever go away? Would she ever stop the wanting? The missing?

The old man's tone grew thoughtful. "Losing family is a hard thing. I had a sister. Gerda. Ten years older she was, and more like my mother than my sister. She never married."

When he fell silent, Fiona lifted her head. "What happened to Gerda?"

He took the pipe from between his teeth and stared at the crows that were flying in to roost on the highest peak of the barn. "She stayed on our parents' farm some miles from here and nursed them through their old age. Afterward I asked her to come live with us, so she wouldn't be alone."

Gray's head came up. "I didn't know that. Why didn't Aunt Gerda come?"

"She said my kitchen wasn't big enough for two women." One side of Broderick's mouth curved in a smile. "She was a wise woman, my sister."

Fiona brushed at a stray wisp of hair. "Is she still living on the family farm?"

When Broderick fell silent Gray answered for his father. "Aunt Gerda died last winter. Pa and I took a wagonload of supplies to her, and found her out in the barn. It appeared she'd fallen after killing a goose for her holiday supper. The temperature had fallen so low, some said it was the coldest they could ever recall."

Despite the heat of a late summer evening, Fiona felt a shiver pass through her at the horrible image of what that poor woman must have suffered, knowing she was alone, and that she would surely freeze to death unless help came quickly.

How much worse it must be for her brother, to know he could have eased her suffering, if only he'd found her in time.

"I'm so sorry, Mr. Haydn."

The old man barely acknowledged her sympathy, and she realized he'd gone somewhere in his mind.

She turned her attention to the wood in Gray's hand. Under his knife it was beginning to take shape. "Is that a dog?"

"Not yet. But soon enough it will be Chester here."

At the sound of his name the hound padded over to rest his head on his master's knees.

"Where did you learn such a wonderful thing?"

Gray shrugged. "I've always seen shapes in wood.

Papa says my grandfather did the same. It passes the time when my chores are finished."

Overcome with weariness, Fiona stood and shook down her skirts. "I'd best get to bed now. I like to write a few pages each night to my mum before I go to sleep."

Gray lumbered to his feet. "I'll string that line in your room first." Setting aside the wood and knife, he picked up a length of rope and a hammer and nails that were lying beside his father's rocker.

As he followed Fiona inside, Flem and Rose were seated at the kitchen table, laughing together. At the sight of Fiona and Gray, their laughter faded.

"What's this? Are you walking the teacher to her door?" Flem saw the color rise to Fiona's cheeks at the same moment that his brother's eyes frosted over. Seeing that Gray had risen to the bait, he couldn't resist adding, "I think she can manage to find her way without your help. Don't you, Gray?"

When Gray didn't bother to answer, Rose shoved back her chair and closed a hand over her older son's sleeve. "Where are you going?"

He paused to stare at the offending hand, then up at her mouth, pursed into a tight frown. "I'm stringing a rope so our houseguest has a place to hang her clothes."

To his retreating back Rose called, "Just so you know—it's my responsibility to say who can set foot in her room and who can't."

With her arms folded over her chest she watched as Fiona opened the door and stood aside for Gray. Satisfied that they would leave the door open until Gray had finished his chore, Rose returned to the table.

Seeing the way Flem was grinning she lowered her voice. "I expect a certain behavior from anyone who comes here to teach our young. After all, what do we really know about this woman?"

He caught her hands in his and lifted them to his lips.

"I know this. She can't hold a candle to you, Ma."

"Oh, you." Laughing, she nodded toward the last of the torte cooling on the windowsill. "You may as well have another piece. It'll be stale by morning."

"If you insist." He waited until his mother crossed the room before getting up from the table to see for himself. From the doorway of the kitchen he could make out his brother standing on a stool, threading a rope from one side of the room to the other, while Fiona stood watching.

Flem quickly dismissed the little twinge of annoyance. It would have been a fine thing to impress the teacher. Still, if he were the one doing that chore, he'd have found a way to use it to his advantage. A peek at her underwear in that pile of clothing, for instance. Or some naughty joke that would bring another flush to her cheeks. But poor, dumb Gray would no doubt just string the rope and run away like a scared rabbit.

"Here you are."

When Rose set down the slice of torte, Flem tore himself from the doorway and settled down at the table.

In her bedroom, Fiona watched as Gray easily pounded in the nails, then secured the rope until it was taut enough to hold her clothes without sagging in the middle.

"Would you like me to help you hang those?" He pointed to the pile of clothing that littered her bed.

"That isn't necessary, Gray. You've already put in a long day."

"So have you."

"I don't mind." As he started away she touched a hand lightly to his arm. "Thank you."

"You're . . ." He stared down at her hand, then caught it in his and turned it over, palm up. "What's this?"

"Nothing. Really." Embarrassed, she tried to snatch her hand away, but he held it fast and lifted the other, as well, studying the raw, red blisters that covered both palms.

"You did too much today. Your hands weren't made for such work."

"My hands are too soft." She could feel the heat rising to her cheeks. That knowledge only made it worse. Now her face was flaming. "It's time they toughened up."

"I've something that will help." He stalked away.

The moment he was gone, Fiona forced herself to breathe. What was it about this silent, solemn man? When he'd taken hold of her hands, she'd been so startled, she'd forgotten how to take air into her lungs.

Within minutes Gray returned with a jar of salve.

"This will sting for a little while." He began to smooth thick, yellow ointment over her skin, taking care to rub it into the open blisters.

Fiona's skin felt as if she'd held it to the fire.

Hearing her little hiss of pain, Gray looked up to see her blink back tears. His tone softened to a whisper. "Only for a minute more, I promise. Then it will start to feel better."

For the space of several minutes he continued holding her hand.

Fiona didn't know what was worse, the burning ointment, or the rush of heat from his touch. Her throat felt so tight, she feared she might never swallow again.

When at last he heard her sigh, he asked, "Feeling better?"

Unable to find her voice, she merely nodded.

"Good." The smile came slowly to his eyes, then to his lips. "I'll leave this salve with you. Use it if the pain wakes you during the night. By morning those blisters should feel some better, and in a few days your hands will be good as new."

"Thank you, Gray. For the clothesline, for the ointment. And for all the help with the school house."

He eyed the pile of clothing littering her bed. "Are you sure you can manage all this?"

"I'm sure."

"All right, then." He turned away. As he started out of her room he paused in the doorway. "If you'd like to sleep late, you could always have Flem take you over to the school tomorrow."

She was quick to refuse. "I'll be ready when you are."

He ducked his head and walked away.

Minutes later Fiona heard the door slam. Then the voices and laughter began once more in the kitchen.

She closed her door and drew the curtains before hanging her clothes. When everything was tidy, she slipped out of her day clothes and pulled on a soft cotton gown for sleeping. She eyed the letter to her mother she'd begun the previous night. The ointment would make it impossible to finish. She would have to write twice as much tomorrow.

After turning back the covers she blew out the lantern. Instead of climbing into bed, she walked to the window and lifted the curtain to stare at the night sky.

"Are you looking at that same moon, Mum? Do the stars seem as close in Chicago?"

In the silence that followed she folded her hands and whispered a prayer. Suddenly overcome with a wave of homesickness, she let go of the curtain and climbed into bed. Curled into a tight ball, she choked back tears until sleep claimed her.

FIONA LAY IN her bed, wondering what had awakened her from sleep. At first the only thing she could hear was the silence of the big farmhouse. But as she grew accustomed to the sounds of the night, she could hear, above the chirr of crickets and the hoot of an owl, the sound of the backdoor closing. Instead of footsteps heading toward the outhouse, these seemed to be heading toward the barn.

Intrigued, she slid from her bed and moved aside an edge of the curtain in time to see Flem leading a horse. Instead of riding, he continued walking until he'd crossed the distance that separated the barn from the house, and from there to the road. Once he was far enough away to go undetected, he pulled himself into the saddle and turned the horse toward town at a fast clip.

Where could Flem possibly go at this late hour? And why?

Not my business, Fiona thought as she returned to her bed. Perhaps there was a girl in town who'd snagged Flem's heart. But what sort of girl would meet a young man in the small hours of the night?

She didn't know. Nor did she care. What Flem did with his time was his own business. Of one thing she was certain: he was the most handsome man she'd ever seen. With that golden hair and those laughing eyes, he would have no trouble finding dozens of young women who would willingly lose their hearts to him.

Within minutes she'd put Flem and his secretive midnight wanderings out of her mind completely as she drifted back to sleep.

FIVE

———◆———

"WHAT'S THIS?" GRAY swung down from the seat of the wagon and crossed the schoolyard to examine the brand new outhouse, where Will was just setting the door on its hinges. "You're finished?"

Will flushed in embarrassment. "I didn't want Miss Downey to have to wait any longer. Flem said I should have done this first."

"No need to worry about what Flem thinks, Will. You're doing a fine job here." Gray noted the freshly sanded bench positioned across one side, with three graduated holes smoothly cut into the wood.

The boy looked pleased. "Miss Downey likes it, too."

"Where is she?"

"Inside." Will nodded toward the schoolhouse.

Gray gave one last glance around the tidy shed before turning away.

He found Fiona standing beside her desk, running her hand lightly across the scarred wood.

As always, he felt a jolt at the sight of her. To cover his nerves he frowned. "It would seem you're ready for your first day of school."

Her head came up, before a look of wariness came into her eyes. "I hope I am."

"I can't see anything left to do."

She gave a soft laugh. "Except maybe to find a more qualified teacher."

"You're going to be a fine teacher."

"How do you know?"

He shrugged. "I just do. You care so much."

"Maybe too much." She stared down at the desktop. "What if I let the children down, Gray?"

He folded his arms over his chest and leaned against the door. "You'd never do that."

"You can't be certain."

"I just have to look at you, listen to you, to know." Suddenly uncomfortable with the direction of their conversation, he straightened. "Come on. Ma'll have supper, and we still have to drop Will at his uncle's."

She hurried across the room and brushed past him, wondering at the little rush of heat when their bodies touched. She stood waiting on the porch as he secured the front door. Will was already sitting in the back of Gray's wagon, with his bundle of tools, whistling to Chester, who was hunting squirrels in the nearby woods. The hound looked up and started toward them at a full run, jumping smoothly into the boy's arms.

Gray helped Fiona up to the high, wooden seat, before climbing up beside her. With a flick of the reins, the horses started across the schoolyard and headed onto the dirt path leading to town.

Gray shot a glance over his shoulder at the boy, who sat with an arm around a panting Chester. "It looks like school will be ready to start right on time."

Will nodded. "All I have left to do tomorrow is clean

up some wood shavings and wash the window."

Fiona shook her head. "I can do that."

"No sense you climbing a ladder, Miss Downey." The boy kept his arm around the hound's neck as they made a sharp turn into his uncle's yard. "After I see to the cleanup, I'll check the roof one last time, to make sure I didn't miss any holes. Don't want rain or snow to spoil your shiny new schoolroom."

As the wagon came to a lurching stop, the boy tossed down his tools and climbed out. At once the dog clambered across to the seat of the wagon, where he rested his head on Fiona's lap.

Gray pressed a coin into Will's hand before picking up the reins. "Tomorrow morning then, Will."

The boy nodded. "I'll be ready." He smiled at Fiona. "Goodbye, Miss Downey. I—"

At the sound of the door opening he turned.

His uncle stepped onto the porch, squinting against the late afternoon sun. "I won't be able to spare Will tomorrow. He's needed here."

Gray nodded. "I understand, Dolph."

"I'll miss you, Will." Seeing the way the boy ducked his head to hide his sadness Fiona added, "Thank you for all your help." As an afterthought she called, "Will I see you Monday for the first day of school?"

Before Will could respond his uncle shook his head. "No time for such things. I've a farm to run. The boy's old enough to earn his keep now."

Seeing the man's scowl, Fiona held her silence, though it was on the tip of her tongue to plead the boy's case. As the horse and cart turned away, she gave a last glance over her shoulder. Will was already inside, the door slamming shut behind him.

"Does Will's uncle really need his help so badly there's no time at all for school?"

Gray shrugged. "Dolph VanderSleet has a hard life for

a farmer. He had only one daughter, and she's living in Ohio now. His wife died four, five years ago. He wasn't expecting to raise his brother's boy."

"Wouldn't you think he'd be thrilled to have someone to keep him company and chase away the loneliness?"

Gray kept a steady hand on the reins as they rolled across the freshly cut field. "Some might. And some, like Dolph, see only the work involved. To them, everything in life is a burden instead of a joy."

A burden.

The thought of it had Fiona clasping her hands together as she pictured in her mind the boy who had worked so willingly alongside her these past days. It had been his skill that had made the start of school possible, and now he wouldn't be allowed to share in the joy of it. That knowledge dulled the keen edge of excitement that had been building inside her.

As if sensing her sadness the hound began licking her hand until she reached over to scratch behind his ears.

Gray shot her a sideways glance. "You're spoiling Chester, you know."

That brought the smile back to her lips. "Do you mind?"

"Not at all. But you might, when he starts shadowing you every time you walk out the door."

"That might not be so bad." She laughed and took the dog's big head between her hands, while rubbing her cheek over his soft muzzle.

Seeing it, Gray went very still, wondering what that soft cheek would feel like against his mouth. That had him frowning and wiping a damp hand across his shirt. He turned the team toward the barn. Once inside he climbed down, then reached a hand to assist Fiona, before turning away abruptly to begin unhitching the horses.

"Goodbye, Chester." She gave the hound one last pat on the head before heading toward the house.

Gray stood beside his dog, watching the way the breeze flattened her skirts against her backside. Then, embarrassed by the direction of his thoughts, he returned his attention to the chore at hand, cursing softly under his breath.

FIONA AWOKE AND lay in the darkness, listening to the stillness of the night. A fresh breeze was stirring the curtains, and she was grateful for the fresh air that cooled the room.

The pork sausage they'd enjoyed for supper had given her a thirst. Sitting up in bed she reached for the pitcher on her nightstand, only to find it empty. With a sigh she got to her feet and picked up the pitcher before crossing to the door.

Following a trail of moonlight across the parlor, she let herself into the kitchen and moved toward the pump that stood at the sink.

"What's this?"

A deep voice caused her to freeze in midstride.

"Flem?" She whirled, and the pitcher slipped from her fingers.

He caught it before it could shatter on the floor, and in one quick motion set it aside. When he straightened, his gaze slid over her, taking in the spill of tangles falling over the neck of her prim cotton nightgown and her bare toes peeking out from beneath the hem of her skirt.

Seeing the way her face flamed, a teasing light came into his eyes. "If I'd known my teacher could look like this, I'd have paid more attention to learning my sums."

"What are you doing up at such an hour, Flem?" She took a step back. "And fully dressed?"

"Such keen powers of observation, Miss Downey." He deliberately stepped closer, causing her to back up again.

"How can I think about staying home and sleeping when there's fun to be had in town?"

"What sort of fun?"

He jammed his hands into his pockets and rocked back on his heels. "Some of the farmers from over the hill in Little Bavaria like to get together and play cards. I'm always happy to relieve them of some of their seed money."

"You play cards for money?"

"You bet." He drew a hand from his pocket and held up a wad of bills. "I'm good at it. See?"

She shook her head. "So much money. Your papa will be so happy to see that."

"Who says I'll show him?"

"You aren't going to share it with your family?"

He gave a low rumble of laughter. "Why should I? What did they do to earn it? Besides, I'd have to admit where it came from, and my poor dear mother would be shocked to learn that her son has engaged in the devil's own work."

"But they could use that money, Flem."

"And you think I can't?"

"What will you do with it?"

"Spend it on things that give me pleasure. That's all money's good for. Didn't you know? Some day I'll use it to take me far away from this miserable hellhole."

Stunned at his choice of words, she merely looked at him.

"Of course, my old hometown is looking a lot better these days. Now that I see how good you look without all those layers of clothing . . ." His hand snaked out, snagging her wrist. "Maybe I could be persuaded to stay at home more often and take my pleasure right here."

She gasped at the stench of his breath and drew back as though slapped. "You've been drinking."

"How very astute, teacher. I'm shocked that you even know what whiskey smells like."

"I've smelled it a time or two, when some of Da's friends paid a call."

His voice lowered with sarcasm. "I suppose your saintly parents would never think to take a sip of spirits. Nor would their perfect daughter."

She stared down at his hand holding firmly to her wrist. "Let me go, Flem."

"What's the matter, Miss Downey? Don't tell me you don't like being touched by a man."

"I don't."

"Liar." He leaned close, his hot breath stinging her cheek. "All women like it, though most of them think they have to pretend not to. It's a game they play."

"It's not a game I'd play. Let me go, Flem, or I'll shout down the entire household."

His smile grew. A smile that had once been charming now caused a tiny thread of alarm to begin twisting along her spine. "No you won't, teacher. And do you know why? Because you're smart enough to know it would cause a scandal, and after Ma was through with all her bluster, you'd be the one to lose your precious job."

He could see at once that he'd hit a nerve. Pressing his advantage, he caught her roughly by the shoulders. Before he could draw her close she kicked him as hard as she could in the ankle.

He swore. But instead of releasing her as she'd hoped, his two hands closed around her throat, and he shoved her against the wall before lowering his face to hers. Against her mouth he muttered, "You'll pay for that."

With a little cry Fiona fought back. Her fingernails raked his cheek, causing him to swear again.

"Why you little—"

Before he could retaliate, he was abruptly yanked away. While Fiona watched in stunned surprise, Gray hurled his brother to the floor. Flem tried to scramble out of his reach but Gray caught him by the front of his shirt and hauled him to his feet, landing a punch in his gut that had him falling to the floor and grunting in pain. With a hiss of fury Gray hauled him upright again.

Seeing Gray's fist raised, Flem held up both hands to protect his face. "No. Don't. I guess I got a little drunk. I didn't mean anything by it."

Gray's voice trembled with a black, blinding rage. "You'll apologize to Miss Downey."

Flem lifted his head and even managed a shaky smile. "I'm sorry, Miss Downey. Truly I am. It wasn't me. It was the whiskey."

Gray gave him a rough shove backwards, where he bumped into the wall and dropped to one knee. Fiona could do nothing more than gape at Flem as he touched a hand to his cheek. Seeing blood on his fingers, he muttered an oath and got to his feet, eager to escape.

Gray thought about going after his brother and pummeling him. It was what Flem deserved. But at the moment, Fiona's welfare was uppermost in his mind.

He turned to her. "Are you all right?"

She nodded, afraid to trust her voice.

"He didn't . . . hurt you?"

She was too close to tears to speak. Instead she merely shook her head.

"I'm glad I got here in time." Seeing her distress, he walked to the pump and filled a tumbler with water.

Fiona was aware that he'd dressed hurriedly, pulling the suspenders of his overalls over his bare chest. His feet, too, were bare, and his hair was mussed, falling over his forehead in a dark spill that gave him a decidedly dangerous look. It was a side of Gray she'd never imagined. For those few moments this gentle farmer had been like a man possessed. Now, though she sensed he was still in a state of high agitation, there was a cautious gentleness to him, as well.

"Drink this." He pressed the glass to her hands and she obediently emptied it.

He set the glass aside and took her hands in his. Despite the heat of the evening they were cold as ice. "You should get to bed now."

"I should. Yes. Thank you, Gray. That's little enough to say. I don't know what I'd have done if you hadn't—"

They both looked up as the door to the kitchen was thrust open and Rose halted in the doorway, her eyes as dark with fury as Gray's had been just moments earlier. In silence she took in the sight of the two of them, standing so close together, Fiona's hands firmly nestled in Gray's.

"So this is how you thank me for my hospitality." She looked Fiona up and down with a hiss of disgust. "I am shocked at your lack of proper demeanor. No decent young lady would allow herself to be seen by a man in this state of undress."

"Mrs. Haydn, it isn't what you think—"

"Not a word. I'm too offended by the sight of you to listen to anything you have to say. Go to your room. I'll decide later whether or not you can be trusted to remain in my home."

"You have to permit me to explain. It wasn't Gray. He was the one who came to my rescue when . . ." Fiona turned to Gray, who was staring at his mother with a look so dark, it frightened her.

Instead of adding to Fiona's explanation he merely nodded toward the door. "Go now." When she looked as though she might argue he said more firmly, "Go."

Reluctantly Fiona turned away. As she hurried toward her room she could hear Rose's clipped words, uttered with venom. "I am not surprised, Grayson. This is exactly the behavior I would expect from you."

Fiona closed the door, shutting off whatever Gray might have said in reply. For a moment she was forced to slump against her bed, fearing her legs might fail her. Her breath was coming in short, painful gasps as she replayed that ugly scene in the kitchen.

Had she overreacted? After all, Flem always seemed harmless enough, with that quick wit and boyish charm. Hadn't he said he was drunk? Why then had she felt as though she'd been fighting for her very life?

Da had often called her his dramatic little actress. Perhaps, in the light of day, this would all seem like a harmless prank.

Still, her heart ached for Gray. Why did Rose constantly berate him, while glossing over Flem's glaring faults? Why was she so quick to believe the worst about one son, while refusing to see any flaws whatever in the other?

Hearing silence settle once more over the house, Fiona got unsteadily to her feet and crossed to the door. Whether Flem's little scene had been harmless or not, she intended to take no chances. She placed a small table holding a basin and pitcher against the door, reasoning that if the door should be forced open in the night, it would cause the pitcher to topple, waking her and everyone else in the household.

Even as she crawled into bed, Fiona was again questioning her sanity. Surely here in this simple farmhouse, living with the family, which stationmaster Gerhardt Shultz had called one of the finest families in Paradise Falls, she was safe from any sort of harm. Of course she was, she reminded herself, over and over again like a litany, as sleep gradually overtook her.

But it was a troubled sleep, filled with dark, disturbing dreams that left her with a vague sense of foreboding.

SIX

❖━◆━❖

FIONA AWOKE TO the sound of frantic activity. Rose stood in the parlor shouting up the stairs. The heavy tramping of feet down the stairs was followed by the rumble of a wagon rolling up to the backdoor.

Minutes later, when Fiona stepped from her room, Rose was in the kitchen, busily wrapping food in linen towels. This day she wore a simple gray gown with a white collar and cuffs. Her hair was pinned in its usual knot at her nape, but over this was a black hat.

Fiona waited for the scolding she anticipated, to be followed by an order for her immediate departure from this house. Instead Rose seemed distracted by her chores. She looked up only long enough to say, "We leave for church as soon as Grayson has Broderick ready."

"You . . . want me to accompany your family to church, Mrs. Haydn?" Fiona struggled to breathe.

"You're the town's teacher, aren't you? You'll be expected to attend services whenever the weather permits."

Rose picked up another towel and carefully wrapped a steaming cake. "Once a month, in fair weather, there is a meal in the churchyard after the service."

Minutes later Flem stepped into the kitchen, whistling a little tune. When he caught sight of Fiona he merely grinned. "Better fetch your bonnet. The wagon's ready to roll."

Rose looked up, then fixed her younger son with a look. "What've you done to your cheek, Fleming?"

"Scratched it on the branch of that old sycamore." He picked up a linen-covered dish. "I'll take that, Ma. Too heavy for you."

When he sauntered away, Rose shook her head. "Men. He probably didn't even think to put witch hazel on it."

She glanced over at Fiona who was standing as still as a statue. "Didn't you hear? Get your bonnet. It's time to go."

Puzzled by this strange turn of events, Fiona hurried toward her room, snatching up her bonnet and a packet of letters for her mother before heading toward the waiting wagon.

In the kitchen Flem was waiting for her. Seeing him, she skidded to a halt.

He merely grinned. "Don't worry, teacher. Ma decided you were just getting a drink of water last night."

"And how did you explain your condition?"

"My condition?" He merely laughed. "You forget. I wasn't even here, teacher. I was already tucked up in my bed. Now let's go before Ma gets her feathers ruffled again."

Fiona followed him outside. She'd been anticipating censure. Instead, she was now being treated like one of the family. She ought to be relieved, but the incident had left her with a sense of unease.

Gray had managed to get his father into the back, where Broderick sat surrounded by cushions and colorful quilts. It was clear, from the high color on the older man's cheeks, that he was embarrassed to be riding alone in the back of the wagon like a sack of grain.

Taking pity on him, Fiona climbed in beside him.

Rose shot her an angry look. "It isn't fitting for the teacher to arrive for her first introduction to the townspeople in the back of a wagon like some helpless cripple."

Seeing one side of Broderick's mouth twist into a snarl, Fiona took his hand and squeezed. "I think we look more like a king on his throne, accompanied by his loyal servant."

That had his frown turning into a lopsided grin. "A king is it?" After a moment's thought he nodded. "I like that."

As soon as Flem and Rose climbed up to the hard seat Gray flicked the reins and the team took off at a fast clip.

Fiona held one hand on her bonnet to keep it from sailing away on the breeze.

As they passed the neighboring farms, Rose had a word for each.

"There's Herman Vogel working his fields instead of honoring the Lord's Day." This was said with a sniff of displeasure.

Gray's hands tightened on the reins. "I think the Lord will understand since Herman has no family left to give him a hand."

Rose ignored her son's comment. "Carl Gustav's fields are looking as sad as his front yard." She shielded her eyes with her hand. "Is Greta Gunther wearing that same old gown? You'd think just once she could make herself something new." She looked down on the old woman who was walking along the side of the road.

To her surprise Gray brought the wagon to a halt and climbed down. "Morning, Mrs. Gunther. May I offer you a ride to church?"

The old woman smiled, revealing a gap where her front

teeth had once been. "Why, thank you, Grayson." She walked to the rear of the wagon and stared at the stranger seated beside Broderick. "Our new teacher?"

Fiona offered her hand as Gray lifted the old woman into the back beside her. "Fiona Downey, Mrs. Gunther."

"Downey? What sort of name is that, my dear?"

"She's Irish," Flem called from his perch beside his mother.

"What a pity." The old woman turned her attention to the man beside Fiona. "How are you feeling, Broderick?"

"None the worse for wear. And you, Greta?"

She peered at him over the rim of her spectacles. "I believe this is the first time I've ever seen you happy at the prospect of attending Sunday services."

He managed a wink at Fiona before turning to his neighbor. "This is the first time I've ever arrived at church like a king in all my regal splendor."

Greta shouted above the clip-clop of the horses' hooves. "Has the stroke affected Broderick's brain now, Rose?"

"Not that I've noticed." Rose adjusted her hat as they rolled along the main road of town toward the church. "But then, how would we know? He's been crazy as a loon for years."

Fiona caught another wink from the old man as they came to a stop in front of the simple wooden building where families had begun to congregate.

While Gray helped his father and the two women from the back of the wagon, Flem and Rose walked arm in arm through the crowd, hurrying forward to talk to the minister.

"Reverend Schmidt, come meet our new teacher, Fiona Downey."

"Miss Downey." The man in the simple black suit accepted her handshake. "I hope you don't mind if I introduce you from the pulpit?"

"If you think it's proper, Reverend Schmidt."

"I do. There's a good deal of curiosity about you."

There was no time for anything more, since the church was already filling up quickly. Rose led the way, with Flem beside her. Broderick leaned heavily on Gray's arm as they started up the aisle. Trailing behind the Haydn family, Fiona could feel the stares of the congregation, and could hear their whispered remarks.

"I heard Mrs. Haydn say that was the new teacher."

"So young. I expected someone older, more respectable, like Miss Hornby."

"This one certainly doesn't look like a teacher."

"From the looks of her, she probably won't last a year."

"Lucky if she lasts a month."

"So thin. Do the Irish starve their young?"

"Too pretty to have a brain in that head."

By the time Rose had led her family all the way to the very front of the church, Fiona's cheeks were blazing. She had only to look around her to see how different she looked from all the other young women. Big, sturdy farm women with plump cheeks and ample bosoms, who stood head and shoulders above her, and all with pale yellow hair tied neatly beneath their bonnets. She was even more aware of her small stature and hair as dark and wild as a gypsy's.

She was grateful to reach her seat. Her relief was short-lived, however, when Flem stood aside and waited until she was seated before settling in beside her. She gave an involuntary shiver at the brush of his shoulder to hers and was reminded once more of their previous night's encounter. Had she only imagined danger? Here, in this house of worship, it didn't seem possible for him to be anything more than a harmless handsome charmer.

With the first strains of the organ, everyone got to their feet.

Flem opened his hymnbook and stuck it in front of Fiona, forcing her to take hold of the other side. When he started to sing, she realized he had a lovely voice— and was only too happy to show it off.

When the hymn ended, they took their seats and the minister mounted the steps to address the congregation. His voice was deep and rich, and he began by asking those gathered this day to join him in offering a warm welcome to their new teacher.

Fiona got hesitantly to her feet and turned to smile at the strangers who were craning their necks to get a good look.

"If you'd step up here, Miss Downey."

Fiona knew her cheeks were as red as apples and prayed that she wouldn't stumble as she made her way up the steps to where the minister stood.

"Our town is grateful to you, Miss Downey, for we've been three years now without a teacher for our children."

"I'm the one who is grateful, Reverend Schmidt. Now that the school is properly restored, thanks to the help of young Will VanderSleet." She looked around, hoping she might coax Will to stand and be acknowledged. Seeing no sign of him she continued, "I'm looking forward to meeting all the children of Paradise Falls tomorrow morning."

When she returned to her seat Flem made a great show of stepping aside to allow her to enter the Haydn pew. It occurred to Fiona that several young women in the congregation actually sighed aloud at the mere sight of him, which deepened his smile considerably.

There was no time to dwell on such things, as the minister began invoking heavenly blessings on the crops being harvested, on the members who had requested prayers for health, for birth, for death, before embarking on a rather long-winded sermon about the wrath of God upon any who would knowingly break the Commandments.

Flem leaned close to whisper, "Do you think God keeps a tally up in heaven?"

Fiona could see the preacher watching them and lowered her gaze, hoping to discourage Flem, but he wasn't to be sidetracked. "I'm betting He figures four days for swearing. A week for stealing. I'm not sure about coveting my neighbor's wife. But I do think it'd be years in the fiery furnace for anyone who committed adultery. What do you think, teacher?"

Fiona was scandalized by his obvious mockery. Still, she could feel laughter bubbling up inside and had to bite hard on her lip to keep it from curving into a grin.

Seeing that his humor was having the desired effect, Flem leaned closer. "If all men's wives looked like our pastor's wife, there'd be no need to threaten hell."

Fiona followed his gaze to the huge woman in the flowing black gown who was seated at the organ. She seemed to have no neck. Instead, there were layers of chins, each jiggling from side to side as she kept time to some imaginary music in her head.

Fiona barely managed to stifle the laugh that billowed up and erupted in a hiccup.

Rose glanced over with a flash of anger.

Instead of heeding his mother's dark warning, Flem pressed the issue. He pretended to pick up the hymnal while whispering, "But if all women looked like Schuyler Gable's new bride across the aisle, I might be willing to risk a few years of hellfire."

Fiona looked up just in time to see a pretty young woman nod to Flem with a smile and a blush before linking her arm with that of the young farmer beside her.

Seeing Fiona's look of stern disapproval, Flem merely winked. "She can't hold a candle to you, teacher."

At his boldness Fiona couldn't hold back the little gasp that escaped. Hearing it, Rose turned and fixed her with a look. When Fiona dared to glance at Flem, he was staring at the preacher with a look of rapt interest. She marveled at how quickly he could change from prankster to devoted follower in the blink of an eye.

As the service continued, Fiona folded her hands primly in her lap and struggled to blot out any distractions, but her mind refused to settle, choosing instead to flit about like a leaf on the wind. From all that she'd observed, there was much more to the town's most admired family than she'd first thought. There was so much anger in Rose, all of it directed at her husband and older son. Fiona had no doubt she would taste that anger as well if she weren't careful to walk a very fine line. Then there was Broderick. The limitations caused by his stroke were bound to affect him. Having to bear the scorn of his wife would surely add to his burden, and it was plain that he and his second son had a prickly relationship. Not that she couldn't understand it. It was obvious that Flem lacked the will to help with even the most basic of chores. What was worse, he seemed to have mastered the art of deception. Here he was, staring at the preacher as though lost in his sermon, when she doubted he was hearing a single word of it. Not that she wasn't guilty of the same offense. She struggled to follow the sermon, but her mind refused.

What was most puzzling to Fiona was Grayson Haydn's position in this family. Though he worked from sun up to sundown, and also shouldered the care of his father, none of this seemed to satisfy his mother. Had something happened in the past to cause this chasm between them? Yet Rose found nothing lacking in her younger son's demeanor. If anything, she seemed determined to gloss over Flem's flaws while seeking out those same flaws in Gray.

Fiona was startled at the sound of shuffling feet as the congregation rose for a final blessing and song before fil-

ing out of the church and spilling into the late morning
sunshine.

In no time the men had set up long wooden planks in
the churchyard, which were soon covered with platters of
sausage and ham, stuffed goose and baked chicken, baskets of bread and biscuits, as well as cakes, pies, and
assorted sweets. After a blessing over the food, there was
a well-ordered parade of families filling their plates and
seeking the shade of several large oaks where blankets
had been spread on the grass.

While women exchanged gossip and family matters,
the men spoke of their crops and speculated on the coming
autumn, and children, happy to finally escape the confines
of church, chased each other in games of tag and hide-
and-seek. The late summer air was filled with their shrieks
of laughter.

Fiona caught glimpses of Flem passing among the tables, flirting openly with the young women. Gray remained on the fringe of the crowd, talking quietly with a
few of his neighbors.

Before Fiona could finish her meal, Rose beckoned her
with a terse command. "It's time you met the right people
here in Paradise Falls."

Fiona set aside her plate and dutifully followed Rose
to where the minister stood talking with several couples.
They looked up with interest when the two women approached.

Rose handled the introductions. "Miss Downey, this is
Reverend Schmidt's wife, Brunhilde."

"Mrs. Schmidt."

After an abrupt handshake, Fiona felt the woman's curious stare.

"You already met Gerhardt Schultz at the train station.
This is his wife, Louise."

"Mrs. Schultz."

Again a quick handshake, with no smile to accompany it.

Fiona turned to the stationmaster. "Would you mind giving these to the conductor, the next time the train comes through town? They're letters to my mother." *Letters.* Such a simple word for the outpourings of her heart, which had gone into every sentence. Fiona had gone to great pains to describe the town, the farms, and the Haydn family, leaving out anything that might be cause for concern, and assuring her mother that her only child had been warmly embraced by these strangers.

"I don't mind." Gerhardt Schultz tucked the envelopes carefully into his breast pocket before turning toward the young couple that had joined them.

Rose handled the introductions. "This is Schuyler Gable and his wife Charlotte. Our new teacher."

"Mr. and Mrs. Gable."

For the first time, Fiona saw the hint of a smile as the young woman offered her hand. "Please call me Charlotte."

"Thank you. My given name is Fiona. Do you have any children who will be attending school?"

"Not yet. But soon, we hope." The young wife cast a sideways look at her husband, whose face flamed under the scrutiny of his neighbors.

As Rose led Fiona toward another group of people she said under her breath. "It's best not to ask such personal questions of those you're meeting for the first time."

"Of course." Chastised, Fiona followed meekly along as she was introduced to so many people, her head was soon swimming.

"This is Emily Trewe, who owns a millinery shop here in Paradise Falls." Rose touched a hand to her hat. "She made this one. And my Christmas hat as well. This is Dr. Simpson Eberhardt."

"Doctor." Fiona gave the bearded man a smile and was

about to say something more when she spotted the old man and boy from the train. "Oh. Excuse me. I see someone I must speak with."

While the others watched, she hurried over to extend her hand to the old man. "I was hoping I'd run into you again. I'm Fiona Downey, the new teacher."

At once the old man whipped his hat from his head and accepted her handshake with a slight bow. "Frederick Dorf. And this is my grandson, Luther, who has just come to live with me."

"Luther." Fiona dimpled. "Will I see you at school tomorrow?"

The boy shot a questioning look at the old man, who nodded. "You will indeed, Miss Downey."

Fiona dropped down to her knees in the grass, so that her eyes were level with the little boy's. "Have you ever been to school before, Luther?"

Too shy to speak, the boy merely shook his head.

"I think you'll be pleasantly surprised, Luther. I'm going to do all in my power to make it an enjoyable experience."

"Thank you, Miss Downey." The old man dropped a hand on his grandson's shoulder and began to back away. "It's kind of you to include us. I'll see that Luther is there."

Before she could say more, he turned and melted into the crowd.

Puzzled, Fiona turned to see what had caused him to end their meeting so abruptly.

Rose stood behind her wearing a scowl that darkened all her features. "Why were you talking to Frederick Dorf?"

"He and his grandson were on the train. They accompanied me on the last miles of my journey here."

"Bringing an innocent child to live such a life." Rose gave her customary sniff of disapproval. "I told you I wanted you to meet the right people here in town. You would do well to remember that you get but one chance to make a first impression."

"What have I done wrong, Mrs. Haydn?"

"You turned your back on my friends to speak to a man who is . . . beneath us."

"In what way?"

The older woman gave a shrug of her shoulders. "There are people who work the land and provide for their families, and then there are those who do not. Come. It's time we started home. Our chores won't get done while we dawdle here."

Fiona followed her to the wagon, where Broderick was already seated in back. Gray hurried over to assist her into the back beside his father, while Flem helped his mother climb to the seat. When all were aboard, Gray flicked the reins and with a creak of leather, they moved smartly onto the road.

As they left the churchyard behind, Fiona studied the blur of faces. It would take a while to sort them out, but she'd made a good start. She ought to be grateful to Rose Haydn for taking the time to introduce her to so many of her friends. Still, Fiona felt a vague sense of unease. She would have much preferred to meet these people without Rose's harsh judgment. It was, after all, what she wanted for herself as well.

She decided to put aside, as much as possible, any preconceived notions about the families of her students and concentrate instead on starting tomorrow with a clean slate.

A clean slate.

She wanted desperately to make a difference in these young lives.

Oh, Da, please give me some of your wisdom.

"Still praying? I'd have thought you'd had enough of that in church."

Hearing Broderick's guttural voice she glanced over to see him studying her with that lopsided smile.

She hadn't even realized that she'd clasped her hands together. Embarrassed, she wiped damp palms on her skirt. "I think I'll need more than prayers to get me through my first day of school."

He lay a hand over hers. Patted awkwardly. "It's going to be fine. You'll see."

"I wish I had your confidence." Despite her doubts, she realized that just having this old man's hand on hers helped ease her fears, at least for the moment.

Almost as though her da was right here beside her.

SEVEN

FIONA STOOD BY the window staring at the darkness beyond and praying it would soon be dawn. She'd been awake for hours, her stomach in knots, her mind awhirl with dozens of thoughts, all of them unsettling.

It had rained shortly after she'd retired to her bed, and she worried that torrential rains would keep the students away from their first day of school. When the rain finally stopped, she latched onto other fears. This was harvest time, and many of the children in Paradise Falls were needed to work the fields. Some desperate farmers, like Dolph VanderSleet, would never consent to their children leaving their chores to attend school. Others, like Frederick Dorf, might be too poor to permit more than an occasional visit to the classroom.

Then there were the children. Some had never been to school. The rest hadn't been there for three years. What were their expectations? Their fears? She wanted to make learning enjoyable, but first she had to get them to step inside the school and leave their fears behind.

Now she must do the same, she reminded herself sternly.

She began to pace, determined to put aside these demons that tormented her. She thought about her father. About the fierce determination that had driven him, first to the shores of a new land, and then from the lowliest jobs he could find, to the one that had brought him such pride and joy.

How had one man, with his thick brogue and stern demeanor, unlocked the key to making his students in this country love and respect him? What magic did he possess?

Oh, Da. Help me reach out to these strangers. Help me to show them the pleasure that can come with knowledge.

By the time the first pale ribbons of dawn streaked the sky, Fiona was washed and dressed and hurrying toward the kitchen.

"Morning." When she stepped through the doorway, Broderick set aside his coffee and gave her a lopsided smile. "Did you get any sleep?"

"A little." At his steady look she managed a weak shake of her head. "Very little."

"There's biscuits and coffee."

She touched a hand to her middle. "I couldn't eat a thing."

"Nerves that bad, are they?"

She nodded.

They both looked up as Gray paused to scrape mud and dung from his boots before stomping into the room.

He glanced at Fiona before picking up a mug of coffee. He turned to his father. "Won't be able to cut today. Too wet."

Broderick nodded. "So I noticed."

It was then that Fiona realized the older man had

shucked his boots, leaving them turned upside down to dry beside the stove. "You started your chores early today."

He merely nodded and continued to sip his coffee.

"Well." When he offered nothing more she turned to Gray. "I'd best start off to the schoolhouse."

"I can take you."

She was already shaking her head. "You said it's too wet to cut. There's no point in going all that way just for me."

"I don't mind." He set down his mug and lay a hand on his father's shoulder. "I'll be back soon to give you a hand in the barn."

The old man nodded.

Fiona followed Gray out the door. The team was already hitched, and as Gray helped her up to the seat, she spied a bouquet of flowers on the hard wooden bench.

"What's this?"

He climbed up beside her and took up the reins. At once Chester was between them, with his front paws resting on Fiona's lap. "Papa picked them for you."

"Your father?"

Gray flicked the reins and the team started across the yard. "He hoped it would ease your worry some."

She lifted the bouquet to her face to hide the tears that sprang to her eyes. "They're beautiful."

And they were. Wild daisies, both white and yellow, pretty pink asters, bluebells, and dahlias as big as dinner plates in every color imaginable. A bouquet so big it filled her arms. And her heart.

She looked over at Gray. "But how could your father pick all these? He would have needed some help."

Gray's lips twitched. "I didn't mind lending a hand. But the idea was Papa's."

Again Fiona was forced to duck her head to hide the rush of emotions.

They drove across the fields in silence. When they stopped at the school, Gray climbed down, then lifted his arms to help Fiona. For the space of a heartbeat she felt a sudden flash of heat, and wondered at the way the earth seemed to tilt as she was held in those big, solid hands.

He set her on her feet and reached for the lunch his mother had packed, handing it to her in silence.

As she turned away he cleared his throat. Fiona paused, keeping her back to him.

"You'll do just fine."

She looked over and absorbed a jolt at the way he was watching her. Feeling her cheeks redden she managed a smile. "Thank you, Gray. And thank your father for me. Each time I feel lost today, I'll look at these and remember his kindness. And yours."

He pulled himself up to the wagon and snapped the reins.

Fiona stood on the porch and watched until a sudden gust of wind had her stepping inside the schoolhouse. She was grateful for the dozens of chores to see to. She hoped they would be enough to keep her fears at bay.

FIONA WAS FEELING more than a little breathless. She'd swept the floor and polished the desktops until they gleamed, even though they were already sparkling. She'd hauled a bucket of water from the stream and filled a pitcher, which she'd set beside a basin on a little table in the outhouse. The rest of the water stood just inside the door of the schoolhouse, with a dipper beside it. The bouquet of wildflowers stood in a second bucket beside her desk. Their fragrance perfumed the room.

In large neat letters she wrote her name on a slate and placed it on her desk.

Her chores completed, she paced from her desk to the door, where she paused to peer about, hoping to hear the sound of a wagon or horse. Seeing and hearing nothing, she paced to her desk, then back again.

What if no one came?

The thought had her going rigid with fear. What if the townspeople had decided that she was too different, too . . . Irish, to be allowed to teach their children?

She pressed her hands to her hot cheeks and stared at the vast expanse of field and forest. Seeing no horse carts or wagons, no sign of children or adults, she let out a long, deep sigh and was just about to turn away when she spied something in the tall grass.

Was that a child's head? Or was she so desperate for a student, any student, that she'd conjured a vision in her mind?

While she watched she saw a figure straighten after retrieving something from the ground. Sunlight glinted off blonde hair as a boy of about ten sauntered toward the schoolhouse, holding a tin bucket in his hand.

A boy. Headed toward the school. Her heart gave a leap of joy before beginning a wild flutter in her chest. As she stepped out onto the porch she caught sight of a cluster of children on the horizon. And behind them, a horse cart bearing several more. They were coming. Her students.

For a moment she was so overcome she had to press a hand to her heart. Then, taking a deep breath, she smiled in welcome.

"Good morning. I am Miss Downey. What is your name?"

There was no answering smile. Only a frown as the boy took a step back from her. "Siegfried Gunther."

"Are you related to Greta Gunther?"

He gave a quick nod of his head. "That's my grandmother." He wrinkled his nose. "She lives with us. She sleeps in my room along with my baby sister."

Fiona thought of her poor mother, forced to share a

room with several nieces. Were they generous? Or did they resent the stranger who was now taking up space in their bed, as this boy seemed to? "I met your grandmother yesterday on the way to church." Fiona held the door. "Come in, Siegfried, and choose a place to sit."

She turned to the cluster of children just reaching the schoolyard and beckoned them inside. As each one entered Fiona introduced herself and asked them to do the same, repeating each name in her mind until it was committed to memory.

The last boy inside was the one who'd driven the pony cart. Taller than the others, taller even than Fiona, he had wind-tossed blonde hair and eyes so pale blue, they seemed made of ice. He took her measure as he brushed past her and walked to the back of the classroom.

Following his lead, the children became unusually quiet, the atmosphere strained as they shuffled about choosing a place to sit. Whenever they caught their new teacher looking at them they ducked their head and studied the floor.

Fiona stood at the front of the room and counted them. Eleven. Eleven students, eager to learn, to grow, to have their young minds challenged.

She wiped her hands down her skirts before picking up the slate from her desk. "This is how I spell my name." She angled it so that all could see. "Now I'll pass the slate around, and each of you may write your name. If you need help, let me know and we'll write your name together."

Fiona handed the slate to a little girl seated at the first desk. "Afton, do you know how to print your name?"

"Yes, Miss Downey," the girl said proudly. "My mama taught me how."

Though it seemed a great effort to press the chalk over the slate, Afton managed her name before holding it up for the others to see.

"That's very good, Afton." Fiona handed the slate to a boy seated behind her.

When the boy stumbled over the spelling of his name, the big boy whispered loudly enough for the entire class to hear. "Now you'll get it, Erik."

"The stick?" Erik visibly paled.

Seeing it, Fiona moved quickly to reassure him. "There is no stick in this classroom. Nor will there be."

"No stick?" The tall boy, whose name was Edmer Rudd, had chosen a seat in the very back of the room. He glanced around in surprise. "How will you make us behave?"

"I intend to appeal to your better nature."

He gave a rude snort. "Miss Hornby said nothing makes children behave like the sting of a switch to their backsides."

It was on the tip of Fiona's tongue to argue the point, but she knew that everything said this day would be repeated around supper tables tonight all over town. Folding her hands behind her back she stepped to the front of the room. "While in this classroom, we will live by the Golden Rule." She glanced around and saw that the children had gone very still, a look of puzzlement on their faces. "We will treat each other the way we would wish to be treated. If we make a mistake, or if we do something that hurts another, we will apologize and do our best to make things right. Can you agree to that?"

The children glanced around uneasily, and seemed to wait for Edmer's reaction. When he merely stared at her, Fiona cleared her throat.

"In time you'll see how easy it will be. My job is to teach you. Your job is to learn. If you don't understand something I've told you, you must let me know so that I can explain it better."

"And then you'll switch us?" Edmer said with barely concealed sarcasm.

When no one laughed, Fiona realized she had her work cut out for her. It would take patience, and a great deal of effort on her part, to persuade these children that she meant what she said. "Perhaps," she said as she sat at her desk, "we ought to go over a few of the rules."

Seeing the suspicion in their eyes she began. "If you wish to be excused to go to the outhouse, simply raise your hand at any time, and you may go."

Edmer gave a snort of laughter. "Miss Hornby used to make us wait until lunchtime. She said we were only using it as an excuse to get out of doing things we didn't like. If you let us go whenever we want, how will you know if we really need to go?"

"It's a matter of honor, Edmer. I expect each of you to know what's best, and to do it." Fiona glanced around. "I've placed a bucket of water, soap, and a towel to be used before returning to the classroom."

"Why?" one of the girls asked.

"So as not to spread germs."

"What's wrong with that? Most of us are German," someone shouted, to the delight of the others.

"So you are." Fiona chuckled. "But I'm talking about germs, not Germans. By washing our hands we can avoid some illnesses. I know you don't think about germs, but since it's one of my rules, I'll ask you to honor it." She pointed. "We have a bucket of water and a dipper there by the door. You are invited to drink whenever you feel thirsty. If anyone didn't bring a lunch, let me know. I have enough to share."

"You'd share your lunch?" Once again, Edmer sounded incredulous. "Miss Hornby used to make us go hungry, so we wouldn't forget a second time."

To hide her sense of outrage, Fiona brushed a speck of dust from her desk and gathered her thoughts. "Now that I'm your teacher, I'll be willing to share my lunch with anyone who has none." She took a deep breath. "I believe I'd like to begin by asking how many of you know how to read."

A few hands went up, and then a few more. Pleased, Fiona opened a book. "Who would like to go first?"

Since no one volunteered, that privilege went to Siegfried Gunther, who managed to stumble through the first page before Fiona thanked him for his efforts. "That was very nice, Siegfried. Now who would like to try?"

Overcoming their shyness of the new teacher, several hands went up and Fiona asked the little girl named Afton to take up where her classmate had left off.

As more of the students read aloud Fiona realized that these children had been denied even the most rudimentary of educations. Though they could manage a few basic words, they could barely work through anything complex.

She hid her disappointment and plunged in with a smile. "I believe we'll put away our reader for now and see how many of you understand sums."

That brought groans from the children until they realized that their teacher was as good as her word, helping them to add and subtract by using colorful stones that she'd collected from the stream, and which she now passed around.

By lunchtime, Fiona had managed to mentally divide the students into several groups, according to their age and ability. To spare their feelings, she decided that she would work on an individual basis with each of them until they'd had time to get into the rhythm of learning.

"Does everyone have a lunch?"

Seeing all the heads nodding, she pointed to the open door. "I believe, since it's such a lovely day, we'll eat in the grass."

Delighted, the children crossed the room to fetch their buckets and followed their teacher into the sunlight.

Fiona chose a spot in the shade of an old oak, and the children gathered around her, sitting cross-legged in the grass as they nibbled on home-baked bread and sharp cheese, hard-boiled eggs, and summer sausage.

She noticed that when Edmer chose a spot already taken by the boy named Erik, he merely stood scowling until Erik shuffled aside.

"While we eat, why don't you take turns telling me about yourselves." Fiona turned to young Luther Dorf, who sat with eyes averted, head down. "Luther, how old are you?"

He stared hard at the grass. "Seven."

"Do you have any brothers or sisters?"

He gave a solemn shake of his head.

"What about your parents?"

"They died when our house burned down. I live with my grandfather now." As he spoke, pale blonde wisps of hair dusted his forehead.

"I'm sorry, Luther." She realized that the boy's journey here, like her own, had been the result of great sadness. "Is your grandfather a farmer?"

"He's a peddler." Edmer announced it in a tone of voice that left no doubt that he considered such a thing far beneath farming. "He lives in a wagon," he added smugly.

Though it was on the tip of Fiona's tongue to remind the older boy about common courtesy, she refrained. Instead she kept her gaze steady on Luther. "It must be interesting to live in a wagon and visit so many towns and villages, Luther."

That had the little boy looking at her with big eyes. "Grandpapa says I'm a big help to him."

"How grand, Luther." Fiona could see the others looking on with interest. "Perhaps some day your grandfather could stop by our school and allow us to see just how the two of you make your living."

A smile bloomed in the little boy's eyes. "I could ask Grandpapa."

"Good. And I'll do the same. I'll speak with him the first chance I get." She glanced around at the children. "There's so much we have to learn."

"Even you, Miss Downey?" Afton looked puzzled.

"Especially me, Afton. While I'm teaching you what I know, you will all be teaching me."

Edmer gave a sneer, which the younger ones quickly imitated. "What are we supposed to teach a teacher?"

"For one thing, you can teach me about life in Paradise Falls. Everything here is new to me, just as the classroom is new to most of you." Fiona gathered up the linen towel and scattered the crumbs for the birds that were perched high above in the tree and was pleased to see some of her students do the same. Tucking the towel into her bucket, she stood and shook down her skirts. "I'll give you a few minutes to run and play, before we have to go back to the classroom."

"Play?"

For a moment the children seemed stunned by her words. Then, when they realized that she was serious, they raced off with shouts and shrieks of laughter and were soon caught up in a game of tag.

Elmer and some of the older children merely stood to one side and watched, refusing to join in the fun.

From her vantage point on the porch Fiona studied the two groups of children, sensing a wariness in the older ones. They'd been bullied by a teacher once, and it was far too soon for them to trust. But at least the youngest of her pupils seemed willing to take her at her word.

She sighed and turned away. For now, for this moment, the panic of the previous night was gone. Perhaps it was the fact that she was finally doing what she'd come here to do. Or perhaps it was merely ignorance of what lay ahead.

Whatever the reason, she felt a sense of calm about what she'd undertaken. There was no going back. Until the school year ended next summer, she was bound to this place, and to these people.

She had a long journey ahead of her. For better or worse, she was determined to stay the course.

EIGHT

———◆◆◆———

"CHILDREN." FIONA COULDN'T believe how quickly the day had flown. "It's time to head home."

Afton and Luther looked up from the slate, where they had been painstakingly printing their letters. The older students, engaged in a game of subtraction Fiona had devised using the river stones, did the same.

As they began collecting their empty lunch buckets and heading toward the door, Fiona followed. On the porch she called, "Will I see all of you tomorrow?"

"Hard to say." Edmer gave a negligent shrug as he moved past her, enjoying the fact that he was almost a head taller than his teacher. "Not if Papa needs me with the haying."

Several of the older children followed his lead, brushing past Fiona quickly and offering similar excuses.

She felt her heart stop. Had she made so little impact that they were already looking for reasons to stay home?

Luther paused and gave her a timid smile. "I'll be back, Miss Downey."

She could have wept. But all she said was, "I'm glad, Luther."

As he began running across the field to catch up with the others, Fiona cupped her hands to her mouth to shout, "I look forward to seeing all of you in the morning."

She stood watching until all but the tallest were hidden by the high grass. Turning away she began to straighten the classroom, wiping down the desktops and slate, emptying the bucket of water by the door, and another in the outhouse.

She eyed the bouquet of wildflowers and considered taking them home. The thought of Rose's disapproval stopped her. It would be better to keep them here in the classroom, where she could perhaps get another day of pleasure from them before they faded.

As she worked, her good nature was slowly restored, and with it, her optimism. The children would be here in the morning. At least most of them. She was certain of it.

Hearing the approach of a horse and wagon, she gave a little laugh and caught up her lunch pail. She couldn't wait to share every moment of this day with Gray. She pulled the door shut, latching it behind her, and turned with a bright smile.

"Flem." She managed to keep her smile in place, though just barely. "What are you doing here?"

"I've come to fetch you home." He leaned down and offered his hand, pulling her easily to the seat beside him.

Her hip brushed his, causing his smile to widen. "So. How many ears did you have to box, teacher?"

"Not a single one." She moved a little away and smoothed her skirts as the horse started off with a trot.

"I'm disappointed. I believe I'd better drop by one of these days and let your students know that it is their solemn duty to annoy their teacher."

"Is that what you did, Flem?"

His smile was quick and charming. "I left that for others. I was always the good boy. Can't you tell?"

She laughed. "I suspect you were very good at leading the others into mischief and then sitting back pretending to be innocent."

He put a hand to his heart in mock distress. "Is that what you think of me? You wound me deeply, Miss Downey. My poor heart may never be the same."

"Are you certain you have a heart, Flem?"

"What a thing to say. Feel the way it beats." He boldly grabbed her hand and held it to his chest. "Oh. Now you have it ticking like a runaway clock." He continued holding her hand, even when she tried to pull it away, enjoying the color that flooded her cheeks.

Fiona was laughing at his antics as they came up over a rise. Her smile faded when she caught sight of Gray kneeling in the dirt, struggling to lift a heavy beam from beneath his wagon. The wood appeared to have broken in two. The weight of it must have been staggering.

He'd unhitched the horse and turned it into a nearby field to graze. In the heat of the afternoon he'd removed his shirt before tackling the task at hand.

Seeing them, he lowered his burden to the ground and got to his feet, shrugging into his shirt before wiping his hands on his pants and walking toward them.

"Looks like that axle's broken," Flem called.

Gray barely flicked him a glance before turning to Fiona. "How was your first day?"

"Oh, it was grand, Gray. I've so much to tell you."

"You can tell him later." Flem flicked the reins, causing the horse to jerk. "I'd say he has his work cut out."

Gray had to step away quickly or be bumped.

As the horse and cart shot forward Flem shouted over his shoulder, "Better not dawdle, big brother. Ma won't like it if you're late for supper."

Fiona turned, about to say something, but she was forced to grasp the back of the hard wooden seat after Flem cracked the whip, sending them flying. She swallowed back her disappointment. She'd so wanted to share this day with Gray. But from the stormy look in his eyes, perhaps it was just as well Flem had come for her instead. Gray seemed in no mood to listen to her silly prattle when he had more important things to deal with.

"Is a broken axle a hard thing to repair?"

"Not if you have the proper tools."

"Does Gray have the proper tools?"

"I didn't ask."

"Shouldn't you have stayed and offered to help?"

"Help Gray?" That had Flem laughing. "Haven't you noticed? My big brother likes to do everything himself. I'd only be in the way."

"But it would seem that two could do the job much faster than one."

"Not if the one is Grayson Haydn. Haven't you heard? According to my father, Gray can walk on water."

Despite Flem's attempt at a joke, Fiona could hear the raw anger in his tone, but as if to prove her wrong, he shot her a boyish smile. As they drew near the barn, he leaned back and let the reins go slack. "I'd love to hear all about your first day at school, teacher."

She glanced over shyly. "Would you really, Flem, or are you just humoring me?"

"Of course I mean it. I want to hear everything." As they rolled into the barn he jumped down before reaching up to assist her. He allowed his hands to linger at her waist for a moment, until she stepped away. "Why don't you stay and keep me company while I unhitch the horse?"

She sighed, feeling the need to tell someone. The excitement of this day was building until she feared it would cause an explosion in her brain.

"Oh, Flem." She sat on a bale of hay and began telling him everything, from her first anxious moments, to the smile given her by Luther at the end of the day.

"If I'd known you were so keen on shy boys, I'd have shown you my true self. I'm really quite shy, you know."

"You don't even know the meaning, Flem. Now let me tell you about Edmer. I think he may turn out to be my biggest challenge of all."

"Then a word of warning, teacher. Edmer Rudd's father, Christian, is one of the richest and most powerful men in Paradise Falls. You'd be wise to treat his son with care."

"I'll not treat Edmer differently than any of my other students, Flem. That wouldn't be fair."

"Fair? Why would you think life would be fair?" Seeing the firm press of her mouth, he shrugged. "Suit yourself. But remember that I warned you. Now, tell me all about Edmer and the others."

Fiona was still talking as they crossed the yard and entered the house. In the kitchen Rose looked up in annoyance at the sound of Fiona's animated voice. At once her young houseguest fell silent.

Flem breathed deeply, turning all his attention to his mother to placate her. "Something smells wonderful."

"I made your favorite. *Roggenmischbrot,* along with roast beef and biscuits."

In an aside to Fiona, Flem translated. "That's sourdough rye bread."

Rose studied her son. "Where have you been?"

"I was heading back from town and offered our teacher a ride home. A good thing. Gray's taking his sweet time out along the south road. If he's not careful, he'll be late for supper."

Fiona shot him a look. When he didn't bother to explain, she said quickly, "Gray can hardly help taking his time, since he's working on a broken axle."

Rose's lips thinned. "Broken axle or no, I'll not hold supper for him. Nor for your father. Where is that man?"

Flem shrugged. "He wasn't in the barn."

"I haven't seen him all afternoon." Rose moved around the table, snapping down plates, knives, forks, spoons as though they were too hot to hold.

Fiona felt a quick rush of alarm. "With his condition he can't have gone far. Perhaps we should go look for him."

"He knows his way home." Rose set down a milk pitcher with a clatter.

"But he may have fallen." Without a thought to where she might begin, Fiona was already out the backdoor when she heard Rose's voice lifted in protest. Ignoring it, she raced toward the barn. Finding it empty, she hurried on toward the smaller sheds beyond, where pigs rooted in the mud and chickens clucked.

"Mr. Haydn. Mr. Haydn." She danced from shed to shed, shoving open doors and peering around before rushing off to the next.

She was halfway across an open field when she heard the sound of a horse and wagon racing up behind her. Seeing that it was Gray, she paused and waited until he pulled up alongside her.

"No one has seen your father all afternoon."

"I just heard when I got home." He offered a hand, lifting her up beside him on the hard wooden seat. As they crossed the field, Gray kept watch in one direction while Fiona studied the other. Because the hay hadn't yet been cut in this field, it was impossible to see beyond the wall of grain for more than a few feet in any direction. Fiona knew that if Broderick had fallen, he would be impossible to find, unless they should hear his voice.

"Mr. Haydn." Cupping her hand to her mouth she shouted into the wind. It snatched her words away as quickly as they were spoken.

"There." Gray pointed at a faint trail, barely visible in the tall stalks. "Someone's been walking."

Turning the horse, he stood up while holding the reins, then suddenly drew back, bringing the horse and cart to an abrupt halt.

They both spotted Broderick at the same moment. He was lying face down, cushioned only by the grain that lay crushed beneath him.

Gray was beside him in an instant, rolling the older man over and checking for a pulse. Fiona saw the relief on Gray's face when his father moaned slightly.

"Where . . . ?" Completely disoriented, Broderick struggled to see who was holding him.

"It's me, Papa." Gray wrapped his arms around his father, rocking him as though he were a child.

"Where . . . are . . . we?"

"The east field. How did you get here?"

His father shook his head. "I was . . . walking. Don't remember."

"When I discovered you missing, I came looking for you. So did Miss Downey."

"Our teacher?" The old man looked up at Fiona, who was kneeling beside them. "I hope I haven't spoiled . . . first day of school."

"Finding you has just made it perfect, Mr. Haydn."

Broderick gave a deep sigh. "I wanted to prove I could . . . walk. Don't remember anything else."

"It doesn't matter now, Papa. I have you. You're safe." Gray struggled to his feet, still cradling his father to his chest. When he reached the wagon he settled the old man gently in the back.

Without a word Fiona climbed in beside him and caught his hands in hers. They were trembling.

"You'll be home soon, Mr. Haydn. Hold onto me until we get there." She wasn't aware that she was crying.

Great scalding tears that rolled down her cheeks and dampened the front of her dress.

Only Gray noticed. He stood a moment, watching the two of them. Then he pulled himself up to the seat and caught the reins. Keeping the horse to a walk, so as not to jostle his father, he headed toward the farmhouse in the distance.

His eyes, narrowed in thought, were hot with a combination of fury and fear.

"HERE, PAPA." GRAY lifted his father from the back of the wagon and strode toward the back porch. Before he was halfway up the steps Fiona raced ahead to hold open the door.

Inside, Rose and Flem looked up from the table.

"What's this?" Rose sprang up, nearly knocking back her chair in her haste.

Gray swept past her and carried his father to the parlor, where he deposited him on the sofa before tucking an afghan around him.

"Tell me what happened." Rose stood behind Gray, who continued to kneel beside his father, vigorously rubbing the old man's hands between both of his until he could feel some heat begin to be restored.

"We found him in the east field, where he'd fallen."

"So far from home?" Rose glanced at Flem, who was standing at the head of the sofa, watching his brother minister to their father. "How can this be?" She pushed Gray aside and sat on the edge of the sofa. "Whatever were you thinking, Broderick?"

Gray closed a hand around her wrist. "Leave him be, Ma. He's too tired right now. He needs to rest."

"What about what I need?" Agitated, she gave her husband's shoulder a rough shake. "You could have died out there, Broderick. Is that what you wanted? To die all alone, never to be found?"

"What do you care?" The old man's eyes opened and he fixed her with a steely look. "Would it matter? Would you shed even one tear, Rose, now that I'm useless to you?"

She jerked back as though he'd struck her. Whatever she'd been about to say was swallowed back. She got to her feet, ramrod straight, and walked out of the room.

No one spoke as her footsteps sounded on the stairs. Upstairs, a door slammed, sending shudders through the house. And then there was silence.

Gray got to his feet. "I'll get you something warm to drink, Papa."

"No." Fiona touched a hand to his arm. "I'll get it. You stay with your father."

In the kitchen, as she set the kettle on the stove, it occurred to Fiona that Rose and Flem had been enjoying their supper. Their plates were heaped with food. Platters of roast beef and potatoes were cooling in the center of the table.

As though it had been just another day.

Had this happened before? Had Broderick often gone off alone? And if so, had it been done out of confusion? Or was there something more here?

Rose's accusation played through Fiona's mind. Was Broderick Haydn's life so painful, his situation so desperate, he would deliberately wander off in the hope of dying all alone?

The thought was too painful to bear. As she spooned sugar into a cup of tea, she pushed aside her fears. It was the stroke. Not only did it destroy his body, but it muddled the brain as well.

She stepped into the parlor and fixed a smile on her lips. She wouldn't dwell on the possibility of anything right now, except the fact that Broderick was home, safe and sound.

But in a small, dark corner of her mind, she couldn't shake the troubling feeling that this was only a brief respite from a terrible storm that was brewing in the Haydn household. A storm that could erupt at any time with such violence, it could strike this family to its very foundation.

NINE

"WELCOME, CHILDREN." AS late summer slid into autumn, the days took on a familiar pattern. Fiona had begun to accept the fact that not all of the children were able to attend school on a regular basis. Some of the older boys were needed on the farms, especially during harvest time. Some of the girls were expected to stay home and help with chores around the house, or care for the younger children while their mothers worked alongside their men. Whenever a student returned, Fiona patiently went over the lessons that had been missed.

She picked up her slate. "Please take your seat, Edmer."

"What if I don't want to?"

His question was followed by a taut silence that had the other students shifting nervously in their desks.

Though Edmer Rudd had missed as many days as he'd attended, it had become clear to Fiona that he was considered a leader among the other children. Whenever he was in attendance, there was a sense of expectancy, as though awaiting the inevitable challenge to their teacher's authority.

She met his stare with a smile. "If everyone did as they pleased, it would be difficult to learn."

"Maybe I don't want to learn."

"Then why are you here?"

"Because my mother said I had to come."

"Your mother sounds like a wise woman. It would seem she wants her son to grow up to be just as wise."

"My father never went to school. Why should I?"

"Many of our parents didn't have the opportunity to go to school." Fiona glanced around at the others. "That makes them all the more eager that we should have what they couldn't have."

"My father says it's a waste of time." Edmer put his hands on his hips and looked around with a sneer. "He said the money the county spends on a teacher would be better spent on a team of mules that could be used among all the farmers during spring planting, and again at harvest time."

Once again Fiona was forced to choose her words carefully, knowing they would be repeated in every kitchen by day's end. "A team of mules would be a fine thing indeed, Edmer. I hope the county will consider it. But eventually mules will grow old and will have to be replaced. If I do my job, I'll instill a love of learning in all your young minds that will be passed on to your children, and your grandchildren, and their children."

"How is that going to help us grow better crops?"

"Perhaps it won't, but by mastering your sums, you'll be able to determine if you're getting the best price for those crops. Some of you may decide to become something other than farmers. Wouldn't it be grand for Paradise Falls if some of you should become doctors, or ministers, or teachers?"

"What if we want to be farmers?" Edmer's tone lifted in challenge. "Are you saying that isn't good enough?"

"Certainly not." Fiona glanced around at the other children, listening to every word of this exchange. "Education gives us the freedom to choose. My da used to say it is a key that unlocks many doors."

While she talked, Fiona moved among them, holding the slate. When she came to Edmer, he held out his hand. She, in turn, glanced at his desk and waited until he'd taken his seat before handing it over.

Pleased that she'd managed to coax him to follow the rules, her smile widened. "Let's begin by learning the name of our President, Benjamin Harrison." She'd written his name on the top of the slate, and asked Edmer to hold it up so they could all see. "It's a very long name, but one that I believe each of you should master. A very wise man once told me that if we are to be good citizens of this great country, it is important that we know the name of the man who is its leader."

While each of her students struggled to complete their assignment, she gave a little sigh of relief. It would seem that she'd managed to avoid a confrontation, at least for the moment. But though young Master Rudd had given up this particular battle, she doubted he was ready to forget the war.

"I CAN'T THANK you enough, Mr. Dorf." Fiona offered her hand, and watched as the old peddler carefully wiped his hands on his shirt before doing the same.

After accepting her invitation to bring his wagon to school, he had graciously permitted each of the students to crawl around inside to see where he and Luther slept, and how they stored so many fascinating items within such a confining space.

Fiona had been pleasantly surprised to find all of her

students in attendance. Perhaps out of curiosity, or perhaps because they didn't really consider this peddler's wagon a classroom, not one student was missing on this day.

To thank Frederick Dorf for opening up his home to them, Fiona had brought enough lunch to include the old man and his grandson. It had taken a great deal of persuasion before Rose Haydn had agreed to the extra food. But, as Fiona had been quick to point out, if Frederick Dorf was as poor as the others believed, it was the least she could do to make up for the inconvenience of taking him and his grandson away from the trail, where they would have been earning some money.

Rose had been outspoken in her protest. "I don't see what good this visit will do. What can children possibly learn from such a man?"

"They look down on him because he earns his living as a peddler."

Rose wrinkled her nose. "And why not? It's a sad, dirty way of life."

Fiona arched a brow. "Have you been inside his wagon?"

The older woman gave a quick shake of her head. "Nor would I want to. Why, do you know that before his wife died, she lived in that smelly, dirty cart, traveling all around the countryside with her man. And now an orphaned grandson. Why should any of us go near it?"

"Because Mr. Dorf provides all of us with his services. Without him, who would sharpen our knives or brings us the bits of ribbon and lace we use to brighten our lives? Gray told me that in the past year alone, Mr. Dorf was responsible for introducing him to a new winter wheat being grown by the farmers in Little Bavaria, and a newer, stronger hitch for the team. Without a peddler, who would sell you the special meats and cheeses he brings from other towns?"

Rose had turned away, unable to come up with an argument.

Fiona wondered what the parents would say when their children reported that the wagon, though small and cramped, had been spotlessly clean, and that every knife, every pair of scissors, every bit of string and twine and ribbon, had been carefully stored in its proper place. Perhaps, she thought, it wouldn't make any difference to most of them, but it had already made a difference to one sad, lonely little boy, who had been allowed, for this precious day, to share his life with his new friends.

Frederick Dorf's words broke through her thoughts. "You will thank Mrs. Haydn for the fine cheese and the strudel?"

"I will." Fiona turned to the children. "What do you have to say to Mr. Dorf?"

"Thank you, Mr. Dorf," they called in unison as they'd been coached before his arrival.

As the old man helped his grandson into the back of his wagon, Fiona saw the pleasure and pride in young Luther's eyes and remembered again why she'd invited his grandfather here. These children had seen, not a poor, dirty peddler as expected, but a small, neat wagon in which an old man and a little boy were managing, to the best of their ability, to make a home together.

When her students were gone, Fiona glanced skyward and seeing the sun already slipping below the horizon, started toward the Haydn farm. After that generous lunch for Mr. Dorf and his grandson, Fiona would hate to incur Rose's wrath by being late for supper, since it seemed to be a particular issue with the older woman.

A WEEK LATER the students were gathered around Gray as he whittled on a block of wood.

It had taken all Fiona's powers of persuasion to get the

shy farmer to consent to visit her school. At first he'd been ill at ease while the children pulled their desks in a circle. Now, as his fingers worked their magic, he forgot his nerves.

"What will it be?" Siegfried Gunther asked.

"I'm not sure yet." Gray kept turning the wood, whittling a bit, then turning it more. "The wood has to let me know what will suit it."

"You mean it talks to you?" This from Edmer Rudd.

"In a manner of speaking. The wood itself decides what is best. Some wood is delicate, and might become a flower or tree. Another piece might be round, and will become someone's face. Or the grain of the wood might be more suitable for an animal." He smiled as he began to see what would work. "I think this will be a great black bear."

The children fell silent as the wood began to take shape before their eyes. After carving the outline of a bear, Gray made a few cuts and whittled a head, eyes, ears. Then he made softer strokes with his knife that looked exactly like fur.

Now the children were so caught up in his skill, and watched with such intensity, Fiona stood back with a smile. This was all that she had hoped for. It was what teaching was all about. That magic moment when a student sees all the possibilities.

At last Gray held up the wood carving. "Well? What do you think?"

"It really is a bear." Afton's words brought nods from the others.

"Would you like it?" Gray held it out to the little girl, who eagerly accepted it.

When he tucked away his knife and got to his feet, Fiona hurried over. "What do we have to say to Mr. Haydn, children?"

They replied in a singsong chorus, "Thank you, Mr. Haydn."

"You're welcome." He grinned at Fiona as she escorted him to the door.

"You see?" She stepped out onto the porch. "That didn't hurt a bit, did it?"

"Not at all." He met her eyes. "You're good with them."

"So are you. Thank you, Gray, for sharing your special talent with my students."

He seemed about to say something more, but instead turned away and walked to his wagon, where Chester sat patiently waiting.

He found himself smiling as he flicked the reins and returned to the fields.

"RAIN'S COMING." BRODERICK was sprawled in the back of the wagon beside Fiona, as the family made its way to Sunday services. Despite the occasional break in the clouds, showing rare bursts of sunlight, Fiona was grateful for the warmth of the blanket tucked around her. The air had a bite to it, warning of what was to come.

The hills around them seemed on fire with leaves of red and gold and yellow, and a heavy layer of frost already glinted on the ground.

Fiona swiveled her head, doing her best to drink it all in. "I've never seen anything so beautiful as this."

Beside her Broderick blinked one eye, while the other stared without seeing. "Don't let it fool you. This land is a woman."

She turned to him with a questioning look.

"So lovely she takes your breath away." He seemed to gather his thoughts before adding, "Then, just when you've lost your heart, she shows her true face."

Fiona knew that the rest of the family couldn't hear

above the clip-clop of the horse's hooves and the wheels of the wagon as they rolled over the deeply rutted road. "And what would that true face be?"

"A cruel beauty. A harsh mistress, demanding all. Giving little."

"I think, despite your words, you love this land, Mr. Haydn."

"God help me, I do." He nodded. "But a word of warning, Miss Downey. Never trust her. When she seems the most beautiful, when you think she could never be lovelier, that's when you must be wary. For she can turn on you and take everything, even your life."

Fiona thought about the story of his sister and shivered. "I'll remember."

She felt the pull of the team against the harness. "I hope we have no more broken axles."

"It wasn't broken." Broderick looked up at the golden leaves above his head. "Gray said it was cut."

"Cut? Why would anyone cut an axle?"

The older man shrugged. "Why indeed? Who would benefit from such an act?"

She tried to remember back to the day, but so much had happened since then, it was impossible. She turned to study Gray and his mother and brother, seated on the front seat of the wagon. Did one of them have an enemy?

Before she could ponder such a thing, their wagon rolled to a stop outside the church. Fiona climbed out and shook down her skirts, while Gray lifted his father and steadied him on his feet. As always, Rose and Flem walked ahead, enjoying the attention of their friends and neighbors, while Gray and Broderick chose to remain in their shadow.

Fiona trailed slowly behind. Now that she'd become familiar with the townspeople, it seemed only natural to pause and smile or whisper a greeting to her students and their parents as she made her way to the Haydn pew at the very front of the church. Though it didn't actually have the Haydn name carved on it, Fiona had never seen anyone else sitting there. As though, she mused, there was an unspoken agreement that this was theirs alone. Was this why Gerhardt Shultz had called them one of the finest families in Paradise Falls? Were they being judged by their loyal attendance at Sunday services? Or had it once been enjoyed by others in their family who were now gone?

Flem stepped out of the pew and waited for her to take her seat before sliding in beside her. She glanced over to see Gray at the far end, with his father beside him, and Rose next to her husband. Gray caught her eye and just as quickly looked away, but not before she saw the slight flush on his cheeks.

As they stood and began the opening hymn, Fiona felt a strange tingling at the back of her neck. As though someone had touched her. She ignored the feeling as she matched her voice to Flem's rich tenor. After two more hymns, the congregation settled down to one of Reverend Schmidt's more notable sermons on the need to bend one's will to that of their Creator. As his words rolled over the assembly, Fiona glanced at Rose and saw the frown line between her brows, a sure sign that she disapproved of the preacher's topic. Fiona stifled a smile. Rose Haydn didn't seem the type to bend her will to anyone, include the Almighty.

An hour later, as they got to their feet for the closing hymn, Fiona felt the tingle once more. As soon as the congregation began to leave, she glanced around and saw, two rows behind her, Edmer Rudd. Beside him stood a man who could only be his father. Taller by a head, muscles sculpted from years of farm work, this man had the same blonde hair and ice-blue eyes. Eyes that were staring holes through her. Beside him was a tall, pretty woman with pale hair pulled into a prim knot and topped with a simple bonnet.

Fiona felt the heat rise to her cheeks as she followed the Haydn family down the aisle. She was aware that Edmer and his parents were walking directly behind her.

When they stepped outside, Gray hurried away to help his father into the back of the wagon, while Rose and Flem moved on to visit with neighbors.

Fiona paused at the bottom of the church steps and extended her hand. "Mr. and Mrs. Rudd. I am Fiona Downey, your son's teacher."

The woman started to extend her hand, then glanced shyly at her husband's scowling face before lowering her hand to her side.

"I know who you are." The man's voice was as chilling as his eyes. "My son has told me all about you."

Out of the corner of her eye Fiona could see people pause to watch and listen. She extended her hand to his son. "Good morning, Edmer."

Before the boy could acknowledge her greeting his father cuffed him on the side of the head, knocking him backward several paces before the boy managed to gain his footing.

When several boys nearby began to laugh nervously, Edmer turned on them with a scowl, his fists raised. "Are you laughing at me?"

The boys quickly disappeared behind their parents, who stared in openmouthed surprise.

Throughout this exchange, the boy's mother glanced nervously around, then stepped back, as though eager to get out of the path of her husband's fury.

Fiona thought to do the same, hoping to avoid any further embarrassment, but Christian Rudd's words stopped her. "We're farmers here. Simple people with simple needs. Knowing the president's name won't put food on our table. We don't need a slip of a girl without a brain in her head inviting a peddler to school and pretending he's worthy of our respect. Or wasting an entire morning watching wood being carved. What we want from our teacher is someone who uses a firm hand to teach our children to read and write, not to coddle those too poor or too backward to learn." He took a step closer, using his height to force her to tip up her head to see his face. "Unless you stop filling our children's heads with silly dreams of becoming whatever they want, you'll find yourself on a train back to wherever you came from."

Fiona could feel her cheeks burning, which only added to her discomfort. She could see Flem and Rose standing together, watching along with their neighbors. Then she spotted Frederick Dorf and his grandson, Luther, looking humiliated. That only firmed her resolve not to back down.

"I was hired to be a teacher to all the children of this town, Mr. Rudd. Not just to those you deem worthy."

"You were hired, Miss Downey, because the town was desperate for a teacher. There's been no one in that school in three long years." He looked her up and down with contempt, then turned so that everyone could hear. "And I say we were better off with no teacher than with one of your kind."

He yanked his son by the shoulder and started away, only to find the path barred by Gray.

"You owe Miss Downey an apology." Except for a narrowing of his eyes, his expression was unreadable, but the tone of his voice left no doubt of the anger simmering inside.

Christian Rudd's chin came up as he shoved his son aside. "She's the one who should apologize. Filling young minds with nonsense. I'll remind you that it was my vote and my money that made it possible for this town to have a teacher."

Gray never moved. His eyes stayed steady on Christian's, but his voice lowered just enough to cause those nearby to flinch. "You will apologize. Whether you do it now, of after I embarrass you in front of your family and this entire congregation, matters not to me. But you will apologize."

No one moved. Children engaged in a game of tag nearby went eerily silent. No babies whimpered. No dogs barked. It seemed, in that instant, that even the breeze had died, so that the autumn leaves no longer rustled about the feet of those watching.

Fiona stood as still as a statue, feeling the blood drain from her face, leaving her temples throbbing.

"You would talk about embarrassing me?" Christian Rudd stood nose to nose with Gray, his face nearly purple with rage. "When everyone knows what sort of man you are?"

"I've faced my own judgment before God and man. Now you will do the same. This good woman has done nothing to you." Gray kept his hands at his sides, though they had already curled into fists. "You will apologize."

In the eerie silence, Christian turned to Fiona, his words as hard as his features. "I apologize."

Unable to find her voice, she merely gave a slight nod of her head as he turned away and started toward his waiting wagon, with his wife and son running to keep up with his long strides.

The rest of the congregation hurried away as well, as though eager to put this awkward scene behind them.

Only Frederick Dorf remained. He walked timidly toward Fiona. His voice trembled. "I am sorry that my visit to your school has caused trouble."

"You have nothing to be sorry for, Mr. Dorf. My students and I learned much from your visit, and that was, after all, the purpose of my invitation."

"Christian Rudd is an important man in this town, Miss Downey. You do not want him for an enemy."

"I don't want anyone to be my enemy, Mr. Dorf. The choice, however, is his, not mine."

When the old man walked away, Fiona turned to Gray, who hadn't spoken a word.

"Thank you, Gray." She hated the way her voice trembled, but there was nothing to be done about it. "But now, as Mr. Dorf said, you have made an enemy of one of your most important townspeople."

"Christian Rudd is important only in his own mind. The man is a bully. Everyone knows it."

"Why do they not stand up to him?"

Gray shrugged. "We tell ourselves we are minding our own business. Perhaps we are. But we all know he bullies his wife and son, and anyone who gets in his way."

He glanced down at her hands, clasped together so firmly the knuckles were white with the effort. "Are you all right?"

Perhaps it was merely relief, or perhaps it was the concern she could read in his eyes. Whatever the reason, she feared that at any moment she might embarrass herself by crying. "I'm fine. But I'd like to leave now."

He put a hand beneath her elbow. Just a hand, but she felt the quiet strength in him and had to resist the urge to turn into his arms and weep until there were no tears left. Instead she merely walked beside him on trembling legs until they reached the wagon.

Gray lifted her into the back, where she settled herself next to his father.

Rose and Flem were already seated up front. They kept their gazes averted, and from the stiff line of Rose's back, Fiona sensed that Rose was not happy being thrust into the middle of this embarrassing scene.

As the horse and wagon moved along the road toward their farm, Broderick drew an edge of his blanket around Fiona's shoulders. She looked over in surprise.

"Cold," he muttered. "Come close. I need your hand."

She placed a hand over his, and he covered it with his other hand before looking up into her eyes. "You must be patient with us. This town's like a baby. Still crawling. You keep forcing us to take little steps. One day, you'll see, we'll be climbing mountains."

She blinked back a tear and managed a weak smile. "Do you think I'll be around long enough to see that?"

"I hope so." One side of his mouth turned up. "Sorry I missed the excitement. There was a time I'd have been in the thick of it."

She sighed. "I'm so embarrassed that the whole town had to witness that."

"You didn't ask for it."

She fell silent a moment before saying softly, "Gray was my champion."

"Not surprised." He gave a grunt of laughter. "Takes after his old man."

TEN

◆━◆✕◆━◆

FIONA'S BREATH PLUMED in the frigid air of the empty schoolhouse. She knelt on the hearth and coaxed a thin flame in the dried grass and sticks she'd heaped on top of the log. Gradually the log began to smolder and burn, and soon she had a fire blazing. Though she was reluctant to turn away from the warmth, she had no choice. Picking up the small hatchet Gray had given her she carried it to the outhouse, where she chopped through the layer of ice that had formed overnight on the bucket of water.

The days had grown shorter, the air so crisp and cold it hurt to breathe it in. In the mornings it was still dark when Fiona left on foot for the schoolhouse, and dusk by the time she returned.

The children often arrived in a single pony cart driven by one of the older boys, and returned home the same way. Those few who lived on farms too far from town banded together to walk in a group, and Fiona often dismissed them early, so that they'd be safely home before darkness settled over the land.

On her way back inside the schoolhouse she filled her arms with as many small logs as she could manage. She was staggering by the time she climbed the steps and deposited them beside the fireplace.

The door was opened on a blast of wintry air.

"Oh." She jumped at the shadow behind her, then gave a little cry of delight. "Will. Will VanderSleet. It's been such a long time. How are you?"

The boy stared hard at the toe of his boot. "I'm fine, Miss Downey."

"Has your uncle given you permission to attend school?"

"No, ma'am." The boy turned several shades of red before he managed to say, "There aren't many farm chores now, with the ground frozen. So I thought I'd come by and see if you might need a hand." He glanced at the meager pile of logs beside the fireplace. "I could chop wood for you. Carry water from the creek."

"That would be grand, Will. But I can't pay you for your hard work."

"Oh, Miss Downey, I don't want pay. I just want to help."

"It would be a great help." Fiona thought a moment. "I know. In exchange for your chores, I'll teach you."

He was already shaking his head. "I won't be able to stay more than an hour. My uncle will expect me back to help in the barn."

"All right. An hour then. Can you read, Will?"

The boy shrugged. "A little. My ma taught me how to write my name before she died."

"That's a start." Fiona drew a desk close to the fire. "Come on. Before the others get here, we'll try a few words on a slate."

"Let me get you more logs first."

Fiona watched as he scampered out the door and returned with his arms laden with firewood. After stacking it neatly beside the fireplace, he took the desk she indicated and began writing a few words on the slate.

When he handed it over for her inspection she looked up. "Where did you learn these words, Will?"

Again that flush on his cheeks as he said softly, "In my grandpa's Bible. He used to read it to us at night. He was the only one who could manage all the big words. Now that he's gone, all I can manage are a few small words."

"Could you ask your uncle to help?"

The boy looked away. "My Uncle Dolph can't read. Neither could my papa. Besides, Uncle Dolph said he doesn't have time for such things."

She sighed. "Then it's up to you, Will. As long as you're willing to work with me, I'll have you reading so well, there won't be any words that will stop you."

"Do you really think so, Miss Downey?"

She heard the plea in his voice and touched a hand to his arm. "Let's not waste another minute."

FIONA TRUDGED UP the lane toward the Haydn farmhouse. In her hand was a lantern she used to light her way.

Hearing the jingle of harness she paused to see a team of horses pulling the big log wagon just topping a ridge. When it came alongside her, Gray drew the team to a halt.

"I stopped by the schoolhouse, but you were already gone."

"You have enough to do, Gray, chopping down trees and hauling the lumber into town." She'd learned from his father that Gray earned extra money every winter by selling logs to the townspeople. "I've told you not to go out of your way for me."

He leaned down and helped her up to the hard wooden seat beside him. "It isn't out of my way. Besides, look how dark it is. It isn't safe for you to be out so late."

"I have my lantern." She lifted the glass and blew out the wick to save precious kerosene.

"But it's cold."

"That just makes me walk faster," she said with a laugh.

They shared a smile as he flicked the reins. The team set out at a fast clip, knowing they were heading toward the barn, where food and water awaited them in a warm stall.

Once inside Gray helped Fiona down. As she turned away he reached into his pocket. "I almost forgot. Gerhardt Shultz said the train came through this morning. The conductor left a packet of letters for you."

"Oh. Thank you, Gray." Fiona took the letters from his hand and stared at them with naked hunger. Then with a little laugh she danced away.

Inside she hurried through the house to her room. Without even bothering to remove her coat or boots she held a match to the lantern and knelt on the floor, where she devoured every word her mother had written.

There was a quick rap on the door, and Flem's muffled voice. "Supper's ready. Ma said you're late."

Fiona's head came up and she flung aside her coat and boots before hurrying from the room. In the kitchen she saw that the others had already begun passing the food.

Rose gave a hiss of disgust, more effective than any words.

"I'm sorry." Fiona ducked her head and felt a tear streaking down her cheek.

Tears? She hadn't even realized she'd been weeping.

Mortified, she rubbed the back of her hand over her eyes before taking her place beside Flem.

"What kept you?" Flem handed her a bowl of steaming potatoes.

"I was reading a letter from my mother." As Fiona filled her plate she could feel Gray watching her while he assisted his father.

"Not a very happy letter from the looks of you."

She twisted her hands together in her lap, wondering how to explain that it wasn't what her mother had said that had her alarmed, but what she hadn't said. It had been such a brief missive. Chicago was cold. Her nieces were busy little girls. She was happy to learn that the Haydn family was good to her daughter.

Not a word about herself. Was she eating? Was she able to sleep while sharing a bed with three lively little girls? Was she still locked in grief over her loss? Had she made any friends in Chicago?

It was Gray's voice that brought Fiona out of her reverie.

"Is this what I think it is?" He shot a look at his mother.

"Bavarian wurst." Rose saw the look of surprise in her men's eyes and was quick to explain. "Brunhilde Schmidt said her husband raved over the wurst she bought from Frederick Dorf. So I thought I'd try one, too."

"Doing business with the peddler, Ma?" Flem laughed. "If you're not careful, you may find yourself being publicly insulted by Christian Rudd."

At that Fiona looked down at her plate.

Rose shoved back her chair and busied herself at the stove, pouring hot water from a kettle into the teapot. She circled the table, filling their cups. "Brunhilde and her husband personally inspected Frederick Dorf's wagon and proclaimed it clean. Certainly cleaner than any other peddler's wagon they'd ever seen."

Flem was chuckling. "Next thing you know we'll be inviting the old peddler and his brat to supper."

"Enough." Broderick set down his cup with such force the tea sloshed over the rim. He waited until Rose had taken her seat. One side of his mouth turned up just enough to hint at a smile. "The Bavarian wurst is good."

Rose's mouth opened and closed, though no words came out.

When the silence became awkward, Broderick turned to Gray. "I'd like to go to the parlor now."

Gray helped his father to his feet, and the two of them shuffled slowly from the room.

When they were gone Flem glanced at his mother. "Did I just hear a compliment?"

"Hush now." Agitated, Rose topped off her tea and sipped, all the while staring into space.

Flem pointed to the apple cake cooling on the windowsill. "Are we supposed to eat that *apkelkuchen,* or did you make it for the horses?"

When his mother didn't answer Flem crossed the room and returned with the cake, which he cut into slices and set on plates, handing one to Fiona, and placing one in front of Rose.

After polishing off two big slices, he turned to his mother, who hadn't even tasted her dessert.

He winked at Fiona. "I guess this would be the time to tell my mother that I have a secret wife, I've sold the farm, I'm taking the money and leaving my family alone and destitute while I pursue a life of debauchery."

Though Rose never even blinked, Fiona was convulsed with laughter. Nobody could make her laugh as easily as Flem.

She pushed back her chair. "I think we should leave your mother alone, Flem."

"I think you're right."

As the two of them walked from the kitchen, Fiona

paused to look back at the woman, still seated at the kitchen table, her tea untouched, her gaze fixed on the spot where her husband had been sitting.

Instead of joining the Haydn men in the parlor, Fiona left them to their privacy and made her way to her room, where she intended to reread her mother's letters. But as she knelt beside the lantern, it wasn't the letters that filled her mind, but the little scene she'd witnessed in the kitchen.

It had seemed such a simple thing. A sausage purchased from a poor peddler. A husband telling his wife the meal had been good. But it had become so much more.

Fiona found herself smiling.

Oh, Da. You once told me that a good deed is like a stone tossed into a pond, sending out ripple after ripple, until the entire surface of the pond is changed. I didn't understand it then, but I do now.

Judging by the look of pleasure and puzzlement on Rose's face, she didn't quite understand it, either. But perhaps she would, in time.

After reading her mother's letters, Fiona bent to her own, filling page after page with stories of her students and the people she'd met in Paradise Falls. As she struggled to bring them to life for her mother, she found herself seeing them in a whole new light.

It had been easy enough to feel compassion for Will VanderSleet and young Luther Dorf, because the harshness of their existence would challenge even the most hardy of souls. She not only admired their efforts, but found herself cheering for them with every step they took.

But now she realized that Edmer Rudd, for all his bluster, was just as much in need of her understanding and her help. She had to find a way to reach the goodness inside him. For only then, when she had done what she could to help all her students, would she consider herself worthy of the title "teacher."

* * *

"WILL YOU BE going into town tomorrow, Gray?"
Fiona stepped into the parlor, where Gray and Broderick
sat staring at the flames of a log fire. Broderick was smoking his pipe. Gray was sipping strong, hot tea, cupping
the mug between his big hands.

It occurred to her that these two men were so comfortable with each other, they needed not a word between
them.

Both looked up as Gray nodded. "I've a load of logs
already in the sleigh. Is there something you'd like me to
deliver?"

She handed him a package wrapped with care in brown
paper and carefully marked with her mother's name and
address in Chicago. "I know it takes a while, and I'd like
this to arrive in time for Christmas."

"I'll give it to Gerhardt in the morning."

"Thank you." She turned away, afraid she might be
intruding on their privacy. "Good night."

"Come sit awhile." Broderick patted the sofa cushion
beside him. "It must be cold in your room. There's no
heat out on that old sunporch, except what drifts in from
the fireplace."

"I don't mind. I've a warm blanket." But she settled
herself beside him and couldn't hide her sigh of contentment as the heat of the fire began to weave its spell. She
glanced around. "Where are Rose and Flem?"

"Ma's baking biscuits for our breakfast. Flem figures
if he hangs around the kitchen he'll snag a few."

Fiona laughed. "He does like his sweets, doesn't he?"

Broderick exhaled a puff of smoke and watched it curl
toward the ceiling. "Fleming has always had a fondness
for all things rich and sinful."

Fiona fell silent, thinking about the number of times
she'd heard Flem sneaking out late at night. No wonder

he couldn't get out of bed until the day was half over. In the past few weeks, he'd been gone more nights than he'd been home. She glanced over at Gray and his father. Did they know? Was it another reason there was such a distance between him and them? Or was she the only one who knew his secret?

Gray drained his cup. "Will tells me you're tutoring him before school."

She flushed. "It's the least I can do. He comes early and helps me with wood for the fire and water from the creek."

"If his uncle finds out, there could be trouble."

She shifted uncomfortably. "I don't want to cause any trouble for Will. He's such a good boy. But he has a hunger to learn, Gray. How can I deny him?"

"I'm not suggesting you should. I just think you ought to be warned that if Dolph VanderSleet should become angry enough, he would make Christian Rudd look like a choirboy."

She shivered, remembering that horrid public scene. She couldn't imagine anything worse.

Gray's words were spoken softly, but with a thread of steel. "If Dolph ever comes to your schoolhouse, I want to know."

"All right." She nodded and reluctantly got to her feet. Though it was warm and snug here in the parlor, she knew she needed to be fresh in the morning. "Good night, Mr. Haydn. Gray."

Once in her room she huddled under the blankets and waited for sleep to claim her. As she drifted, she thought how wonderful it would be to fall asleep on the sofa, in front of a roaring fire, with the sweet smell of Broderick's tobacco filling her lungs. And, because she was too weary to pretend otherwise, she knew what would make the dream perfect. The deep voice of Gray washing over her as she slept. But that was a foolish wish. With all that he had to attend to around this farm, there could hardly be any time left over to give even a single thought to a foolish young woman who was allowing her imagination to carry her much too far.

If Grayson Haydn knew what she was thinking, he would no doubt be horrified.

ELEVEN

———◆◆◆———

As THE DAYS of December raced by in a blur of lessons, Fiona could sense a change in her students. Even though Christmas in this small farming community was a simple affair, spent mainly in church and filled with religious symbolism, there was room for simple gift-giving as well, which added an air of expectancy.

Over lunch the children talked of nothing else.

"Guess what I'm making for my grandfather, Miss Downey?"

"What, Luther?"

The boy lowered his voice. "A strip of fine leather, to repair his harness. I've been curing a piece of pig's hide for weeks."

"What a lovely gift. He's going to love it."

The boy flushed with pride.

"I'm crocheting a doily for my mama," Afton said proudly.

"Did your mama teach you to crochet?"

The little girl shook her head, sending golden curls dancing. "My grandmamma taught me, before she died."

"That will mean so much to your mother." Fiona glanced around. "What about the rest of you? Do you have surprises for your family?"

Siegfried Gunther described the steps he and his father were sanding for his mother, which would be added to the base of their porch when the snow melted.

Fiona noticed that Edmer was standing to one side of the room, listening without joining in. To draw him into the conversation she called, "What about you, Edmer? Have you thought of anything for your parents?"

He shook his head and tried to affect a look of boredom. "I can't think of anything they don't have."

"It must be grand to have everything you want." She smiled. "Maybe, if you listen, you'll hear them mention something they've always hoped for."

He shrugged and pretended to be busy writing on the slate, but it occurred to Fiona that he seemed more withdrawn than usual, and she found herself wondering if he had recently tasted his father's famous temper. Edmer had been gruff with the other students, a sure sign that he was feeling edgy.

She wished she knew how to reach this unhappy boy. Though she longed to speak with his mother, she feared that a visit to his farm might provoke another round of anger from Christian Rudd. Anger he might decide to visit upon his long-suffering wife and son.

"It's tempting to sit and dream about the things we'll give those we love for Christmas. And I must say that I'm proud of you for caring more about the things you'll give than those you hope to receive." She stood and beckoned them back to their desks. "Now it's time we got on with our work."

*   *   *

"HERE, WILL." FIONA handed the boy her slate. "I believe you've mastered enough words to write a story."

He looked up from the fireplace, where he'd stacked logs for the day. Wiping his hands on his pants he accepted the slate and took a seat. "What will I write about?"

"Write about the things that interest you. Tell me about the tools you've learned to use, and what you can make with them."

At once he bent to his task while Fiona walked around the room wiping down desks and arranging them close to the fire in preparation for another day.

It gave her such joy to teach this boy. Will had a quick mind. She needed to tell him something only once and he remembered it. After mastering syllables, there seemed no word that could stump him. He was now reading with more skill than any of her students.

She took an apple from her lunch pail and cut it in two, placing half on Will's desk. He idly picked it up and ate while continuing with his work on the slate. A short time later she placed the second half in front of him, and he polished that off as well.

She gave a little smile of satisfaction. When she'd discovered that the boy left home each morning without eating breakfast, she'd begun sharing what she had. To save him any embarrassment she'd told him that Rose Haydn packed more food than one person could possibly eat. It had taken some persuasion, but he now accepted her offerings without protest.

He looked up. "I'm finished. Would you like to hear it?"

"Yes, please." She looked over his shoulder as he read the story from the slate.

They were both so engrossed in what he'd written, they failed to hear the door open until they heard Edmer's voice. "What're you doing here, VanderSleet?"

Both Will and Fiona turned to him with matching looks of guilt.

"Will . . . offered to bring in some logs for the fire."

Edmer glanced at the neat stack, then back at the slate in Will's hand. "I heard the words you were speaking. How did you learn to read like that?"

"I'd better go, Miss Downey. My uncle will be expecting me." Will got to his feet and handed the slate to Fiona before crossing the room to fetch his shabby coat. Without a word to Edmer, he was gone.

"I didn't hear your pony cart, Edmer." Fiona began quickly wiping the slate.

"My father bought me a pair of snowshoes, and I wanted to try them out." He watched her frantic efforts to erase the evidence of Will's lesson. "Siegfried Gunther said he'd pick up the other students in his father's wagon."

"That's nice of Siegfried." Fiona set the slate on her desk and turned away. "Since you're early, perhaps you wouldn't mind carrying a bucket of fresh water to the outhouse."

"I don't see why I should. My father said that's your job, Miss Downey."

"It is, yes." Fiona caught the slight flush on Edmer's cheeks and felt a sense of satisfaction in knowing that he had the good grace to be embarrassed by his imitation of his father. She gave a cool nod before picking up the bucket and heading toward the door. "While I'm gone, you can begin writing the new words you learned yesterday."

Fiona stepped out the door and glanced around, wondering which way Will would have gone. Probably through the woods, in order to avoid being seen by the approaching students.

As she crossed the snow-covered schoolyard, she gave a long, deep sigh. The timing of Edmer's arrival couldn't have been worse. Knowing how much he enjoyed causing trouble, there was the very real possibility that he would reveal Will's secret. She had no idea how Dolph VanderSleet would react to that knowledge. Hadn't Gray warned her of his temper?

She whispered a little prayer that just this once, Edmer would show more wisdom and compassion than had been shown to him.

TWO DAYS LATER Fiona arrived at the schoolhouse to find Will already chopping wood for the fire.

"Will." She was so happy to see him, she could have hugged him. Instead she merely held the door while he carried an armload of logs inside. "Does this mean your uncle approves of you coming here?"

He wiped his hands on his faded pants. "Nothing's changed, Miss Downey. I left home before he was awake."

"I see." She shrugged aside her unease and moved about the room, preparing for another day. "Why don't we begin with sums?"

Will took the slate from her desk and began adding the columns of numbers she dictated. No matter how many rows of numbers she gave him, he always managed to come up with the correct total.

They both looked up when the door was thrown open and Edmer Rudd came rushing inside, holding two pieces of shattered wood.

"Edmer." Fiona hurried to his side. "What happened?"

"Nothing." He turned away in embarrassment. "I didn't figure you'd be here again, VanderSleet."

"Edmer." Fiona caught him by the shoulder and turned him to face her. "How did you get that bruise on your temple?"

"My father . . ." He pulled away.

"What about your father?"

Edmer shrugged. "Do you remember when you told me to listen to my parents and see if there was something they really wanted for Christmas?"

Fiona nodded.

"I heard my mother telling my father she'd like a pretty shelf in the parlor to display my grandmother's figurines. I went out to the barn to plane some wood. But when my father saw what I was making, he told me it was too ugly to ever be allowed in his house. I . . . said things that made my father angry. He cuffed me on the side of the head. I wanted to hit him back, but I knew I couldn't. So when he left . . ." He stared down at the broken pieces of wood.

Fiona sighed. "You hit the shelf instead, and broke it."

He tossed aside the pieces of wood. "It doesn't matter. My father was right. It's too ugly to hang in our house. My ma would have laughed at me for even trying."

"That's not so, Edmer." Fiona felt such a welling of sorrow at the defeated look in his eyes. With a hand on his arm she said softly, "There isn't a mother in the world who wouldn't be proud of something made by her son out of love. Now, let's look at all that happened and see if there are lessons to be learned."

"Lessons?" Both Will and Edmer spoke the word in unison, looking at her as if she'd grown a second head.

"Each thing that happens to us in this life is meant to teach us something." She tapped a foot, as she mused. "I would say that the first lesson here is that anger begets anger."

"I don't understand." Edmer looked at Will, who seemed equally puzzled.

"Your father said something that made you angry, so you responded in kind. Because he's bigger, your father reacted to your angry words with his hands. Because you're smaller, you couldn't retaliate, so you waited until he was gone and took out your anger on the gift you'd planned to make for your mother. How could all of this have been turned around?"

Edmer's temper flared. "My father could have told me he was proud of me, instead of making fun of my gift."

Fiona nodded. "That's true. The two of you could have worked together to make something for your mother. But since that hasn't happened, what can you do now to make it right?"

Edmer kicked at the broken pieces of wood. "I can burn these and forget about my stupid gift."

"Oh, Edmer, don't you see. We always have choices in life. We can choose to make something right, or we can make a bad situation even—"

Whatever else she was about to say was forgotten at the sound of booted feet coming up the steps.

Edmer quickly turned away to hide his tear-streaked face from the others. Will VanderSleet set the slate on Fiona's desk and hurried to pull on his coat. Amid the laughter and chatter of the arriving students, he tossed more wood on the fire before slipping quietly away.

IT WAS THE day before Christmas Eve, and to everyone's joy, it was snowing. Great, fat flakes that dusted hair and eyebrows and melted on tongues. Knowing that the children's eagerness couldn't be contained on this, their last day of school before Christmas, Fiona suggested they spend an extra half hour in the snow before returning to their desks.

The boys were busy tossing snowballs, while the girls were flopping on their backs in the drifts making angels.

With every shriek of laughter Fiona's smile widened. It was so good to hear the joyous sounds of children.

She stepped out onto the porch to summon them inside and nearly collided with a burly figure.

"Mr. VanderSleet." At the dark look in his eyes she took a step back.

He was holding firmly to his nephew's wrist. "I've been told the boy's been coming to school, where you've been teaching him. What gives you the right to go against my wishes?"

"I'm sorry. I know you said he was too busy to attend school, but I didn't think you'd mind, as long as I didn't keep him away from his chores."

"Liar." He dragged Will close and flung him against Fiona, knocking them both against the door. "You're two of a kind. Liars. And sneaks, as well. I should have known this was where he was sneaking off to so early in the morning."

When Fiona straightened, she drew Will behind her. "If you want to blame someone, blame me, Mr. VanderSleet. I should have known better. But Will assured me that he was keeping up with his chores. This boy has a bright mind. He's as good with his mind as he is with his father's tools."

"My brother was too lazy to farm. He figured he could get by doing for others. And now his boy's no better. Thinking he can live off me while breaking my rules. This is what happens to those who break my rules." He closed his hand into a fist and lifted it to her face.

Though her pulse was pounding, Fiona refused to back away. Instead she lifted her chin and faced him squarely. "If you want to hit someone, Mr. VanderSleet, hit me."

His fist shook, and it was clear he could barely contain his fury. "Oh, you'd like that, wouldn't you? You'd go crying to the town council and I'd have the whole lot of them on my doorstep. Reverend Schmidt. Doctor Eberhardt." He reached around her and snagged Will's arm. "I'll hit someone, all right. And next time, he'll remember who puts the food on his table and the roof over his head."

As they turned away, Fiona started after them, her

mind whirling with every horrible scene she could conjure. Without being aware of what she was doing she tugged on Dolph VanderSleet's sleeve.

He turned on her with a look of such darkness she almost lost her nerve. Then, steeling herself, she said breathlessly, "I beg of you, Mr. VanderSleet. Don't hurt this boy. He's been hurt enough by the loss of all those he loved."

"Since coming here you've stuck your nose into things that don't concern you. You run your school, teacher. I'll run my own family." His eyes narrowed, and he pushed her aside before turning and dragging his nephew away.

Fiona was forced to stand by helplessly while they disappeared into the woods. When at last she turned toward the schoolhouse, she realized that the children had huddled together to witness the entire frightening scene in strained silence. Only Edmer stood to one side. The moment she caught his eye, he lowered his head and turned away from her, and she knew. With terrible certainty she knew that he'd been the one to seal Will's fate.

FIONA BANKED THE fire and closed the door of the school, setting the brace before starting toward the Haydn farm. She'd dismissed the children early, and though her heart was heavy, she'd managed to wish each of them a happy Christmas before sending them on their way.

She saw Gray's wagon lumbering toward her and knelt to scratch Chester's ears as the dog bounded up. When she straightened, she realized that Gray wasn't alone in the wagon. Seated beside him was Will. Seeing the bruises on his cheek she let out a cry.

Gray brought the wagon to a halt and climbed down before hurrying to her side.

"How did you . . . ?" She peered over his shoulder at Will. "Where did you . . . ?"

He held up a hand to stop her. "Word travels too fast in Paradise Falls. By now everyone in town knows about your encounter with Dolph. I hurried over to his farm to see that Will wasn't punished too severely."

"Oh, Gray. Look at his poor face."

As she started to push past, his hands at her shoulders stopped her. "You mustn't fuss over the boy. It will only embarrass him more."

"Fuss? Fuss?" She slapped at his hand, but he held her fast.

"Listen to me. Unless we find a way to resolve this thing between Will and his uncle, he could find himself with no home."

"No home! Would your mother . . . ?" She saw the quick shake of Gray's head and knew the answer before she'd even finished the question. "Surely there's someone."

"There is no one who will go against Dolph VanderSleet. We must find a way for him to resolve this thing with his nephew."

Fiona hung her head. "I can't bear to think of Will going back to his uncle's home."

"I asked him if he wanted to return. He said he does. Remember, that is his only home. It was home to his father and grandfather, as well."

At the mention of his grandfather, Fiona's eyes went wide. "Oh, Gray. There may be a way. That is, if Will is truly determined to return."

When she told him what she had in mind, Gray shrugged. "I can't believe it would make any difference to a man like Dolph. But anything is worth a try." He walked with her to the wagon and helped her up to the seat beside Will.

The boy ducked his head, and Fiona bit back any words of comfort. If Gray were right, it would be better to pretend that she couldn't see the result of his uncle's anger.

As they drew near the VanderSleet farm, Fiona found herself whispering a fervent prayer.

Oh Da. Help me to say and do the right thing, so that Will and his uncle can get beyond this anger.

When the wagon came to a halt, the door slammed and Dolph stepped onto the porch. "Came back for more, did you?" He glared at the young woman seated beside his nephew. "You're not welcome on my land, teacher."

"I'm sorry, Mr. VanderSleet. It won't happen again. I hope you'll accept my apology. I thought I was doing a good thing by teaching Will to read. He told me the only thing he wanted to do was read the Bible, the way his grandfather had."

The man's eyes narrowed with disbelief. "My father was a great man in the old country. Many came to him to have their family documents read aloud. Are you suggesting that in just a few months you could make this boy as smart as that?"

"I can't make anyone smart, Mr. VanderSleet. All I can do is share the little knowledge I have. What I'm saying is that Will has been blessed with a good mind. With enough education, he has the potential to become a great man like his grandfather. Perhaps you would permit him to read to you from the family Bible?"

The man looked from his nephew to the teacher, before turning on his heel and striding inside. Minutes later he stepped out, carrying the heavy, leather-bound Bible. When he beckoned, Gray helped Fiona down from the wagon seat, while Will scrambled down behind her.

When they climbed the steps Dolph flipped open the Bible and shoved it toward Will. "Read."

Will merely stared at the words until his uncle poked a finger in the middle of the page. "You will read this. Now."

"It's . . ." Will swallowed. "It's the Book of Psalms." He cleared his throat and glanced at Fiona, who managed a weak smile of encouragement.

"Give up your anger, and forsake wrath; be not vexed, it will only harm you."

Dolph snatched the book from his nephew's hand and studied the words, though both he and his nephew knew he couldn't read. "You aren't making this up?"

"No, sir."

He handed back the Bible and gave a curt nod of his head. "More."

"For evildoers shall be cut off, but those who wait for the Lord shall possess the land."

Dolph slowly nodded as the familiar words washed over him. "I remember my father reading that. It was one of his favorites. Maybe that's why the book opened to this page." He glanced over Will's head to where Gray and Fiona stood. "I'd forgotten how much I missed the sound of my father's voice, reading from the Bible."

He lowered his head, deep in thought. An ominous silence settled over them. Finally he lifted his head and took a deep breath before saying, "Would you come in?"

Fiona turned to Gray, who shook his head. "Another time, Dolph. We'll be going home to supper now."

The older man nodded. "Another time then." He turned and opened the door, holding it for his nephew. "Come in, Will. It's cold outside."

Will paused a moment, then closed the Bible and followed his uncle. At the door he turned. "Goodbye, Miss Downey. Mr. Haydn." Almost as an afterthought he called, "A happy Christmas to you."

Gray put a hand beneath Fiona's elbow. As he escorted her to the wagon he muttered, "I believe it might just be a happy Christmas now, thanks to your quick thinking."

TWELVE

———◆———

"FLEMING." ROSE HAD been up since dawn, shouting orders at her men to fetch wood, stoke the fire, or go to the root cellar in search of dimpled apples and rarely used spices. "I need these apples peeled."

"Yes, Ma." Flem whistled a little tune while he set to work.

"What can I do, Mrs. Haydn?" Fiona came to a skidding halt in the doorway and stared around in fascination.

A sideboard was piled high with more food than Fiona had ever seen at one time. Braided breads dotted with dried fruits and nuts. Loaves of steaming pound cakes wrapped in rum-drenched linen towels. Strudel, dusted with sugar. Pies and tarts filled with custard and cherries and sweet dark pumpkin.

The wonderful aroma of cinnamon and licorice and anise permeated the air. Was there any doubt that it was Christmas Eve?

Rose removed yet another loaf of bread from the oven

and set it by the window to cool. "I want you and Gray
to begin delivering these to our neighbors."

"Oh, how grand. Do you bake something for everyone?"

"Of course. It's our tradition. Now go and get ready."

Fiona danced away to fetch her coat and shawl. When
she returned Gray was helping his father into his boots.

"I don't know why you insist on going along." Rose
pounded a lump of dough, then turned it and pounded
again. "You'll only slow the young people down."

"I don't mind taking him, Ma." Gray helped his father
to his feet, before fastening his coat. "It'll do Papa good
to visit with our neighbors."

Rose arched a brow. "And sip their lager. I know what
you're up to, Grayson Haydn. Do you think I won't know
your father's been drinking?"

"It's Christmas Eve, Ma." Flem dipped his finger in
the bowl of frosting before brushing a kiss over her cheek.
"You wouldn't want to break with tradition now, would
you?"

She touched a hand to the spot, leaving a dusting of
flour, and relented, as he'd known she would. "Just see
that your father returns in time for supper. I'm cooking a
goose."

"Wouldn't miss it." Broderick leaned on his son's arm
as the two started out the door.

Instead of helping his father into the back of the
wagon, Gray lifted him up to the hard wooden seat. Once
Gray and Flem started loading the back of the wagon with
sweets, Fiona understood why. By the time they'd finished, there was enough to feed the entire town of Paradise Falls, with some to spare.

Gray helped her up, settling her between him and his
father.

She turned to see Flem disappearing inside. "What
about your brother?"

"He'll stay and do Ma's bidding."

"And eat everything in sight," Broderick added with a sigh.

As Gray flicked the reins she turned to him. "Will we really be able to deliver all of this in one day?"

"We'd better. We'll need the back of the wagon for Papa to sleep off the beer on the ride home."

Beside her, Broderick merely chuckled. It occurred to Fiona that she'd never seen the old man this happy.

Their first stop was at their nearest neighbor's farm.

"Since his wife died, Herman Vogel lives alone," Gray explained as they pulled around to the backdoor. "He has long talked about going to live with a daughter, but so far there's been no one offering to buy his farm."

A stooped old man with a thatch of white hair atop a face as wrinkled as the apples in the root cellar stepped out of the barn and crossed the yard to their wagon.

"Happy Christmas, Herman," Gray shouted.

"And a happy Christmas to you, Grayson. Broderick." The man peered at Fiona through cloudy, milk-blue eyes. "Our teacher?"

"Fiona Downey, Mr. Vogel," she called. "And I wish you a happy Christmas, as well."

"The same to you, miss." He whipped his hat from his head and stood watching as Gray climbed down and retrieved several bundles wrapped in linen cloth.

"Ma sent you some wurst and *leberkase*. And a strudel."

"My thanks to your kind mother." The old man managed a warm smile. "Will you come in and share a glass of lager?"

Before his father could answer Gray gave a quick shake of his head. "We thank you, Herman. But we have many more farms to visit before the day is over."

He flicked the reins, and Fiona turned to watch as the old man climbed the steps to his porch. When they were out of earshot she said, "That was kind of your mother."

Gray nodded. "Ma loves Christmas. It's her time to shine. And Flem's," he added. "If Flem had his wish, every day would be Christmas."

Beside Fiona, Broderick gave a grunt of displeasure. "He eats and drinks as though every day is."

The three of them were laughing as they stopped at the next farm, where Greta Gunther wiped her hands on her apron and persuaded them to come inside to sample her chicken, wurst, and wonderful dark bread, all washed down with sips of beer. When Fiona hesitated, Greta offered her strong black tea instead.

By the time they'd visited the sixth farm, Fiona was protesting that she couldn't eat another bite, while Broderick, after sampling half a dozen lagers, was happily humming a little tune.

"Where to now?" Fiona asked as Gray settled his father on the high, hard seat.

"It's the VanderSleet farm." Gray flicked the reins.

Fiona clasped her hands together tightly, steeling herself against the knowledge that she might have to look at fresh bruises on Will's face.

Oh, Da, I don't know what I'll do if the anger is back.

As their wagon rolled to a stop the door opened and Dolph stepped onto the porch.

"Good day." Gray swung down and walked to the back of the wagon. "Ma has sent *mettwurst* and *roggenmischbrot*."

He walked up the steps and placed the linen-clad parcels in Dolph's hands.

"I thank you." Dolph looked over at Broderick and Fiona. "Will you come in? I have lager."

Before Gray could refuse Broderick had taken hold of Fiona's arm. "Of course we'll come in."

Gray lifted his father from the wagon and helped him up the steps, while Dolph held the door. Just then Will came around the side of the house. When he saw them he broke into a wide smile.

"Miss Downey. Look what my uncle has given me for Christmas." He held up a small rusty saw. "It belonged to my grandfather."

"Oh, Will. How marvelous." Fiona turned to his uncle. "That was kind of you, Mr. VanderSleet."

Dolph merely shrugged. "I thought the boy should have it, since he's more handy with tools than I am."

Once inside Dolph invited them to gather around the rough wooden table while he proceeded to cut into a wheel of cheese and brown bread before passing around glasses of lager.

Because she didn't want to insult her host, Fiona took a sip and was surprised at how good it tasted.

"Will." Dolph glanced over at his nephew. "Why don't you entertain our guests by reading something?"

While the others enjoyed their food and drink, the boy opened the Bible and chose a passage at random. As he read, Fiona glanced at his uncle, who sat with eyes closed, and a smile upon his lips.

At length he opened his eyes and nodded to his nephew. "That was good, Will. Almost as good as when my father read it to me. I think," he added, "this will be the best Christmas in this house since my father left us."

Fiona was grateful for the beer. It helped her swallow the lump that had somehow become lodged in her throat.

They stayed as long as they dared, before announcing that they still had to go to the Rudd farm to deliver food before going home to supper. As they made their way to the wagon, Will disappeared inside the barn, returning moments later with something wrapped in a length of faded blanket.

"Would you mind giving this to Edmer?"

Gray nodded as he assisted his father. "Put it in the back of the wagon with the food, Will."

They left with shouts of happy Christmas ringing in
their ears. When they were once more on the road, Fiona
turned to Gray. "I can't quite believe the change I'm seeing in Dolph VanderSleet."

Gray nodded. "If I hadn't seen it with my own eyes, I
wouldn't have believed it either." He gave her a nudge.
"You might want to hold on to Papa. All that lager will
soon have him nodding off."

"Not a chance." The old man laughed, though he
seemed perfectly content to allow Fiona to loop her arm
through his. "I'm having too much fun."

They were still laughing as they rolled up to the Rudd's
big, sturdy farmhouse. Up close Fiona could see that it
was the most prosperous in Paradise Falls.

Once again she braced herself for whatever was to
come. She had neither seen nor spoken to Edmer's parents
since that horrible scene outside the church.

After bringing the team to a halt Gray touched a hand
to Fiona's arm. "I know you're concerned, but whatever
Christian may be thinking, he'll be civil. After all, it's
Christmas Eve, and we've come bearing gifts."

She managed a trembling smile. "I hope you're right,
Gray."

"Trust me." He lifted her down, then did the same for
his father, keeping an arm around the older man's shoulders when he felt him stagger just a bit.

Both Christian Rudd and his wife Lida were standing
in the doorway as Fiona followed Gray and his father up
the steps.

"Welcome to our home." Lida Rudd held the door and
Christian took Broderick's arm, helping him inside, while
Gray returned to the wagon to retrieve the food.

Lida Rudd tentatively offered her hand to Fiona. "Welcome to our home, Miss Downey."

"Thank you." Without hesitation Fiona returned the
handshake.

Gray sprinted up the steps and handed the linen-wrapped parcels to his hostess. "Ma baked you something special."

"We've been looking forward to Rose's linzer torte. Please, give your coats to Christian and come to the parlor." Lida led the way into a big room where a cozy fire blazed on the hearth.

In no time they were being served yet more cheese and brown bread and tall glasses of dark beer.

"Would you prefer lager or tea, Miss Downey?"

Fiona laughed. "I think I'd better have some tea now. Though I confess to liking the taste of lager."

"You've never tasted it before?" Lida poured tea and handed her guest a cup.

"Today was my first." Fiona sipped and looked up as Edmer stepped into the room. "Happy Christmas, Edmer."

The boy avoided her eyes. "Happy Christmas, Miss Downey."

"I almost forgot. I have something for you, Edmer." Gray set down his glass and stepped out of the room. When he returned he explained, "We just came from the VanderSleet farm. Will asked us to give you this."

"This is from Will?" The boy looked puzzled. "Are you sure it's for me?"

"That's what he said."

As Edmer stared at the parcel his mother said gently, "Go on, Edmer. Open it."

While the others looked on the boy knelt on the rug in front of the fire and unrolled the length of faded blanket.

"What is it, Edmer?"

"It's . . ." He stood and held out a piece of wood that had been perfectly sanded, the ends painstakingly scrolled like delicate seashells. "It's for you, Mama. I heard you say that you wanted a shelf for your mother's figurines. I tried to make you one, but I ruined it. I didn't think I had anything to give you, but now . . ." He fell silent when he saw the look on his mother's face.

"Oh, my." Lida Rudd ran her hand over the smooth finish and turned to her husband with shiny eyes. "Christian, have you ever seen anything so beautiful?"

Christian touched a hand to the smooth wood before glancing sharply at his son. "I didn't realize Will VanderSleet was such a good friend of yours."

"I didn't realize it, either." Edmer's cheeks were suffused with color, his eyes blinking rapidly, as though fighting tears.

To the astonishment of everyone, he rushed from the room and fled up the stairs.

In the silence that followed Christian turned to his wife with a scowl. "Order our son down here at once, or I'll go up there and teach him some manners."

Lida Rudd turned as pale as the shelf she was holding. "Please, Christian. It's Christmas time." She turned to Fiona with a pleading look. "Miss Downey, can you tell us what has happened?"

Fiona set down her tea and got to her feet. "Would you mind if I spoke with Edmer?"

When Christian started to refuse Lida put a hand on his arm, then just as quickly lifted it, astonished by her own boldness. "If you think you might help."

"I'll try." Fiona left the room and climbed the stairs, following along a narrow hallway until she paused in the doorway of the boy's room.

Edmer looked up from the bed, then away, furiously rubbing at his eyes. "You have no right to be here."

"Your parents are concerned, Edmer."

"I'm fine." He swallowed. "Tell them I'll be down in a while."

"Very well."

As Fiona turned away the boy said gruffly, "Why would Will do something nice, after what I did to him?"

She paused, then turned, choosing her words carefully. "Maybe it's because he wants to be a ripple in a pond."

He frowned. "I don't understand."

Fiona met his troubled look with a smile. "It took me many years to understand. If you'd like, we'll talk a while, and see if we can make some sense of it."

It seemed hours later, though it had been only a few minutes, when Fiona and Edmer descended the stairs and walked into the parlor, where the others were eating in silence. Everyone looked up as they entered the room.

Edmer glanced first at his father, whose eyes were fixed on him with fury, and then at his mother, eyes downcast, hands trembling.

While Fiona took a seat beside Gray, the boy squared his shoulders. "You probably heard that Mr. VanderSleet punished Will for going against his wishes and attending school."

Christian Rudd nodded. "In his place I'd have done the same."

Edmer swallowed before saying, "I'm the one who got Will into trouble with his uncle."

"What do you mean?" Christian's hands were already curling into fists at his sides.

"I told Mr. VanderSleet that Will was sneaking off to school early in the morning."

"Why would you do that, Edmer?" Lida glanced uneasily at her husband.

The boy shrugged. "I was angry with Pa. He'd made fun of my attempt to make you a shelf. And maybe I was jealous of Will."

His mother touched a hand to her mouth to stifle her little cry. "When you have so much, how could you possibly be jealous of a poor boy with no family?"

Edmer shook his head. "You don't understand. Will can do so many things. There isn't anything he can't do with his tools. And I heard him reading to Miss Downey. He never even stumbled over the words."

"Was that reason enough to cause him trouble?"

Edmer shook his head. "I thought so at the time. Now I'm sorry for what I did. But don't you see? Even after all I did to Will, he didn't try to get even. Instead, he made you that shelf."

"Why would he do such a kind thing?" Lida twisted her hands.

After a quick look at Fiona for reassurance, Edmer took a deep breath. "Miss Downey has been telling us that we can change what we don't like by . . . becoming tiny stones in a pond."

"More nonsense?" Christian turned to Fiona with a scowl. "What's that supposed to mean?"

She merely smiled. "Your son will explain."

"Miss Downey told us that instead of getting back at someone who has been unkind to us, we can change their hearts by doing a kindness in return. And that's what Will did."

Broderick set down his lager and belched. "In my day it was called turning the other cheek."

In the awkward silence that followed, Lida crossed the room to touch a hand to her son's arm. "I love my gift, Edmer."

"Will made it."

"But you were the one to think of it. For that reason, I'll always treasure it."

Gray helped his father to stand and noted that he was listing slightly. "We have to get home now. Ma will have our hides if we're late for supper. She's cooking a goose."

They were all aware that Christian Rudd hadn't moved. Even when they walked to the front door, he remained in the middle of the parlor, watching as they slipped into their coats and scarves.

It was left to his wife to see them out.

"You'll thank Rose for me, Broderick."

He leaned heavily on his son's arm. "I will."

"And thank you, Gray. Miss Downey." Her voice trembled slightly. "I wish you all a happy Christmas."

"Happy Christmas, Mrs. Rudd. Edmer." Fiona looked beyond them to Christian, whose eyes were narrowed on her like twin beams of ice. "Happy Christmas, Mr. Rudd."

She turned away, expecting no reply and hearing none. And found herself wondering if these two would, when their house was once more empty of company, answer to a bully's fists.

THIRTEEN

———❖———

"I WIN, MA." As Gray and his father stepped into the kitchen, Flem held out his hand and was rewarded with a cookie. With a laugh he took a bite before explaining. "Ma was worried that you'd be late. I told her that no matter how many lagers you shared with the neighbors, there was no way you'd be late for Christmas Eve supper."

"I raised a smart son." Face flushed, Broderick lowered himself to his chair and waited for Gray to remove his boots and coat.

"So." Rose turned from the stove. "How many beers did you have?"

"Too many." Broderick grinned. "But how could I refuse, when our neighbors kept asking me to raise a toast to my talented and very generous wife?"

Rose couldn't keep her smile from blooming. "They liked my gifts?"

"They loved them, Ma." Gray hung their coats on a

hook by the door and was careful to wash his hands and roll his sleeves.

"I've set the table in the parlor." Rose led the way, and Fiona caught her breath at the dazzling display of silver and crystal, winking in the glow of dozens of candles.

"Oh, Mrs. Haydn. This is . . ." She looked around. "Words fail."

Pleased, Rose indicated the sofa and chairs that had been moved close to the fire. "Supper will be ready soon. But for now, we'll have some elderberry wine to warm you from your travels. Fleming, you pour."

Flem poured burgundy liquid from a crystal decanter into small fluted glasses and passed them around on a silver tray.

Broderick lifted his glass. "As always, we drink first to those who have left us."

As the others sipped, Fiona felt a quick, hard tug on her heart and had to dip her head to hide the grief that she knew would be in her eyes.

Oh, Da. How I wish I could hear, just once more, the sound of your voice, with that wonderful music of Ireland in every word. And to feel again your arms, so strong and warm, around me.

When she'd composed herself she took a sip. The wine was sweet and glided down her throat like liquid honey.

"To us." Broderick shot her a smile. "And to those we wish were here with us."

Again that quick tug, and she found herself hoping that her mother was sitting warm and snug, sipping wine with family, and feeling safe and loved.

Safe and loved. It was what Fiona wished, more than anything, for her mother.

Keep her safe, Da. Safe and treasured by those who are with her now.

While Broderick proposed yet another toast, Rose slipped away to the kitchen and returned carrying a huge silver platter on which rested the biggest goose Fiona had ever seen.

"Flem. Gray." Rose pointed with the carving knife. "You may fetch the rest of the food."

"What about me, Mrs. Haydn?"

"You help Broderick to the table."

The old man winked at her as she set aside her glass and helped him to his feet. In the time that it took to get him seated, the table was groaning under the weight of more food than Fiona could imagine. Mashed potatoes and buttery gravy. Golden egg noodles. Cabbage and glazed beets and tiny carrots and two kinds of beans. Rolls and so many slices of bread, some dark brown, and others dotted with bits of fruit and nuts.

As they took their places, Flem walked around the table, topping off their glasses with more elderberry wine.

After passing the platters and filling their plates, they bowed their heads as Broderick said curtly, "We ask a blessing on this feast."

"Oh, Mrs. Haydn." Fiona couldn't help exclaiming over each bite she took.

Rose made her usual protest. "It's just simple food."

As soon as the words were out of her mouth, they all burst into gales of laughter. In fact, they laughed throughout the entire meal. By the time they had polished off slices of rum-soaked pound cake and tiny fruit tarts, the Haydn family had laughed and talked more than Fiona had heard in all the time she'd shared their home.

Broderick sat back and lifted a napkin to his mouth. "I believe this is the finest Christmas Eve supper yet, Rose."

"Thank you, Brod . . ." The words suddenly died in his wife's throat.

Everyone turned to look at her, but she was staring at her husband as though seeing a ghost.

"What's wrong, Ma?" Flem got to his feet.

Rose pointed and made a strangled sound. "Your . . .

hand. Broderick, you're holding your own napkin."

The old man merely smiled. "So I am. I wondered when someone would notice. I've been working on it for some time now."

Fiona realized that he hadn't once spilled any of his lager throughout the day, but until this moment, she hadn't given it a thought.

Rose shook her head in disbelief. "Doctor Eberhardt said there was nothing to be done about a stroke."

Broderick shrugged. "Somebody should have told me sooner. I've been walking every day, and every day going a bit farther than the day before."

That, Fiona realized, would explain his tumble in the fields that frightful day. He'd been pushing himself to the limits, in order to retrieve the strength he'd once had.

"Now," he added with a lopsided smile, "if I only I could get my face to work again."

Rose stared at him. And though her expression never changed, there was a softness to her voice that hadn't been there before. "Your face looks fine to me, Broderick."

In the silence that followed, Fiona glanced from one to the other, feeling as though she were violating their privacy. The look that passed between them was almost too sweet to bear.

Flem got to his feet and circled the table, filling their glasses yet again. "I believe it's time to celebrate."

Without waiting for them to respond he crossed the room and removed the fringed scarf that covered the piano. The others picked up their glasses and gathered around as he played familiar carols. At first they gave voice haltingly, but as the music grew more lively, so did their singing, until even Broderick and Rose joined in.

When they ran out of Christmas carols, Rose said, "Play that song you've been talking about, Fleming. The one that you said Mr. Sousa wrote."

Without missing a beat Flem launched into a rousing

John Philip Sousa march that had them stomping their feet.

When he was finished, Fiona clapped her hands in delight. "That was wonderful. Oh, Flem, I had no idea you could play like that."

"I have all kinds of hidden talents." With a wicked grin he shoved away from the piano and picked up a sprig of mistletoe.

Holding it over his mother's head, he kissed her soundly.

"Oh, you." With a pretty blush, Rose gave him a shove. "Don't waste your kisses on me when there's someone your own age to enjoy."

That was all the coaxing he needed to walk to Fiona and hold the mistletoe over her head while he brushed her lips with his. She knew her face was as red as the berries, which only made her face flame more. And though his parents merely laughed, she could see a steely look come into Gray's eyes.

She pushed quickly away and fluttered her hand like a fan. "I believe I need to sit down."

"We all need to sit," Rose said.

Before his mother could sink into a chair Flem grabbed her and began waltzing her around the room, all the while singing at the top of his voice. Though Rose pretended to push away, it was obvious that she was having the time of her life.

Fiona marveled at the change in Rose. She was like a schoolgirl, blushing and laughing as though flirting with a lover.

Finally Rose managed to push free of her son's arms. "Enough. I need to catch my breath. Dance with our teacher."

"No, Flem." But though Fiona protested, he had no intention of letting her be. Instead he dragged her to her feet and whirled her around and around until her head was spinning. When at last he stopped, she sank gratefully onto the sofa beside Broderick.

"You two make a handsome couple. I've always thought the girls in this town were too silly for Fleming. He deserves someone with a good mind as well as a pretty face." Rose turned to her husband. "Don't you agree?"

Across the room Fiona saw Gray standing perfectly still. When he caught her looking his way he busied himself lifting his glass and taking a long drink before setting it on a side table.

Flem filled his father's glass and his own before saying, "Who would like to be first to open my gifts?"

Without waiting for a reply he handed his mother a small box. She opened it to reveal a pretty enameled brooch in the shape of a rose.

"It's for your Sunday dress."

"Oh, Fleming. It's beautiful."

He grinned. "I knew you'd like it. A rose for a Rose."

He handed his father a pint of dark beer. "For tomorrow."

Broderick studied it. "Did you buy this in Little Bavaria?"

Flem nodded. "I was over there the other day and remembered that you once said they make the best beer in America."

"The most expensive, too."

Before Broderick could say more Flem handed a package wrapped in brown paper to his brother.

Gray opened it and held up a leather belt.

"Hand-tooled," Flem said proudly. "There's a farmer in Little Bavaria who makes the finest leather goods." With a grin he added, "I think you'll like it better than that length of rope you've been using."

Gray laughed and offered his hand. "You're right. I thank you."

"I saved the best for last." Flem handed a tiny package to Fiona.

When she opened it, she gave a gasp of pleasure. "Oh, Flem. A comb for my hair."

He took it from her hand and set it in a tangle of curls. "Hair this pretty ought to be adorned."

"Thank you." She got to her feet. "If you'll wait a minute, I'll bring out my gifts."

She hurried away to her room and returned with several parcels. "These are from my mum. She wanted to thank you for making me welcome in your home."

Rose opened some tissue and held up a pale pink handkerchief edged with delicate lace. "Oh, this is far too fine to ever use." She examined the lace. "I've never seen anything so fancy."

Fiona dimpled. "Mum will be so pleased. Though her hands aren't as steady as they used to be, she still makes the finest lace." She turned to the others. "These are also from Mum."

The three men opened their packages to find identical knitted gloves and made a great show of trying them on and praising the quality of the work.

"These are from me." Fiona handed Rose a lovely pink shawl, edged with darker pink roses and pale green leaves. "I've been knitting it for weeks."

Rose couldn't hide her pleasure, even while protesting that it was far too fine to ever use.

For the men Fiona had knitted scarves. "Yours is black, Mr. Haydn. I made yours, Gray, to match your name." She shyly handed him a soft, dove gray one before turning to Flem. "And yours matches your personality. Flamboyant red," she added, to the laughter of everyone.

All three of the men quickly wrapped them around their necks to show them off.

"They're perfect," Rose proclaimed. "And just the right colors for each of you."

"I made one for myself in bright yellow," Fiona said, "to cheer me on these dark winter days." Feeling festive, she draped the yellow scarf around her neck.

"I believe that just leaves our presents." Broderick turned to his oldest son. "Where have you hidden them?"

Proudly wearing his scarf, Gray walked upstairs and returned carrying several parcels.

Rose opened hers to find a bolt of pretty fabric in a pale pink flowered design. "So you can make yourself a new dress," her husband explained.

"It's beautiful. And it will go perfectly with my new shawl and handkerchief."

Gray handed his brother a parcel, and Flem tore off the brown paper to find sheet music.

For a moment he looked incredulous. Then with a grin he glanced over at his brother. "Scott Joplin?"

"He's a new songwriter. I thought you'd like his music. I had to send away for it from a catalog."

Flem hurried to the piano and studied the music before tentatively touching the keys. Within minutes he was pounding out a toe-tapping tune that had them all clapping their hands.

When he was finished he squeezed Gray's shoulder. "Thanks. It's the best gift ever."

"It's from Papa, too."

Flem walked to his father and bent down to kiss his cheek.

Gray handed his father a small parcel. "I made this for you, Papa."

Broderick unwrapped it and held it up. "A new pipe."

"I carved it last week."

His father examined the intricate carving. "It's almost too grand to use." He stuck it between his teeth. "But I'll force myself."

Everyone shared in the laughter as he said to Gray, "Now let's give Miss Downey her gift."

Gray set a big box in front of Fiona. She knelt on the floor and tore aside the brown paper before peering inside. "Slates?" She began lifting out several small, neatly framed slates. "How many are there?"

"An even dozen," Broderick said proudly. "Gray framed each of them by hand."

"Oh, my. I can't think of anything I would have loved more. However could you have known?" With a little laugh Fiona set them aside and hurried over to press a kiss to Broderick's cheek. When she turned to Gray he flushed and quickly stuck out his hand, as though afraid she might kiss him, too.

She took his hand between both of hers, and then, unable to resist, she brushed her lips over his cheek. Just the slightest touch, but she felt a rush of heat all the way to her toes. "Thank you, Gray."

"Well." Rose sat fingering the lace of her handkerchief. "I believe we could all make do with another sip of elderberry wine."

Flem was quick to pour, then he sat on the floor at his mother's feet and drew up one knee, while Gray stood by the fire, staring into the flames.

Rose's voice grew dreamy. "I remember when you boys were about four and six. You waited up until past midnight hoping for a glimpse of Father Christmas."

Flem chuckled. "I was determined to stay awake the whole night. The next thing I knew, it was Christmas morning, and I was in my bed."

Gray laughed, remembering. "We'd made a pact to keep each other awake. Every time you dozed off, I'd give you a nudge. But when I finally fell asleep, and felt a nudge, it wasn't you trying to wake me, but Aunt Gerda, who'd spent the night. She was the one who carried you to your bed. And when I realized I'd have to face Father Christmas alone, I decided I'd rather be in my bed, too."

"You? Afraid?" Flem shook his head in amazement.

"That has to be the first and last time that has ever happened to the fierce Grayson Haydn."

Gray merely grinned.

"What about you, Miss Downey?" Broderick sipped his wine. "What was Christmas like at your house?"

"There was never a Christmas Eve as lively as this has been." Fiona couldn't help laughing as she allowed herself to go back in her mind. "My mum always made soda bread and a lovely beef roast with boiled potatoes and cabbage. We would exchange gifts and then Da would read to us."

"What did he read?"

"The Sonnets of William Shakespeare were favorites of ours. We all shared a love of reading. But we were especially fond of the English poet, Robert Browning. Da loved reading his poems to us."

"Do you recall any of them?" Rose prodded.

"I do. Yes." She set aside her glass and thought a moment. Then in a soft voice she began. "The year's at the spring, and day's at the morn; morning's at seven; the hillside's dew-pearled. The lark's on the wing; the snail's on the thorn; God's in His heaven—all's right with the world."

She paused, fighting for composure. The pain, sharp and swift, had come over her with no warning, and now she felt tears prickling her lids.

"I'm afraid I must beg your forgiveness, but it's been a long and wonderful day, and now I must say goodnight." She got to her feet, praying she could hold back the tears until she was safely out of sight. "I wish you all a very happy Christmas."

She heard their voices echoing that wish as she picked up her lantern and hurried from the room.

Once inside her room she closed the door and set down the lantern before slipping out of her dress and petticoats.

Shivering in the cold she pulled on the heavy cotton night-gown and turned toward her bed.

There was a tissue-wrapped package resting on her pillow. Inside was a small book of poetry by Elizabeth Barrett Browning, *Sonnets from the Portuguese.* With a little gasp of pleasure she opened the book to find it inscribed simply with the date, and the name Grayson Haydn.

"Oh, Gray." Stunned and happy beyond belief, she clapped a hand to her mouth, then looked down in dismay at her nightclothes. It was too late to go back in the parlor and thank him for this wondrous gift. She would have to wait until tomorrow.

She climbed beneath the covers and opened the book to a random page before beginning to read.

The face of all the world is changed, I think, since first
I heard the footsteps of thy soul move still, oh still,
beside me as they stole betwixt me and the dreadful
outer brink of obvious death, where I, who thought to
sink, was caught up into love, and taught the whole of
life in a new rhythm.

Fiona blew out the lantern and closed the book, pressing it to her heart. Strange. She had been dreading the thought of spending her first Christmas alone with these strangers in this faraway place. Now, they were no longer strangers, and the town of Paradise Falls didn't seem so very different from the place she had once called home.

Above all else, she knew she had found a good and true friend in the man who had just given her this most precious gift. She would cherish it, and him, for a lifetime.

FOURTEEN

———◆◆◆◆◆———

CHRISTMAS MORNING DAWNED cold and crisp, with new snow falling like a blanket of gauze over a soft, blurred landscape.

Fiona washed and took great care while dressing. For Christmas services she chose her best Sunday dress, a soft ivory wool with a high, simple neckline and long, tapered sleeves. Over this she wore an ivory shawl which her mother had crocheted in a clever cabbage rose design. Instead of brushing her hair in its usual neat knot, she decided to wear it long and loose, and pinned to one side with the mother-of-pearl comb Flem had given her. As she studied her reflection in the looking glass, she decided that, with her hair falling around her face in such a fashion, she looked entirely too daring and not at all like a teacher. Before she could change her mind, there was a knock on her door and Flem's muffled voice was calling her to breakfast.

She set aside her looking glass and hurried to the

kitchen, where the others had already gathered.

Broderick sat at the head of the big kitchen table, sipping tea. Though he still wore a towel tied around his neck, his drooling was much less pronounced. As he sipped, more of the tea went down his throat than spilled down his bib.

Gray was busy washing up, after seeing to his chores in the barn. His boots stood beside the stove, frosted with snow and dripping on a rug. He stood with his back to the room, his sleeves rolled to the elbows. Fiona studied the way his shirt stretched tightly across the muscles of his back and wondered at the dryness in her throat.

Broderick set down his cup when he spotted her. "Well, don't you look pretty."

Gray turned just as Flem called out, "I see you're wearing my comb."

Embarrassed, she touched a hand to her hair, hating the flush she knew was on her cheeks. "I'm thinking I'll take it out before we leave for town."

"Why?" Rose set a platter of sausage in the middle of the table.

"It seems too . . . frivolous for the town's teacher to be wearing."

"Nonsense." Broderick glanced at his oldest son as he took his place at the table. "What do you think, Gray?"

Gray took his time reaching for the platter of sausage and placing several on his father's plate before helping himself to some. "It's Christmas Day."

"Exactly." Flem took the platter from his brother's hands and held it out to Fiona. "Even a teacher is allowed to be frivolous on Christmas, don't you think, Miss Downey?"

She dimpled and speared a sausage. "I suppose so." She glanced over at Gray. "I wanted to thank you . . ."

Before she could finish he held up a hand. "The slates were from both Papa and me."

"Yes, but—" She saw the quick shake of his head and realized that he would be horribly embarrassed to have her mention aloud his other gift. Thinking quickly she amended, "The slates are really a gift to all my students, as well. A gift that will be appreciated for many years to come. I can't tell you how much they mean to me."

Flem pretended to be wounded. "Does this mean you like them more than my comb?"

Fiona laughed. "I love the comb, Flem, and whenever I want to be frivolous, I shall wear it."

"I'll take that as a sign then." He glanced around the table. "Whenever we see Miss Downey wearing a comb in her hair—"

He looked up at the sound of a horse and cart. "Someone's here." Pushing back his chair he peered out the window. "It's Christian and Edmer Rudd."

He threw open the backdoor and the two stomped up the steps. Christian was carrying a large, linen-wrapped parcel. When he stepped into the steamy kitchen, he removed his cap and called out greetings to all.

"Happy Christmas." He set his bundle on a sideboard and opened the wrapping.

"Is that a smoked ham?" Rose crossed the room to examine it more closely.

"That it is. Edmer and I went around to Frederick Dorf's this morning and bought all he had brought from Little Bavaria."

"You . . . went to his wagon?" Rose couldn't hide her surprise.

"I spied it yesterday in a field just outside of town. I knew that even Dorf wouldn't be out and about on Christmas Day. And I thought, since Little Bavaria sells the finest hams around, and Frederick Dorf is the only peddler to bring them to our town, I'd present them to my friends and neighbors on this happy day."

"They are much appreciated. Come." Rose stared

knowingly at her sons. "We've plenty of room at our table. You must eat something."

Gray and Flem got to their feet and hurried to the parlor, returning with two additional chairs. When Christian and Edmer were seated, Rose began passing them platters of sausage and eggs and slices of bread warm from the oven.

Christian was in a fine mood. After indulging his hearty appetite, he sat back, replete, sipping strong hot tea. "We invited Dolph and Will VanderSleet to supper after services. Lida would be pleased if you would join us as well."

Rose's glance took in Fiona. "That would be five additional guests at your table."

He avoided looking directly at Fiona. "We have room. Lida has asked Reverend Schmidt and Brunhilde, and young Schuyler Gable and his wife Charlotte, as well."

Rose gave a slight nod of her head, and Broderick spoke for all of them. "We would be happy to come, Christian."

Edmer glanced shyly at Fiona. "You'll come too, Miss Downey?"

She nodded. "I would be honored."

"Good. Good." Christian pushed away from the table and his son followed suit. "Now we must be off to deliver the rest of these hams." He nodded to each of them in turn before picking up his coat. "We'll see you at services."

When they were gone Rose studied her husband over the rim of her cup. "I don't believe I've ever seen Christian Rudd in such a mood. What do you think has come over him?"

Broderick touched a napkin to his mouth. Such a simple thing, but it had been such a long time since he'd been able to do even the simplest things for himself. He set it down and smiled at his wife. "Perhaps he is learning how to be a stone in a pond."

Rose looked perplexed. "I don't understand."

Broderick merely smiled. "Neither does Christian. But at least he's willing to learn."

"I'LL NOT RIDE in back of the wagon on Christmas." Broderick stood on the back porch and made the pronouncement as Gray drove the team from the barn.

Rose shot him a look. "Then who will ride in back?"

"I care not." He glanced at Flem as Gray brought the wagon to a halt. "Why don't you and Miss Downey ride in back?"

While Gray looked on Flem gave a wicked grin. "A wonderful idea. How about it, teacher? Want to sit in the hay with me?"

Before she could reply Gray interrupted. "If you think you're ready to drive the team, Papa, maybe you and Ma would like to ride alone? Flem and I can take Miss Downey in the little sleigh."

Rose could see that her husband was itching to drive the team. She placed a hand on his arm. "I leave it up to you, Broderick. Are you feeling strong enough?"

He nodded. "We'll see you at church." After scrambling up to the hard seat, he reached a hand to his wife.

When they were gone Gray turned toward the barn. "It will only take a few minutes to hitch old Strawberry to the sleigh. Want to give me a hand, Flem?"

Fleming shook his head. "I'll just stay here with Miss Downey while you take care of it."

He watched his brother walk away before turning to Fiona. "Alone at last. I thought they'd never leave."

While she laughed softly at his words he studied the comb, winking like the snowflakes that were falling around them. "I knew just how that would look in your hair."

"It's beautiful, Flem." She touched a hand to it. "I do love it."

"I'm glad. I wanted to impress you."

"Why?"

At her simple question he caught her by the chin and stared down into her eyes. When he realized that she was serious, he broke into a wide smile. "You don't know, do you?"

"Know what?"

"That you're beautiful. I've always loved being around beautiful women. I like looking at them. Flirting with them. Teasing them." He leaned close and puckered his lips. "Kissing them."

She drew back as though he'd slapped her. "Don't say such a thing, Flem."

"What?" He stared at her "That you're beautiful? Or that I'd like to kiss you?"

"Both. You're too bold. You make it sound . . . like some sort of silly game. I'm not interested in flirting. Or . . . anything else you might have in mind."

"So prim and proper, aren't you, Miss Downey? Know what I think?"

"I don't care what you think." She started to turn away but he grabbed her by the arm and forced her to face him.

"I think all that prim and proper starch in your petticoat is just playacting, to hide the passionate heart that beats inside."

She stared down at his hand as though it offended her. "Let me go, Flem."

He tightened his grasp and leaned close. "And if I don't?"

Just then they heard the jingle of harness. Flem withdrew his hand, breaking contact, and took a step back.

By the time the horse and sleigh paused by the porch,

Flem was smiling and whistling a little tune, as though he hadn't a care in the world. He settled Fiona in beside Gray, then sat next to her, tucking a fur throw over their laps.

Gray flicked the reins. With the wind whistling past their faces, and the snow falling softly in their hair, the horse and sleigh moved smoothly over the fresh mounds of snow.

While Fiona rode in silence, Flem seemed more cheerful than usual as they made their way to town, where, it seemed, everyone in Paradise Falls had come together for a joyous Christmas service.

"OH, FLEMING." LIDA Rudd clapped her hands. "Play us one more tune. Please."

After a festive supper, everyone was seated in the Rudd's parlor, the women enjoying tea while the men drank dark beer and tapped their toes to Flem's rousing music.

Charlotte Gable had fallen under his spell, giggling and blushing like a schoolgirl when he'd singled her out to turn the pages of his sheet music. From her vantage point, Fiona watched as Charlotte's young husband, Schuyler, became more and more withdrawn. While the men drank their beer and talked about their farms, Schuyler merely scowled at his wife as she sat close beside Flem on the piano bench.

On a rug in front of the fire Edmer and Will huddled together, heads bent in quiet confidence. It occurred to Fiona that these two boys had become unlikely allies. Perhaps in time, they might even become friends. And that could change them both.

Feeling relaxed and content, Fiona accepted a second cup of tea from her hostess. "You've a lovely home, Mrs. Rudd."

"Thank you, Miss Downey."

"And the Christmas supper was grand," Rose chimed in. She glanced over at her husband, who was beginning to show the strain of such a long day. "But I do believe it's time we headed home."

Lida Rudd lowered her voice. "Broderick has made a remarkable recovery, hasn't he?"

Rose nodded. "Dr. Eberhardt told me at services that he was astounded by the improvement he has seen in the past months. He has no idea what the future holds, since Broderick has already surpassed all expectations."

"You must be proud of your husband."

Rose gave a thin smile. "He's a stubborn man. Too stubborn to allow even illness to rule his life."

"I would call that most fortunate for you," Lida said with a laugh.

Rose set aside her tea and crossed the room to whisper to her husband.

Minutes later Broderick stood and offered his hand to his host. "I thank you for this lovely supper, Christian."

The rest of the guests took this as a signal to end their visit, as well.

Fiona followed Gray and his family to the door, where, after retrieving coats and scarves and gloves, everyone prepared to take their leave, with Reverend Schmidt and his wife in the first wagon, and Dolph and Will VanderSleet following close behind.

Schuyler Gable looked around before saying to his hostess, "Where has my wife gone?"

Before Lida could begin to search for her missing guest, Charlotte and Flem stepped from the parlor. Though the young woman's face was flushed, and her demeanor clearly flustered, Flem merely smiled and held up his sheet music. "I almost left this behind."

Lida Rudd put a hand on his arm. "Thank you again, Fleming. Your music added so much to our evening.

Why, if I hadn't known you all your life, I'd think you were a professional musician."

His smile became dazzling. "You couldn't have paid me a higher compliment, Mrs. Rudd."

As their family started toward the waiting horses the crisp night air rang with the sound of their happy voices calling out their goodbyes to their hosts.

Gray settled Fiona in the sleigh before climbing in beside her. Flem walked to the other side. When he was seated, and had tucked the fur around them, Gray flicked the reins and the horse started up, keeping a short distance behind the lantern that swayed on the back of their father's wagon.

They had gone some distance before Flem began chuckling.

Gray glanced over. "What is amusing you?"

"Schuyler Gable. If he doesn't take better care of that pretty little wife of his, he may lose her."

Gray's voice became dangerously soft. "Schuyler Gable is a good friend, Flem."

Flem's voice turned sullen. "What's that supposed to mean?"

"We'll talk about this when we're alone."

"No. We'll talk about it now. Say what you're thinking, brother."

Gray sighed. "There is a line you cannot cross with a man's wife."

Flem threw back his head and laughed. "What if the wife is more than willing to step across?"

"She's young. Unsure of her role as a bride. Someone like you can easily dazzle her."

"Someone like me?"

Gray snapped the reins and said through clenched teeth, "All that charm."

"You make it sound like a vice. At least you're willing to admit I'm charming."

"Oh, you're charming, Flem, and you know how to use it. But Schuyler and his wife deserve better from you."

"Why? Because I didn't want to marry her? If I'd asked her, she'd have been mine instead of his, and he knows it."

"Maybe. But you didn't ask her, did you?"

"Why should I? Why would I want to tie myself to one woman for the rest of my life, when I can have them all?"

Gray suddenly swore and reined in the horse. Though they came close to colliding with the wagon in front of them, he managed to bring the horse to a halt just in time.

He was out of the sleigh in an instant and racing ahead to his father's side. Minutes later he returned, slightly out of breath.

"You'll have to drive the sleigh, Flem. Papa's too weary to handle the team any longer."

As Gray walked away and pulled himself up to the wagon seat, Fiona's heart plummeted. This beautiful day had just come to an abrupt, and most unpleasant, end.

FIFTEEN

———◆◇◆———

BY THE TIME Flem brought the sleigh to a halt at the barn, Gray was unhitching the team from his father's wagon. He barely looked up from his task. "You might want to see if Ma needs a hand with Papa. I'll unhitch Strawberry for you."

Flem seemed grateful to escape the unpleasant chore. After helping Fiona out of the sleigh, he hurried to the house, leaving her to fold the fur lap robe and set it aside. That done, she watched as Gray took out his still-smoldering anger on the harness, tossing it over the rail of a stall with such force she feared the leather might split.

Her first thought was to leave him alone with his dark mood. He seemed in no frame of mind to accept something as unimportant as her meager thanks, but there might never be another time for her to express her appreciation. She settled herself quietly on a bale of hay and watched as he turned the horses into their stalls and saw to the dozens of small tasks required for their comfort.

He seemed to take particular pleasure in stabbing a pitch-fork into a mound of hay and scattering it into each stall, before pouring water from a bucket into each trough.

Finally he slammed the last stall shut, unhooked the lantern from a peg on the wall, and turned.

That was when he spotted Fiona sitting as still as a barn cat in the shadows.

His voice was harsher than he intended. "It's too cold to stay out here. You should be indoors, by the fire."

"I'm not cold, Gray. Besides, I wanted a moment alone to thank you for that lovely surprise."

He looked ill at ease at the mention of his gift. "I saw it in the catalog when I was searching for Flem's music. I hoped it would be to your liking."

"Liking? How could I not like something so thought-ful?" She gave a little laugh and closed her eyes, quoting from one of her favorite poems.

How do I love thee? Let me count the ways. I love thee to the depth and breadth and height my soul can reach, when feeling out of sight for the ends of being and ideal grace. I love thee to the level of every day's most quiet need, by sun and candlelight . . .

As her voice trailed off she opened her eyes to see Gray staring at her in a way that had her heart stammer-ing. "What is it, Gray? What's wrong?"

He shook his head and turned away. "Nothing. I'm glad my little surprise pleased you."

"Oh, Gray." Without thinking she crossed to him and lay a hand on his arm. "I thought nothing could please me more than the slates. But when I found that book on my pillow, I was moved to tears. I thought . . ." She shook her head, sending dark curls dancing around her face. "I thought I would feel so miserably alone this year, so far from home and family, without Da and Mum. But all that changed with your gift." Impulsively she stood on tiptoe and brushed a kiss over his cheek.

She was aware that he'd gone very still. In his eyes was a strange, almost haunted look. Then he blinked, and the look was gone.

Alarmed that she had offended him by her boldness, she took a quick step back. "Goodnight, Gray. Thanks to you, this has been a truly wonderful Christmas."

With a swirl of skirts and petticoats she danced away, leaving him to stare after her.

For the longest time he merely stood watching, until she disappeared inside the house.

When at last he picked up the lantern and started across the yard, a figure stepped from the darkness and watched his departure through narrowed eyes.

FIONA SLIPPED INTO her cotton nightdress and turned down the covers of her bed, but instead of blowing out the lantern, she left it burning while she opened her precious book and began to read.

The words of Elizabeth Barrett Browning's love poem were so beautiful they brought tears to her eyes.

She understood the kind of special love the poet wrote about. Had witnessed it every day of her life between her Da and Mum. What's more, her parents had loved her just as freely, and had expressed that love for their only child without restrictions.

But what she was feeling for Gray was unlike anything she'd ever felt before. It was neither the comfortable love she'd felt for her parents nor the pleasant love she'd felt for friends.

Just what was she feeling for Gray? How could it possibly be love, when she felt so quivery inside? When he touched her, she felt hot and cold and almost sick to her stomach. These feelings churning inside her were so new, so frightening, she wasn't quite sure what to make of them.

What about Gray's feelings for her? Whenever he looked at her, there was no warmth in his eyes. No smiling curve of his lips. Instead, he seemed always tense and angry. As though everything about her made him want to turn away.

Only a fool would mistake such outward expressions of discomfort for love. And yet, what else was she to make of his gift?

She pressed the book to her heart and closed her eyes, thinking back to that impetuous moment when she'd kissed Gray's cheek. He'd been startled, of course. But there had been something else in his eyes. Something so dark, so intense, it had caused her heart to leap like a flame in dry straw.

Oh, Da. With a sigh she leaned over and blew out the lantern, before drawing the blankets around her shoulders. *How will I ever know whether this thing I'm feeling is love, or just gratitude for the kindness of a friend?*

She could feel herself drifting on that soft cloud of contentment that was a prelude to sleep. Suddenly she was alert. A sound had her eyes snapping open. She lay a moment, hearing the distant scrape of the barn door, and then the muffled hoofbeats that could only mean that Flem was heading out on one of his midnight excursions.

"Oh, Flem." Her muttered words were tinged with exasperation. "Even on Christmas night?"

Minutes later silence descended once more and she huddled under her blanket, willing herself to sleep.

THE DREAM HAD Fiona's lips curving into the merest hint of a smile. She was walking the campus of Bennett College with Da, who had stopped Mrs. Murphy to boast that his daughter was a fine and gifted teacher.

At the sound of Mrs. Murphy's brogue, Fiona hugged her arms about herself and thought how much she'd missed that lovely sound.

Mrs. Murphy opened her mouth to say something else, but the words were lost when Fiona's mattress suddenly shifted, as though something heavy had settled on it.

"What . . . ?" She was instantly awake.

Her protest was cut off as a hand closed over her mouth. In a suffocating panic she pried at the offending hand, but her strength was no match for the one holding her down.

"Don't be afraid." Flem's voice, little more than a whisper, had her eyes going wide.

"Flem." As he removed his hand she sucked in several deep breaths. "You're drunk."

"Maybe. A little. But not so drunk I don't know what I want. You want it, too, Fiona Downey. You're just too innocent to understand what you're feeling. But I can help you."

As he lowered his face to hers she pulled away with a little cry.

"Stop." She sat up and pushed against him, before making a desperate scramble to escape. But before she could slip out of bed strong hands closed around her shoulders, pinning her roughly to the mattress.

"Don't fight me." He straddled her, pressing her body beneath his while he fumbled with the front of her night-dress. "You'll like this, teacher. It'll be far more enjoyable than doing sums on a slate."

"Flem. No. You mustn't—"

He closed a hand over her nose and mouth, effectively silencing her cries. The more she fought him, the harder he pressed, until she could feel herself beginning to lose consciousness. Spots danced in front of her eyes, and she could feel herself floating. Floating.

With her last breath she fought him, her body bucking

beneath his, until she managed to free one arm and brought her fist to the side of his head.

He swore and released his hold on her. That was all she needed to swing her legs over the side of the bed and make a dash for the door.

Before she could open it he gave her a rough shove and stepped in front of the door, barring her way.

Fiona picked up the porcelain pitcher from her nightstand and raised it by the handle like a sword. With her breath coming hard and fast she hissed, "Get out of my room or I swear to heaven I'll smash this against your face. How will you be able to explain that to your mother?"

Her words seemed to sober him instantly.

As the fog cleared from his brain he stared at her as though he couldn't believe what he was seeing. All the way home he'd worked himself into a frenzy, thinking about the way she would fight him until, lulled by his obvious charms, she would melt against him and give him what every girl eventually gave him.

"You really don't want me?"

If she weren't so desperately afraid, his words would have been laughable.

She kept the pitcher raised for emphasis. "I don't want you, Flem. Not now. Not ever. If you dare to touch me again, I'll go to your father. Now get out of my room or I'll shout down the household."

He watched the rise and fall of her chest as she struggled against the tears that were threatening. Then he shook his head, as though still unable to accept the truth. "It's Gray, isn't it?"

When she said nothing, he scowled and turned away to pull open her door.

Seeing that he was truly leaving, relief poured through Fiona, and she sank to her knees, before dropping the pitcher and burying her face in her hands.

Before taking his leave Flem turned and shot her that familiar charming smile. "It would seem you've set your cap for a slow, plodding workhorse, teacher. A pity, when you could have taken a much more enjoyable ride on a sleek, frisky racehorse."

As he turned, he caught sight of Gray standing at the foot of the stairs. Thinking quickly, he pulled Fiona's door closed and touched a finger to his lips. "I wouldn't bother our teacher right now, big brother. After a quick tumble, the ladies always need their rest."

"Liar." Gray's eyes were hot with fury. "Don't say such things about her. Don't you ever speak of her that way."

"Maybe you'd like to ask her yourself." Growing bolder by the minute, Flem chuckled. "Go ahead. But I warn you—you risk embarrassing our sweet little teacher. She would prefer the rest of the world think of her as an innocent."

He saw Gray's look of disbelief, followed by one of uncertainty. That only had him prodding more. "You mean you never noticed? Under that prim shawl beats the heart of a very passionate woman."

Gray's hand shot out, fisting into the front of his brother's shirt. "If you say anything more, it will be the last word you ever speak." His voice was strangled. "I swear it."

Feeling the way Gray's body was vibrating with a building rage, Flem lifted his hands in a gesture of surrender. For the space of a heartbeat he thought he'd pushed Gray too far, and feared he might yet taste the fury he knew his older brother capable of. He watched as Gray fought back the simmering heat until, at last, his fingers uncurled and he took a step back.

As Flem turned and started up the stairs to his room, his smile returned. Once again he'd managed to turn Gray's timing to his own advantage.

Oh, it couldn't have been more perfect.

*   *   *

THE ANGER PULSING through Gray was like a great, black wave that all but blinded him. He wanted, needed, to lash out at someone or something. To use his fists in a knock-down, drag-out fight that would cleanse him of this building fury.

His first thought was to knock on Fiona's door and demand to know if his brother had lied. Of course he'd lied. Fiona was too good, too honorable, to have done what Flem implied.

He strode across the room, then came to an abrupt halt, plagued by sudden indecision. How could he possibly knock on Fiona's door and risk causing her embarrassment?

He stood just outside her room and listened for any sound that might signal she was still awake. He could hear nothing through the closed door.

He remembered the first time, when Flem had tried to force himself on her in the kitchen. She'd seemed so relieved to have someone come to her aid. But this time Flem had seemed so smug and satisfied.

Too smug. Too satisfied.

How could he believe anything Flem told him? Hadn't his younger brother proved time and again to be a most accomplished liar? Still, there was no denying that he was pleasing to the eye and had learned how to use his considerable charm to his advantage with women. Most women, in fact, couldn't resist Flem.

But Fiona? She seemed wise beyond her years, and immune to the shallow charms of the likes of Flem.

Gray stepped closer and strained to hear anything out of the ordinary. If she were to sigh, to pace, to call out, he would go to her in a heartbeat. He waited, wishing for some sign that she needed him.

Needed.

What he needed was the truth. If he learned that his brother lied, he would first comfort Fiona, and then confront Flem with the truth, before having the satisfaction of the fight his hot blood craved.

Hearing nothing, Gray turned away and made his way to the backdoor, still battling both fury and disbelief. Because anger was easier to deal with, he decided what he needed was a long walk in the frigid darkness.

AFTER FIONA'S TEARS had run their course, she tried to stand, but her legs were too weak to support her. *Not surprising*, she thought as she crawled across the room to her bed, considering what she'd been through.

As the shock of her attack sank in, she gathered the covers around her and wondered if she would ever feel warm again. She felt chilled clear to her bones.

She could still feel Flem's hands on her. Could still feel the panic that had swept her when she'd thought she would surely suffocate.

She heard a sound outside her door and sat up in the darkness, frozen with fear. New doubts assailed her. Had Flem returned? How could she possibly defend herself a second time? She should have taken steps to see that he couldn't force his way in again.

Though every movement was an effort, she slipped out of bed and grasped the edge of her night table, pressing all her weight against it as she moved it inch by painful inch across the room and in front of her door.

That done she stood perfectly still, listening for anything out of the ordinary.

Was that the sound of someone breathing just beyond her door? She thought so, though she couldn't be certain. She stood there for as long as she could. When the cold and the exhaustion finally forced her back to bed, she huddled under the blankets, too afraid to close her eyes.

Oh, Da. Tears welled up and she brushed at them with the back of her hand. *Help me stay strong and vigilant, in case Flem should come back.*

She replayed every terrible moment in her mind, wondering if she'd done anything to invite such a lewd attack. She had never given Flem any reason to think she wanted him. And yet, he'd seemed absolutely astonished when he'd finally come to the realization that she was willing to do battle to protect her virtue.

Did he think himself so handsome and charming and irresistible that no woman would ever refuse his advances?

She thought back to his defense when Gray had criticized him for his flirtation with Charlotte Gable. He had acted as though he had every right to another man's wife. If that were true, then he would surely think he had the right to any unmarried woman, as well.

Fiona had witnessed time and again how he used his charm with his mother. There was nothing he couldn't have, if he made up his mind to it. He'd boasted that it had been so since he was just a boy. Was that when Fleming Haydn had decided that the rules by which others lived didn't apply to him?

As the hours dragged on, the shock of what she'd been through took their toll. Just before dawn she fell into a troubled sleep.

SIXTEEN

——◆◆◆◆——

FIONA AWOKE, GRATEFUL that there was no school scheduled. Moving at a snail's pace she managed to wash and dress. As she poured water from the pitcher into the porcelain basin, she paused to stare at it, grateful that she hadn't had to use it against her attacker.

The simple act of tidying the bed linens had her studying the bed through new eyes. What had once been her refuge had almost become a horror. In the light of day it was difficult to imagine that she'd been imprisoned in this small space, fighting for her life.

She shivered and sank down on the edge of the bed until she could compose herself.

The incident with Flem was still so vividly etched in her mind, she wondered how she would ever be able to put it aside.

Would Flem have behaved differently if he hadn't been drunk? Or did the liquor just magnify the flaws that already existed in his personality? Whatever the reason, she knew that she would never again be able to sleep unless she took measures to protect herself. Broderick was the logical one to confide in, because of his authority in the family, but she feared that something this upsetting might bring on another stroke. There was no way she could share such a thing with Rose. That left only Gray, and the thought of telling him what had happened was too painful to imagine. Still, she feared for her life if she didn't take steps to bar Flem from ever assaulting her again.

As she made her way to the kitchen she heard the sound of voices raised in anger.

She was surprised to see Flem dressed in his Sunday best. Usually, after a night of drinking and gambling, he slept until midafternoon. Yet here he was, standing beside the stove, facing his parents who were seated at the table. Fiona was grateful that he barely flicked her a glance before returning his attention to something his mother was saying.

"What do you mean, you're leaving?"

Before Flem could respond Gray stomped in from the barn and set his boots to dry after hanging his coat by the backdoor. When he'd finished washing up, he took a seat at the table without a word to anyone.

When he caught sight of Fiona he looked away with a frown.

Broderick set down his cup with a clatter. "Where would you go?"

"Any place that doesn't have farms." Flem took his time pouring tea and sipping.

Fiona turned away, intent upon returning to her room, so that the family could have this discussion in private.

Before she could leave Rose set down a plate with a terse command. "Eat."

Feeling trapped, Fiona picked at her food in silence.

"Just like that?" Broderick looked up at his younger

son. "You come in here and announce you're leaving, just like that?"

"It's something I've wanted to do for a long time. It's no secret that I hate this place. I hate farm chores. I want to go where there's laughter and music and..." He drained the last of his tea. "Life. I want to live life, not just watch it pass me by."

"I ask you again." Broderick met his son's eyes. "Where will you go?"

"Chicago." Flem spoke the word almost reverently.

"Chicago." Broderick spat the same word as though it offended him. "It would seem you've given this a great deal of thought."

"I have. There are places there where I could play my music. You heard Mrs. Rudd last night, Papa. She isn't the first to say I play like a real musician." He turned to his mother. "You've told me, Ma, that you had dreams of going places and doing things when you were my age. Well, I have dreams, too. It's time I went after them. Why should I walk behind a plowhorse all day and shovel manure every night, when I could be a musician?"

Rose avoided her husband's eyes, aware that he'd turned to her with a scowl. "How will you get to this Chicago?"

"I'll take the train. I checked with Gerhardt days ago. There'll be one in town today."

"Today?" Rose's breakfast was forgotten. She set aside her fork to stare at her son. "How will you pay for this train ride to Chicago?"

Broderick's cup was halfway to his mouth when Flem answered. "I have money." He reached into his pocket and pulled out a wad of bills. "Lots of money."

Tea sloshed everywhere as Broderick set his cup down with a thud. "How did you come by all this money?"

Flem's smile was pure charm. "The men of Little Bavaria might be good enough farmers, but they're lousy gamblers."

"Gambling?" Broderick shoved back his chair, staring at his son with a look of black fury. "You would risk my money by gambling?"

"It's not much of a risk. I told you. Those farmers—"

"Not a risk? Not a risk?" Broderick brought a fist down on the table so hard it sent dishes rattling. A plate smashed on the floor, but no one paid any attention as shards of glass scattered everywhere. "You've watched your mother and me struggle every day to keep this farm going. Your brother works like a mule so that we have enough for each spring's planting. And you're off risking it all on the turn of a card. When do you do this gambling?"

"At night. I don't like to sleep at night so I—"

"No!" Broderick's voice lowered with anger. "You don't need to sleep at night, since you sleep most of the day while others do your work." He pinned his son with a dark look. "Where do you gamble?"

"Usually in Little Bavaria." Flem added casually, "At someone's home."

"Whose horse do you ride?" Broderick demanded.

"Yours, Papa."

"Mine. And whose money do you steal to do this gambling?"

"I don't steal I—"

"Whose money do you steal to do this gambling?"

"Yours, Papa. But I hardly ever lose. Here." With a look of arrogance he began peeling off bills and tossing them into the air, where some fluttered to the table, others landed on the floor. "That should more than pay you back for what I used to get started on my fortune."

A bill floated down, brushing Broderick's sleeve. He shook it aside before turning to his wife. "You tell me, Rose. What kind of son steals the sweat of all those he claims to love, for his own pleasure?"

Rose simply stared at her son, unable to take it all in. When she could find her voice she managed to whisper, "Why, Fleming? How could you do this to me? To all of us?"

"I have dreams, Ma."

"Dreams." She was shaking her head. "How could you put your dreams ahead of what is right?"

"Do you want me to stay, Ma?"

"You know I do, Fleming, I can't imagine—"

He held up a hand and stopped her. "For what? To become what you've become? Look at you, Ma. You told me you once had dreams of a grand life. You were going to travel, see the world. What happened to that life, Ma? Is this what you wanted? To wash clothes and bake strudel until you're too old to get out of bed?" His hand closed around the wad of money and he jammed it deep into his pockets. "I want more. I want—"

"You told us." Broderick's eyes were narrowed on his younger son. "You want music and laughter, regardless of the cost to those you leave behind."

"That's right. I don't care about the cost. I want it all. And I'll have it in Chicago. I want to wake every day feeling alive. Sharing some excitement with people who feel the same way."

He turned to his brother. "You haven't said anything yet, Gray. Not that I'd expect you to take my side in this. When it comes to family arguments, I always know where you stand. Squarely with Papa and always against me."

Gray calmly finished his breakfast and set down his fork. "Then I don't need to say a word, do I?"

Rose pinned Gray with a look. "Did you know about this?"

He shook his head. "Flem doesn't confide in me, as you well know. But I can't say I'm surprised." He turned to Flem. "If you've already talked to Gerhardt about the train schedule, you've been planning this for some time.

I noticed a carpetbag out on the porch when I was coming in from the barn. I assume you're ready to go today, with or without Papa's permission."

"I'm eighteen years old. I don't need anybody's permission to live my life. I figure if I leave now, I can walk to town in time to board the train in an hour."

Rose started to cry. "You're really leaving me, Fleming?"

He walked over and brushed a kiss to her cheek. "I'm not leaving you, Ma."

"You can't. You can't leave me all alone here. You can't, Fleming." She wrapped her arms around his neck and hugged him so fiercely he cried out and was forced to pry her arms from around him.

It took all of his strength to hold her at arm's length. He studied the wild-eyed look of her as though seeing a stranger. "It isn't you, Ma. I'm leaving this place. This farm. This godforsaken town. There's nothing for me here."

After enduring the scene in silence as long as he could, Gray shoved aside his empty plate. "No challenges left, is that it, Flem? You've conquered everything and everybody in Paradise Falls?" Though he hadn't intended to, he glanced at Fiona.

His meaning wasn't lost on Flem, who gave a quick, dangerous smile. "That's right, big brother. Everything and everybody."

Fiona left her meal untouched and pushed away from the table, determined to give this family the privacy they deserved.

Before she could escape Flem crossed the room and caught her roughly by the shoulders. "Leaving before you can offer me a fond goodbye, Miss Downey?"

At the mere touch of him she went rigid with shock. Sensing that she was about to claw at his face, Flem pinned her arms at her sides and, with his family watching, kissed her full on the lips. Stunned and horrified she fought free and wiped a hand over her mouth, as if to erase the foul taste of him. "How dare you?"

When she looked over at his family, she realized that they had already turned away, as though embarrassed to witness something so intimate between their son and their houseguest.

He covered her challenge with an exaggerated sigh. Then, to add to her humiliation he said, "I know how much you wish you could come with me, but as I've told you before, I travel alone."

The look of impotent fury in his brother's eyes was all that was needed to assure Flem that his parting shot had hit its intended target.

He was actually grinning as he called a final goodbye to his family before casually strolling out the door. While they watched in stunned silence he picked up his carpet-bag from the back porch and started across the yard, all the while whistling a little tune.

Reeling under the sting of this final humiliation, Fiona fled to her room, unaware that her reaction confirmed in everyone's mind that she was grieving the loss of someone dear to her.

SEVENTEEN

———◆◆◆◆———

WINTER DESCENDED UPON the land with all its fury, painting a bleak, bitter landscape. The fields of the Haydn farm, like the hills beyond, lay frozen under a blanket of ice and snow. The air was now so frigid it shot icy darts to the lungs of anyone who dared to breathe it in too deeply.

The only creature up and about when Fiona left for school each morning was Chester the hound, who roused himself from sleep in the hay to wag his tail from the doorway of the barn as she began her long, silent journey to school. Her students arrived in pony carts and sleighs, wrapped in fur robes and swathed in scarves that left only their eyes uncovered.

Each morning she and Will VanderSleet chopped through thick layers of ice in the creek to fill the buckets of water. Logs burned continuously during the day, and the children gathered close to the fireplace for warmth.

A simple visit to the outhouse required many minutes

of preparation for her students, as they pulled on boots, coats, scarves, and mittens. When they returned, they stood in front of the fire until their backsides were warm enough to sit at a desk.

With each passing day Fiona grew more eager to escape the Haydn farm and take refuge in her work. Life in the Haydn house had become one of strained silences, broken only by the occasional quarrel between Rose and Broderick. Gray had become distant and sulky, and Fiona's shy attempts to draw him into conversation had been met with defeat.

Though she had gone over every moment of that fateful morning in her mind, she could come up with no other logical explanation for his behavior except Flem's kiss. Somehow Gray believed that she had invited it. What was worse, Flem's words had been calculated to make his family believe that she had wanted to leave with him. But why? Was this retaliation for having rejected his advances? Or was there something more here? Could it be something deep and dark and hurtful between Flem and his brother that made him want to strike out in such a mean-spirited way, using her as the weapon?

She didn't know what hurt more. The fact that Flem had succeeded in driving a wedge between her and Gray, or the fact that Gray thought so little of her.

This much Fiona knew. Flem had managed, in one simple act, to forever change those who loved him. The Haydn family, which had only recently begun to experience joy and laughter, were now even more subdued and distant than ever. Rose was so miserably lonely without Flem, who had been her only joy, that it seemed her poor heart was shattered beyond repair. The gulf between Rose and her husband seemed wider than ever, and she now found fault with everything Gray did, with even more venom than before.

Late at night, while Gray and his father sat in stony

silence by the fire, and Rose brooded in the kitchen, Fiona huddled alone in her cold room and pondered how Flem could have done this to people he claimed to love. What made a person so occupied with self, he would pursue his own pleasures at any cost?

She had begun to surmise that it was something he'd learned at his mother's knee. Once he'd discovered that his charming smile and insincere flattery could get him anything he wanted, he simply used those gifts on everyone he met.

She pushed aside thoughts of Flem. Added to her worry over the Haydn family was the fact that she'd received no letters from her mother in many weeks. She could think of only one reason why her mother wouldn't write, and that was illness. The thought that her mother might be sick and suffering, far from the comforts of her familiar home and loving daughter, was almost more than Fiona could bear.

She drew the blanket around her shoulders and started yet another letter to her mother.

Dear Mum

   You and Da would be so proud of the progress I'm making with my students. The two oldest lads, who were once at odds, have now become good friends, and the two of them have been helping me prepare the schoolroom each morning. All the students can now read at least a little, and they're getting better at their sums.

   I'm saving my money, Mum, so that when school is out I can send for you. I'm hoping I can find a room in town to rent, so that we can be together. I can't wait to see you again. It's been too long.

Fiona was horrified to see a tear slip onto the page and smear the words. She hadn't even realized she was crying.

She sniffed and wiped at her eyes, before blotting the moisture from the paper.

With a sigh she put aside her letter and crawled into bed. It was so cold her teeth were chattering. She huddled under the blankets and prayed she could soon escape into blessed sleep.

FIONA WAS IN her room preparing some challenges for her students. During these long, isolated days, without a brief respite outdoors, they tended to grow restless. She'd found that by challenging their minds, the hours flew by faster.

She looked up at the tap on her door and was surprised to hear Broderick's voice calling her to supper. When she hurried to the kitchen she found Rose serving the table, and Broderick seated as his usual place.

She glanced around. "Aren't we waiting for Gray?"

Rose, who had been sulking for days after a particularly bitter dispute with her husband, set a platter of wurst and sauerkraut in the middle of the table. "He knows what time we eat."

Broderick helped himself to the food before passing the platter to Fiona. "He was taking a load of logs to town."

"That's no reason to be late for supper." Rose snapped the kettle down on the stove. "Why can't he think about the rest of us?"

Broderick sighed. "He can't make the farmers who are buying the logs work faster, just because his mother wants him home for supper."

Rose took her place at the table. "Then he ought to get an earlier start in the morning."

"If he started any earlier it would be the middle of the night."

Rose slapped the table. "Why must you always defend him?"

Broderick set down his fork. "Why must you always criticize him?"

The object of their discussion stomped up the steps and threw open the door, bringing with him a blast of frigid air. He had to lean against the door to secure it.

When the latch was fastened he turned. "Sorry I'm late."

"And well you should be." Rose glared at him. "Your boots are leaking all over my clean floor."

He removed them and set them on a rug by the back-door before hanging his coat and scarf. While he rolled his sleeves and washed his hands in a basin he said, "I stopped by the station to see if Gerhardt had any mail."

Rose touched a hand to her heart and Fiona could see that the poor woman was desperately awaiting the rest of his news.

Gray turned. Seeing them both watching him he shrugged. "I'm sorry. There was nothing."

As he took his place at the table and reached for the platter Rose's pent-up emotions exploded. She shoved away from the table and got to her feet, staring at her son as though he were a complete stranger. "I can't bear this any longer."

Gray and his father merely stared at her.

She paced to the stove, then back to her chair, while the others watched in silence.

"I can't bear not knowing what has happened to Fleming."

Broderick sat back in his chair. "What do you intend to do about it?"

Rose paced to the stove, turned, and walked back to the table. "Grayson must go to Chicago and find Fleming."

"And where do you think I should look, Ma?" Gray filled his plate.

"Someplace where there is music and laughter." She began pacing again, talking to herself. "Fleming is an accomplished pianist. By this time he will have secured himself a place to work and a place to live. If there is a symphony, perhaps he is working there. I'm sure his fellow musicians would help him find a clean, respectable place to live." She nodded, pleased with the image that presented. "Yes, something fashionable. I'm sure of it."

Gray began to eat, but before he'd managed two bites, his mother snatched the plate away. "How can you sit here and calmly eat when your brother may be going hungry?"

"You just said you believe he has a job and a place to live."

"I pray it's so." She stalked to the stove and set aside Gray's plate absently. "I need to know. I'll die if I don't know what's happened to my son."

"And what do you want me to do when I find him?"

She turned. Her eyes burned like twin flames, making her pallor even more pronounced. "You must convince him to come home."

"You want him to leave his job with the symphony and his . . . fashionable quarters, and just come home?" He made a sound that might have been a laugh or a sneer. "And if he won't?"

She clenched her fists. "You've always been bigger and stronger. You can force him to come home with you."

"Force him. You want me to toss him over my shoulder like a sack of grain and carry him home." Gray turned to his father. "Is this what you want?"

Broderick gave a long, deep sigh. "I don't know. If your mother is right, and he's found his dream, I don't believe he will return, even by force. But I want you to try. God knows, there'll be no peace in this house until your mother is assured in her mind that Fleming is safe."

Without a word Gray shoved away from the table and walked out of the room. Minutes later they could hear his footsteps as he climbed the stairs. Several hours later, when Fiona went to her bed, he was still in his room. Whether brooding or packing, no one knew.

AS SHE DID every morning, Fiona carried her lantern to the kitchen to fetch her lunch before leaving for the schoolhouse. Gray stood at the stove, filling a cup with strong hot tea. It gave her a jolt to see him, clean-shaven, his dark hair carefully combed, dressed in his Sunday best.

A frayed carpetbag stood by the door.

"It's true then? You're going to Chicago?"

He didn't bother to turn around. "Was I given a choice?"

Fiona stood a moment, watching him lift the cup to his mouth and drink, all the while keeping his back to her.

From her pocket she withdrew the envelope she'd intended to leave on the kitchen table. "I've written my aunt's name and address. I was hoping you might be willing to visit, just long enough to see why my Mum hasn't written."

He turned then and gave her a long, steady look. "How long has it been since you heard from her?"

"Christmas." She carefully schooled her features and fought to keep her voice from trembling. "If she is ill, I need to be assured that she's being cared for."

"Of course." He accepted the envelope just as Rose and Broderick stepped into the kitchen.

It was plain that they'd been arguing. Rose's face was flushed, her mouth a thin, tight line of anger.

Like Gray, his father was dressed for traveling. "If you'll fetch the wagon, Grayson, I'll drive you to the station."

"There's no need, Papa. It's dark, and you'll have to return alone."

The older man straightened his shoulders. "Old Strawberry and I know the way. We could make it there and back in our sleep." He turned to Fiona. "We can drop you at the schoolhouse on our way."

"That will take you too far out of your way, Mr. Haydn."

"We have time." He glanced at his son. "Go on now."

Gray relented, knowing there was no way of changing his father's mind. A short time later, when they heard the approach of the horse and wagon, Fiona and Broderick stepped outside and joined Gray on the high, hard seat.

Rose remained on the porch. Her voice was as brittle as the frozen branches of the trees in the yard. "Don't come home without your brother."

When Gray made no reply she shouted, "Do you hear me? Don't come home without Fleming."

Fiona shot a sideways glance at Gray, but was unable to read anything in his stony countenance. She thought of the tears and the almost loverlike embraces Rose had lavished on her younger son, yet for this son there wasn't so much as a kind word as he embarked on the same journey.

Gray flicked the reins and the horse started forward. When Fiona turned, she could see that Rose had already fled the cold and had returned to the warmth of her kitchen.

"It's just her way," Broderick said softly.

Gray didn't bother to respond.

They rode the rest of the way to the schoolhouse in silence. When Gray brought the horse to a halt, he climbed down and held out a hand to assist Fiona.

She stared up at him, wishing for something, anything, to ease the tension between them. In the end all she could manage was, "I wish you a safe journey, Gray."

"Thank you. I'll do my best to find your mother."

"I can't ask any more than that. I'm grateful to you, Gray. I hope and pray you find her in good health."

Hearing the way her voice trembled, he touched a hand to her arm and seemed about to say something. Seeing the hopeful way she was staring into his eyes, he took a step back and climbed up beside his father.

She stood watching as the wagon was swallowed up by the darkness. Soon the only thing she could see was the swaying of the lantern, until even that disappeared from sight.

EIGHTEEN

———◆·■·◆———

"DID I HEAR the wagon?" Rose nearly dropped the loaf of bread she was lifting from the oven. She set the pan down and hurried to throw open the backdoor, smoothing her hair and stripping aside her apron.

Fiona walked out onto the porch to stand beside her.

They had received word from Gerhardt Shultz that the train from Chicago would be arriving this day. Broderick had already driven the horse and wagon to town, leaving his wife to take out her nerves in the kitchen. She had been cooking since early morning, preparing all of Flem's favorite foods. The air was perfumed with the fragrance of chicken and wurst, breads dark and light, and sauerkraut. Both a bundt and a strudel were cooling on the windowsill.

Rose shielded the thin winter sun from her eyes. "Do you see anything?"

Fiona nodded. "I do. Yes."

Rose gave a nervous little laugh. "You see? I wasn't imagining things."

When the horse and wagon finally pulled up the lane and turned into their yard, the two women could see that there were only two figures aboard.

Before it had even come to a halt Rose launched herself off the porch and raced toward her older son, who climbed wearily from the wagon seat. "Where is Fleming? I told you not to come home without your brother."

"Come inside, Ma." He helped his father down.

The moment Broderick was out of the wagon he caught his wife's hand and led her toward the house. Though she protested, she moved along at his side.

Gray reached into the back of the wagon for his carpetbag, before turning. When he did, he caught sight of Fiona standing alone on the porch, twisting her hands together nervously.

He climbed the steps and avoided her eyes as he held the door, leaving her no choice but to walk ahead of him. Once inside he seemed to take forever setting down his bag and stripping off his heavy coat before carefully hanging it on a peg by the door.

When he turned, he took a deep breath before saying, "I think you should all sit down."

Rose was suddenly wary. "What is it, Grayson? What terrible things do you have to tell?"

"Ma." He glanced at his father, who eased Rose into a chair.

Fiona followed suit, her eyes never leaving Gray's. Gray got down on his knees in front of her.

His voice lowered. "I went to the home of your aunt."

Fiona's eyes went wide. "You saw my mother?"

"I'd hoped to. I was . . ." He shook his head. "I'm sorry. I was too late."

"Too late? I don't under—"

He spoke quickly, hoping to spare her any more pain.

"You were right in surmising that your mother had become ill. Your aunt said it started with a fever, and quickly moved to her lungs. The doctor said it was pneumonia." He reached into his pocket and removed an envelope. "Your mother had begun a letter to you when she took ill. Your aunt thought you might want to read her last words."

Fiona stared at the envelope in his hands without reaching toward it. "Her last . . . ?"

"Your mother is dead, Fiona. She was buried two days before I arrived." Gray thrust the envelope into her hands and awkwardly patted her shoulder. "Your aunt sent along a box of her belongings. I'll bring them to your room later."

Fiona clapped a hand too her mouth, her voice little more than a whisper. "This is my fault. I should have been there with her."

Gray reached for her, closing his big hands over hers. "It was nobody's fault. Your aunt said your mother seemed very frail when she arrived in Chicago. It was her belief that your mother lost her will to live after losing your father."

She shook her head in denial. "But I could have given her some of my strength, if only I'd been there with her. Don't you see? I was all she had left. And I deserted her."

"You didn't desert your mother. You did what you had to do." Gray could see her eyes glazing over with shock and grief. At a loss for words he stood and filled a cup with water before handing it to her. "Drink this."

She did as she was told, emptying the cup in one long swallow without even being aware of what she was doing.

In the silence that followed Broderick turned to his wife. "Grayson found where Fleming was living."

"Oh, praise heaven." Rose lifted a hand to her quivering lips. "Tell me it was worthy of him. How did he look? Is he happy? What sort of job did he find?"

Gray exchanged a look with his father, and it was plain that they had already spoken at length about how much to tell Rose. Even though they would sugarcoat the truth, her heart was bound to be broken.

Broderick spoke for both of them. "Fleming has changed, Rose."

Her head came up. "What do you mean, changed?"

"Grayson found him playing a piano in a club."

"A gentleman's club?"

"Of sorts. He's staying in a room above it, with a group of pretty unsavory people."

Rose sniffed. "How many people?"

"Maybe a dozen or so."

Her eyes narrowed on her son. "In one room?"

Gray thought of the rat-infested tenement, the stairs littered with filth and broken bottles and sleeping drunks, and merely nodded.

She got to her feet, her eyes blazing. "Why are you spreading such lies about your own brother? Fleming has no need to live in a crowded room. He has plenty of money."

"Rose." Broderick put a hand over hers. "His money is all gone."

"Gone?"

Broderick said softly, "Tell your mother."

Gray glanced at his father before saying, "Flem might have been good enough to beat the farmers in Little Bavaria out of a few dollars at poker, but he was no match for the gamblers he met in Chicago."

She pulled away from her husband and fisted her hands at her waist. "They cheated him of his money? And you did nothing to stop them?"

"By the time I got there, the money was gone. Not that Flem seemed to care."

"How can you say such a thing? Why wouldn't he care?"

"Like Papa said, he's changed."

Her chin lifted. "How has Fleming changed?"

Gray shrugged. "Whiskey can dull a man's mind."

"Whiskey?" Rose stiffened as though she'd been struck. Slowly her shock turned to righteous anger. "How could you return without the brother who needs you, now more than ever?"

"I did what I could, Ma. I told him I'd been sent to Chicago to bring him home. We had a pretty nasty time of it." Gray paused, and decided not to go into details about the vicious, knock-down, drag-out fight that had ensued. At one point he'd found himself facing half a dozen pair of fists. The only salvation for Gray had been that most of Flem's friends had been too drunk to do too much damage, but at one point he'd found himself facing the tip of a razor-sharp knife in the hands of a hulking gambler who'd threatened to carve him into pieces.

"When I left that day, I told Flem I'd be returning in the morning to take him with me to the train." Gray turned to Fiona, who had listened to the entire narrative without expression. "That's when I went to locate your aunt's house."

He saw her fingers tighten around the envelope.

With a sigh he returned his attention to his mother. "The next morning, when I went back to Flem's room, he was gone. One of his roommates told me that Flem said he'd rather live in the meanest of Chicago's gutters than return to Paradise Falls."

Rose's anger was so palpable, she was trembling. She pointed a finger at Gray. "I don't believe you. I don't believe you even found your brother." She nodded her head for emphasis as she turned to her husband. "That's it. That's what this is about. He couldn't find Fleming, and he decided to cover it up with this horrible lie." Her voice lowered for emphasis. "He's always been jealous of Fleming. Even when they were just children, he knew."

"What did I know, Ma?"

She turned to Fiona, completely ignoring her son. "Did you know that when Fleming was born, people used to stop me just to admire my beautiful baby? By the time he was two he had long golden curls and the face of an angel." She paused for a moment, remembering. "He was seven when Broderick took him to the barn and cut off all his beautiful curls." She rounded on her husband. "I thought I would never be able to forgive you for such a cruel act."

"Cruel? Rose, the boy was being taunted by the other boys in town."

She nodded. "Because they were jealous." She turned back to Fiona. "I knew that he was special. I always told him so. He'd been blessed with so much more than other children, and as he grew to manhood it became obvious to everyone. No man in Paradise Falls was more handsome, or charming, or talented. Women, no matter what their age, couldn't help falling under his spell. If the men were cool to him it was only because they were jealous of all that he had. You know what I'm saying is true. I saw the way you looked at him."

Fiona was too shocked to do more than shake her head in denial, but Rose had already turned away to flick a dismissive glance at Gray. "I should have never sent you to fetch your brother, knowing that your jealousy would only cause you to spread vicious lies about him."

Broderick closed a hand over her upper arm. "Rose, listen to me."

"No." She pulled away, her eyes glittering with fury. "You listen to me. I refuse to believe anything Grayson has said about his brother. Fleming will return home one day, rich and successful. And when he does, he will prove the lies that have been spread about him."

Gray turned his back on his mother and picked up his carpetbag. Without a word he strode out of the kitchen.

Moments later they heard his footfall on the steps as he climbed the stairs to his room.

In the silence that followed Broderick clasped Fiona's hands, and noted that they were as cold as death. "I'm so very sorry about your mother, Miss Downey."

She said nothing as she bowed her head.

Broderick glanced at his wife, who stood with arms crossed over her chest, staring blankly out the window. "Our young guest has suffered a grave shock. She needs something to warm her."

Rose didn't turn. "And what about my shock?"

He sighed and crossed to the stove, spooning cabbage soup into a bowl. When he placed it in front of Fiona, she merely looked at it. Placing a spoon in her hand, he said gently, "Eat."

She dipped the spoon into the bowl and lifted soup to her mouth.

"Good." He sighed. "Again."

She did as she was told, as he'd known she would.

He continued coaxing her until the bowl was empty. Then he helped her to her feet and said, "Go to your room now, Miss Downey, and read your mother's letter. It will help you to deal with your loss."

He led her out of the kitchen and waited until he saw her door close. Then he returned to his wife's side, wishing he could force Rose to behave the way he'd just now forced their young houseguest.

But perhaps it would be easier for Fiona Downey in the long run. She was merely dealing with death, while Rose was facing something far worse. The waste of all those fine, bright dreams for her favored young prince had now gone up in ashes and smoke.

Dearest Fiona
    With every breath, I feel my strength slipping away.
I hate the thought of leaving you. But you will never

be alone. You have your father's sure and steady pur-
pose, and his fine mind, and his strength of will. Know
also that you have all my love. Your father and I will
remain with you in spirit always.

Gray knocked on Fiona's door and waited. When he
heard no response from inside her room, he tentatively
opened her door. She was sitting on the edge of the bed,
so as not to muss it, holding a single piece of paper.

"I've brought your mother's things." He crossed the
room and set down a trunk.

When he straightened, she barely glanced over. "Thank
you, Gray."

He knelt in front of her and could see that her eyes
were dry. She was sitting perfectly still, as though holding
herself together by a mere thread. He could see the effort
she was making to dam up all of the feelings threatening
to break free.

He took her hand in his. "Your aunt wanted you to
know that your mother didn't suffer. She just closed her
eyes and went to sleep."

When Fiona said nothing he added, "And she particularly wanted me to tell you that your mother's last words
were about you, and how proud you made her."

Despite her efforts one big wet tear slid from the corner
of her eye and spilled down her cheek.

She wiped at it with her free hand until he stopped her.
"Let the tears come."

She turned her head away.

"Don't be ashamed to cry." He drew her up and gathered her against his chest. "When we lose someone dear
to us, we have a right to our grief."

"Oh, Gray." The cry was torn from her lips before her
slender body shook with great, heart-wrenching sobs.

Now that she'd begun, she wept from the depths of her
soul, letting all the pain and anguish of the past months

mingle with the razor-sharp pain of this latest loss. She cried for the father she had adored, and the gentle mother who had been her angel. She wept for all the fine, loving memories of her past that could never be repeated in the future. And she wept for herself, giving vent to all the loneliness of the past months, and her fears for the unknown that lay before her.

Finally, when the tears had run their course, she took a deep, shuddering breath and stepped back. "I got your shirt all wet."

"It doesn't matter. It will dry." He pulled a clean handkerchief from his pocket and offered it to her.

She dried her tears and began twisting the pale linen square around and around her finger. "Thank you, Gray."

Now that he'd offered his comfort, he looked ill at ease. "I'll leave you now to go through your mother's things. Papa said you should come later and eat something more."

"How is your mother?"

He paused in the doorway, amazed that even now, in the depths of her own grief, she would care about another. "She's in her room. Papa is with her."

"Gray."

He turned.

Fiona took a deep breath. "I'm truly sorry for all that you had to go through. It must have been horrible for you, not only learning about my mother's . . ." She swallowed. "My mother's passing, but then to have to deal with Flem living in that horrible place and refusing to come home."

His expression never changed. But there was a softness in his tone. "You believe me?"

"Of course I believe you, Gray. Why would you lie about your own brother?"

He merely stared at her for long silent moments before saying softly, "Thank you."

He spun away and closed the door.

Fiona stood listening to the sound of his retreating footsteps, before turning her attention to her mother's trunk. Now that she'd shed her tears, her mind seemed clearer, sharper—as was her pain.

She sat back on her heels and thought again about that scene in the kitchen between Rose and her son. Though Fiona could sympathize with Rose's loss, her heart went out to Gray.

She admired his stoic acceptance, even while she cringed each time he was forced to endure yet another lashing of his soul at the hands of his own mother. What kind of man could survive such torture without once striking back? And what, she wondered, would happen if he should finally reach the end of that long-suffering patience?

She hoped she would never have to learn the answer.

NINETEEN

———◆━◆◆◆━◆———

FIONA SHOOK SNOW from her hair as she climbed
the steps to the farmhouse. Inside the kitchen, she was
assaulted by the smells that had become so familiar to
her. Bread baking. Wurst simmering in a pot. The air redolent with rich spices and seasonings.

Rose looked up from the stove and cast a disapproving
glance at Fiona's boots, dripping on the floor. Without a
word Fiona removed the boots and set them on a rug
before hanging her coat.

More than two weeks had passed since Gray's return
from Chicago, and though Rose continued to cook and
clean, she had exchanged less than a dozen words with
her oldest son.

Broderick spent all his time in the barn, hiding out
from his wife's seething anger. Gray had begun chopping
trees before dawn, and then hauling them to town, returning in time for supper. Fiona often heard the rattle of the

wagon as it passed her windows while she was just getting out of bed.

In order to overcome her grief, Fiona immersed herself in the classroom. She had paired each of her older students with a younger one, to assist in reading and sums. To her delight, everyone seemed to benefit from this, with the older ones taking pride in the accomplishments of their partners, and the younger ones working even harder to please their tutors.

Her greatest pride came from the way these diverse children had begun to accept one another. The friendship between Will and Edmer had spilled over to the others. Afton and Luther Dorf had begun forging a bond of trust, with Afton helping Luther with his words and accepting his help figuring sums.

Just as Broderick stepped into the kitchen they heard the rumble of Gray's wagon.

"Bitter out there tonight," Broderick muttered. He turned to Fiona. "You must be half-frozen after that trek across the hills."

"I am, yes." She held her hands over the open burner to warm them, and glanced up when Gray entered.

He went through his ritual without a word, kicking off his boots, hanging his coat, rolling his sleeves and washing his hands.

"Supper's ready." Rose carried a platter to the table and the others gathered around.

Broderick had just uttered the blessing when they heard the jingle of harness.

Rose clapped a hand to her mouth. "The train. I thought I heard it earlier. Fleming's come home. This must be Fleming." She shoved back her chair and rushed across the room while the others got to their feet and watched.

When she yanked the door open, Gerhardt Shultz was standing on the porch.

In her disappointment it took Rose a moment to remember her manners. "Come in, Gerhardt."

He stepped in and stared hard at the floor. "I've come . . . with news."

"Of Fleming?" Rose turned to her husband with a look of triumph. "I told you. Hurry, Gerhardt. What is it?"

"There's been an accident in Chicago." The stationmaster cleared his throat.

"Fleming's been hurt." She caught the end of her apron and twisted it around her hand. "What happened?"

"Now, now." Gerhardt held up a hand. "We don't know if it was Fleming. I just thought you ought to know that someone, a young man, was hit by a train in Chicago."

"A train? But how? Oh, my poor darling." Rose clapped a hand to her mouth. "How bad is it?"

The man turned to Gray and Broderick, avoiding the look in Rose's eyes. "The engineer said there wasn't a thing he could do. He saw several men weaving in and out along the tracks. He blew the whistle, and one man deliberately dropped down until he was lying right in the path of the train. Like he was daring the train to hit him."

"No. No. No." Rose spoke the word like a litany of denial. "It wasn't Fleming. I would know if he had died. I would feel it here." She pressed a hand to her heart and closed her eyes, listening to the steady, throbbing beat. "It wasn't Fleming, Gerhardt. You've made a terrible mistake."

The stationmaster hung his head. "I hope you're right, Rose. The authorities will do their best to identify the young man. They went through his clothes, but found nothing."

Rose's head came up sharply. "Then why did you bother to bring us this news?"

The stationmaster shrugged in discomfort. "Someone said that Fleming had been seen drinking whiskey while playing the piano in a beer garden nearby."

"A beer garden?" Rose huffed out a breath. "Fleming found work playing music in a gentleman's club."

"I only know what I'm told, Rose. A young man reported that Fleming often challenged his friends to lie down on the tracks, and one or two had done so on other occasions. But this night they were too drunk to know whether Fleming had actually joined them, or if he'd had time to jump to safety. Someone saw a man running away just before the train struck, but he didn't come back to volunteer any information."

"If Fleming's friends had been in peril, you know as well as I, Gerhardt, that he would have been the first to come to their aid."

The stationmaster looked hard at the floor. "Yes, well . . . as soon as I know more, I'll come by with the news."

"Thank you, Gerhardt." Broderick offered his hand and the stationmaster awkwardly accepted it before turning away.

When the door closed behind him, the others stood in silence, listening to the jingle of harness as the horse and wagon departed.

"It wasn't Fleming. It wasn't." Rose stood twisting her apron around and around her hand. "They've made a terrible mistake. I would know if my own son was dead." She looked at her husband. "I would."

Broderick lay a hand on her shoulder, his voice gruff with feeling. "You aren't the only one who's worried sick, Rose. He's my son, too. And Grayson's only brother."

"Grayson!" She stepped away from her husband's touch, her eyes narrowed on her older son. "I suppose you're satisfied now."

"Rose." Broderick reached out for her. "Stop this."

"Why? Why should I stop?" She drew back, her face twisted with pain and rage. "It isn't fair. Fleming is my whole life. My beautiful, talented son. Everyone knows that it's so. And now his reputation is being destroyed by these vicious, evil rumors of beer gardens and drinking whiskey. Why?" Tears spilled over, streaming from her eyes. "Why would anyone say such a thing about Fleming? Oh, why did he leave me? He never should have gone away." She jabbed a finger in Gray's chest, then doubled her fists and began pummeling him. "Why did it have to be Fleming? Why? Why? Why couldn't it have been you?"

In the stunned silence that followed her outburst, Gray grabbed her wrists, stilling her movements. His eyes were as dark as thunder.

Like one who'd been clubbed, Broderick stumbled across the room and slumped into a chair, staring at his wife with a look of horror and revulsion, unable to believe the words that had come from her lips.

Fiona pressed a hand to her mouth to keep from crying out.

Without a word Gray released his mother and walked to the backdoor where he retrieved his coat and boots. He walked out the door without looking back.

As the door slammed behind him, Fiona turned away and fled to her room to hide the bitter tears that were scalding her eyes.

JUST BEFORE DAWN Broderick was sipping his tea in silence, while Rose sat across from him at the table, looking pale and drawn.

Fiona hadn't managed any sleep. She'd huddled in her bed, listening in vain for the sound of Gray's footsteps on the porch.

Where had he gone? Was he out there somewhere in the bitter cold, too proud and too battered to return to the shelter of his home? And what of his poor shattered heart? For surely his heart must have been slashed to pieces by the hateful words flung in anger by his mother. What son could endure such pain from the one who'd given him life?

"Tea, Miss Downey?"

She glanced over at Broderick, who looked suddenly old and drawn. "Thank you, no. I couldn't manage a drop."

She laced her boots and was busy pulling on her coat when she heard a horse's hooves. Without realizing it she clutched a hand to her heart, whispering a prayer that it would be Gray. As if in answer, he stomped up the porch and stepped into the kitchen.

For one long moment he looked at her, before looking away. But in that brief second she saw, not defeat, but something very like pride and fierce determination.

Broderick scraped back his chair and stood, laying a hand on his son's sleeve. "I've been worried."

"No need." Gray carefully removed his boots and hung his coat. "I'll stay only long enough to pack my things."

"Your things?" Rose shot him a challenging look. "Where do you think you're going?"

He ignored her, choosing instead to address his words to his father. "It's time I made my own way. I've bought Herman Vogel's farm. I made him an offer last night, and he accepted. He said as soon as he can make arrangements, he'll leave to join his daughter. In the meantime, I'll move in and give him a hand with whatever he needs."

Broderick nodded. "You chose well. He has a fine, sturdy house. Rich soil. It's a good farm. All it needs is someone to work it."

"And what about this farm?" Rose was on her feet now, slamming down her cup for emphasis. "How are we supposed to survive with Fleming missing and no one but a crippled old man left to work the land?"

Gray saw his father wince at his mother's cruel choice of words. "Don't worry, Papa. With my farm adjoining yours, I'll be able to plow and harvest your fields along with my own. You know I would never desert you."

"I know, son. This is the right thing to do. You deserve a place of your own. A chance to follow your own dream." Broderick surprised them both by drawing an arm around Gray's neck and drawing him close to mutter thickly, "You have my blessing."

"Thank you, Papa." Gray kissed his father's cheek before walking out of the room and up the stairs.

When Fiona left for the schoolhouse, Rose was slamming pots and pans around the kitchen, while Broderick stood by the window, staring off into the distance.

A short time later, as Fiona drew near the school, she saw a horse and wagon heading across the field toward the Vogel farm. Running alongside was Chester, the sound of his baying shattering the morning silence.

She knew that she ought to feel happy for Gray. He would finally be free of his mother's constant harping. Free of the hateful comparison between himself and his brother. Free, finally, to build something all his own.

It was pure selfishness on her part, she knew, but the joy she ought to feel for him was marred by the knowledge that she would no longer be able to see him, sleepy-eyed, brooding, first thing in the morning, or to watch him, sleeves rolled and shirt straining across his shoulders as he washed before supper each night.

How would she bear not hearing his voice? Not seeing those big, work-roughened hands wrapped around a cup of tea after a day in the fields?

She wanted to be happy for him, and was, she told herself firmly. But as she began another round of morning chores, her poor, battered heart refused to cooperate.

TWENTY

QUIET AS A tomb.

Fiona shivered at the thought. Grief seemed to surround the Haydn house like a shroud. If she'd found the loneliness difficult before, it was now oppressive. Without Gray to act as buffer, his parents rarely spoke, except when it was absolutely necessary.

At first she'd tried to break the uncomfortable silence at the supper table with talk of her day. She'd shared little stories of her students, of their misadventures and silly pranks. Gradually she realized that no one was listening. Not Broderick, who ate quickly and silently, before fleeing to the parlor, where he sat in front of the fire smoking his pipe and staring morosely into the flames. Not Rose, who more often than not shoved her plate aside and busied herself at the stove until the others were driven away, leaving her alone with her gloom.

Though both their sons had left them, their ghosts remained, separating these two lonely people into prison cells from which there seemed no escape.

As Fiona made her way through the parlor to her room, Broderick looked up and removed the pipe from his mouth. "Days are getting longer."

She glanced at the lace-covered window, surprised to see the sun just setting. "I hadn't noticed."

"It'll be spring soon."

"Spring." She spoke the word on a sigh.

"Sick of winter, are you?"

She nodded. "It seems to last much longer here in Paradise Falls."

"In all of Northern Michigan." He stretched out his long legs toward the fire and crossed one foot over the other. "Got time to sit a spell?"

"I guess I could." She settled herself in the big overstuffed chair beside his, grateful for the warmth here in the parlor.

"What was winter like in Bennett?"

"It could be cold and snowy, but not as much as here. I've never seen this much snow before. Mountains of it."

He huffed out a laugh. "Good for snowshoes. This was a mild winter compared to some."

"Mild?" She looked over to see if he was serious.

"My father used to say, beware a mild winter. It pays a call in springtime with a vengeance." He blew out a puff of smoke and watched it curl toward the ceiling. Then he looked at the pipe in his hand, studying the intricate carving on the bowl. His tone grew thoughtful. "Grayson was named for my father. He's a lot like him— good with his hands. An artist, I suppose, in his own way. Keeps his thoughts to himself. Strong as a mule, and just as stubborn. Loyal—if he gives his word, he'll never take it back." He paused a beat, speaking more to himself than to her. "I miss him." He looked up, and seemed surprised to have revealed so much. "I sense that you do, too."

Fiona swallowed. "I do. Yes."

"Well." He set the stem of the pipe between his teeth and turned to stare at the fire, lost in thought.

He never even seemed to notice when Fiona left him alone to go to her room. Once inside she turned down the bed linens and drew the draperies against the cold night air that whistled past the panes. She undressed and slipped into her nightgown before removing the pins from her hair. As she ran a brush through the thick curls she thought about Broderick's question. She'd answered him simply enough, but it hadn't nearly conveyed her true feelings. There were times when she ached to simply see Gray's face. To feel those dark eyes skimming over her, sending her heart into that quick dance it always took whenever he looked at her. She longed to reach out and touch that lock of hair that constantly spilled over his forehead in the most appealing way. To hear his voice—low, gruff, terse. To watch the softness that came into his eyes, into his voice, when he cupped Chester's head between those big hands.

As she crawled between the covers she felt a sense of shame. There were times lately, it seemed, that she was grieving more for the loss of Gray than for her own dear mum.

GRAY SET DOWN his plate and watched as Chester finished the last pieces of wurst before licking it clean. The hound had already been fed in the kitchen, but he was always willing to have seconds. That done, he rested his chin on Gray's knees and looked up into his eyes.

"That's all there is." Gray scratched behind his dog's ears before picking up a block of wood from the table beside his chair. While he ran his fingers around the shape of it, Chester curled up on a rug in front of the fire and closed his eyes.

Gray reached for his sharp knife and began whittling. He'd eaten his supper in the parlor, in front of the big roaring fire. That was one of the privileges of having his own place. Ma had never allowed them to eat anywhere except at the table. The kitchen was for every day. The dining room was only for Sunday supper, and then only if they had company. She'd never allowed her rules to be broken.

Except for Flem, who broke them constantly. But that never counted in her eyes.

Gray set down the wood and picked up the cup of steaming tea from the table beside his chair, staring around as he sipped. This was a good room, big, sturdy. The floors were made of oak cut from the nearby forest and polished to a high shine. The fireplace had been made of fieldstone, hand-hewn by Herman Vogel and his father, who had come with his family from Bavaria more than fifty years earlier. The kitchen was a delight, with a huge wood-burning stove and a fancy, intricately carved table and six chairs brought from the Black Forest, though how the Vogel family had managed to bring them all this way, Gray couldn't imagine. Herman had left most of the family belongings behind in his determination to make the trip to his daughter's place in one wagon. Beds and dressers in the three upstairs bedrooms. Chairs, rugs, a faded sofa. He'd even left the dishes in the cupboards, and the blackened pots and pans. The only things he'd insisted on taking had been the paintings of his ancestors that had graced the walls, and the wedding quilt his wife had sewn before their marriage more than fifty years ago.

Gray studied the faded spot on the wall above the fireplace. Maybe one day he would have a painting there. A painting of a woman. He could all but see her, skirt flattened against her legs as she walked across a field of daisies. Thick dark hair swirling around the face of an angel, fair skin and eyes as blue as a summer day, reed slender, her head barely reaching his shoulder.

It annoyed him that he could see her so clearly. All he needed to do was close his eyes and she was here with him.

He picked up the wood and started cutting, shaping. He liked having his own. He liked doing what he wanted, when he wanted.

He hoped his father wasn't too lonely. Knowing his mother, she would make things miserable until her temper had run its course. It gave him some comfort to know his father had Fiona there for company.

His hand paused. He could see her. Smell her. Hear that lilting brogue.

It was true that he liked having his own, but if he were to be honest, he'd like it better if he had someone to share it with. Not just anyone. But it would do no good to dream about Fiona Downey. He'd seen the misery in her eyes when Flem had left. Had seen the way she grieved, the same as Ma. She couldn't help falling in love with Flem. All women did.

Annoyed at his thoughts, he bent to his work, cutting, whittling, until he could see the wood begin to take on the shape he wanted. He would think about springtime, and the things he would do around the farm.

"MAY WE GO outside after lunch, Miss Downey?" Afton looked up from her slate, sending yellow curls dancing.

"That's a grand idea, Afton." Fiona opened the door, allowing the breeze to rush in. She could all but smell spring in the air. This morning she'd almost forsaken her coat in favor of a shawl, but she'd decided to be practical.

Another few weeks and she would be able to put away her scarf and gloves and coat altogether.

It was early April and the snow had been melting for a week now. Each time the sun came out, more water dripped from the roof of the schoolhouse, forming icicles overnight that nearly reached the ground. The children made a game of breaking them off and using them like javelins to see who could toss them the farthest.

"I'm finished, Miss Downey." Luther set his lunch bucket beside his coat and raced outside in his shirt-sleeves.

"So am I." Afton followed suit, leaving her coat on a peg by the door and dancing down the steps.

Soon the schoolyard was filled with the sounds of children laughing and shouting as they climbed trees and chased each other in a game of tag.

Because they'd been confined inside throughout the long winter, Fiona decided to allow them a little extra time outdoors to run off their energy. She was wiping down the slates when the door slammed shut with such force it startled her. When she leaned into it, she was forced to use all her strength just to push it open.

When had the wind shifted from east to north?

She looked up and was startled to see big fat snowflakes drifting about.

Putting her hands to her mouth she summoned the children inside.

"Just a few more minutes, Miss Downey." Edmer, upside down, was swinging by his knees from the branch of a tree.

"The air's grown cold." She clapped her hands to get the attention of those who'd raced beyond the outhouse in a game of tag. "I think you'd better come inside now, and we'll stoke the fire."

"I'll help." Edmer swung down from the tree and raced inside. Whenever Will wasn't at school, Edmer had become Fiona's official assistant. What had once seemed a chore to him now was done with a sense of pride.

He tossed a log on the fire and poked at the glowing coals until flames began to lick along the bark.

When all of the children were inside, Fiona latched the door against the wind and they resumed their classes. They were especially eager because one of their assignments had been to ask their parents and grandparents to tell them something of interest about their early lives in faraway countries. These tales were then shared with the class. Luther couldn't wait to talk about his grandfather's childhood in a tiny hamlet in the Alps.

Though the wind picked up, whistling past the window, rattling the door, they were so engrossed in their work they took no notice until they heard the jingle of harness.

Minutes later there was a pounding on the door. Fiona hurried over to release the latch. The wind blew the door from her grasp as Christian Rudd, his hair and coat frosted white, stepped inside in a rush of snowflakes.

"Storm coming." He nodded toward the row of coats and boots. "Better get the children dressed. I'll see them all home."

"I'm grateful." Though Fiona was startled by the amount of snow that had fallen, she had no time to think about it as she herded the children into their warm clothing before waving them toward the waiting wagon.

"You'd best bank that fire and get started for home, Miss Downey."

"I will. Thank you, Mr. Rudd."

He pointed to the lantern beside her desk. "You'll need that."

She laughed. "I hardly think so. It's midday."

"Trust me." In quick strides he pulled himself up to the seat of the wagon and took up the reins. "This time of year the weather can turn in the blink of an eye. You'd be wise to secure the door and the shutters over the window before you leave. Best not to dawdle."

She waved him off and called goodbye to the children before turning away.

Following his advice, she secured the shutters over the window. When she stepped inside the school, it took all her effort to close the door against the north wind that nearly whipped it out of her hand.

She banked the fire and slipped into her coat. Picking up the lantern she thought about what Christian Rudd had said. Though she thought it silly, she would trust his wisdom in these things. Using a small stick held to the hot coals, she lit the wick. With her gloves in place and her bright yellow scarf wrapped around her head, she stepped onto the porch and firmly latched the door.

As she walked down the steps she noted that the snow was already ankle high. How could this be? Hadn't it only begun within the hour? Or had she lost track of time?

With the wind and snow blowing against her face, she was forced to lower her head and hunch over to avoid the worst of it. But even that didn't help for long.

Before she'd walked half a mile the sky was so dark she could barely see a few feet in front of her. To make matters worse, the snow was now over her boots. The hem of her skirt was wet and heavy as it slapped against her legs.

To keep her mind from the cold, she thought about the fine supper that would be awaiting her at home. Rose had said she would be making cabbage soup. Just another mile or so and she would be snug and warm in the Haydn kitchen.

The snow seemed to be falling faster now. A thick wet curtain of icy chips that stung her eyes and battered her face until she couldn't feel her lips. Her fingers had long ago gone numb, and she stepped up her pace, desperate now to reach the warmth of home.

The temperature was dropping so quickly the wet snow soon turned to swirling daggers that blinded her. Her petticoats and skirt were beginning to freeze to her legs.

She heard a sound like thunder, and beside her a tree limb crashed to the ground, snapping into frozen shards. Startled, she managed to avoid being hit. But minutes later she stepped into a snowbank that was waist high and found herself lying face down. The lantern slipped from her hand.

Dazed, she pushed herself to a sitting position. Lifting a gloved hand she stared in horror. With the loss of her only light, and the snow swirling around, it was impossible to see even her own hand in front of her face.

This was no ordinary snowstorm. She was caught in a blizzard, and plunged into darkness, with no idea where the Haydn farm could be, or which direction would take her back to the shelter of the school.

TWENTY-ONE

———◆———

GRAY SWIPED AN arm over the sweat on his brow. He'd spent the morning cleaning the barn to his liking. It wasn't Herman Vogel's fault that it needed so much work. The old man had simply been overwhelmed by all the chores that went into keeping up a farm of this size. As his father was fond of saying, farming wasn't for the old or the faint-hearted.

Now, after forking fresh hay into the stalls and filling the troughs with water, Gray looked around with a sense of pride. It might not be completely to his liking yet, but by this time next year he'd have put his personal mark on it. He wanted to add a workbench, where he could repair harness and equipment. And maybe even a storage cabinet for his tools.

When Chester bounded into the barn Gray looked over and began to laugh. "Where did you find that much snow? You must have been digging around the woodpile, looking for foxes."

The hound shook himself and settled down on a pile of fresh hay to chew at ice balls that clung to the pads of his paws.

Gray glanced at the open doorway and was surprised to see the curtain of snow, so thick it obliterated the house only a few hundred yards away. He'd been so absorbed in his chores he'd had no idea the weather had turned so bitter.

"Good thing we didn't go to town." He stepped out and whistled to his dog to follow before leaning his weight into the big barn door. "A storm this bad, we could have ended up stuck along the trail. I feel sorry for anyone who gets caught in this."

He was halfway to the house before the realization dawned.

Fiona. She would have been at school this morning. With no warning of what was coming, she would be trapped there with her students.

He raced back to the barn and began to harness the team.

FIONA WAS SO cold she could no longer feel her feet. Her face had long ago gone numb, as well. Her clothes were crusted with ice and snow, the weight of them pulling at her, threatening to drag her down with every step she took. The thought of giving in and lying down was so tempting. She'd heard of blizzards, but this was the first time she'd ever experienced one. She'd heard the tales of men freezing to death in the snow if they dared to stop, and so she forced herself to keep moving, though by now she was thoroughly lost.

In the blinding white landscape, nothing looked familiar. There were no buildings, no unusual trees or boulders by which she could mark her progress. Just endless snow, snatching at her hair.

She'd lost her scarf somewhere. Snagged by the branches of a tree, or perhaps blown away on a gust of bitter wind. She'd been too cold to notice.

She had been walking for what seemed hours. She should be close to the Haydn farm by now. Though the blowing snow stung her eyes she cupped her hands around them to peer about, hoping to spot the barn. As she did she stepped on something buried in a drift. Dropping to her knees she fished around for it and held it up, then gave a little cry of dismay as recognition dawned.

It was the lantern she'd dropped so very long ago. She'd walked all that time for nothing. She was back where she'd started, halfway between school and home.

"No. Oh, please. No." Overcome by exhaustion and despair, she buried her face in her hands.

GRAY WAS OUT of the wagon as soon as the team had pulled up to the schoolhouse. After bounding up the porch steps, he could see that the door had been firmly latched from the outside and braced with a timber.

He felt a sense of relief. Fiona and the students were gone. He walked around to the side and saw that the shutters had been drawn over the window and firmly latched. A good sign that Fiona had understood the measures needed in the face of a storm of this size.

He returned to the wagon and headed the team toward home. Chester huddled close, resting his head on Gray's lap.

Gray absently patted the hound. "I know. We'll both be grateful to be inside, warmed by a fire, and enjoying a good supper, won't we, old friend? Especially now that we know the teacher is safe at home."

The words had no sooner escaped his lips than he spied something through the haze of snow. Something bright yellow, fluttering from a branch. He was out of the wagon and racing through the snow. As he snatched it up, he gave a muttered oath before tucking it inside his coat. There was no denying that it was Fiona's.

He'd never been much of a believer, but the words of a childhood prayer played through his mind as he headed into the storm.

Be with me in the hour of my need.

"OH, DA." FIONA'S teeth were chattering so hard she could barely get the words out, but it seemed important that she address her last words to her beloved father. She was certain the end was near. She'd walked as far as she could manage. The weight of her frozen clothes, and the fact that she could no longer feel any part of her body, made her realize that she'd done all she could. For the past half hour she'd been thinking about Broderick Haydn's sister, Gerda, who had frozen in her own barn, just steps away from the comfort of her own home. What had he once said to her? He'd compared the weather to a woman.

A word of warning, Miss Downey. When she seems the most beautiful, when you think she could never be lovelier, that's when you must be wary. For she can turn on you and take everything, even your life.

"Oh, Da. I'm so cold. And so tired. I didn't expect to join you and Mum so soon. But if it's to be, then I'm ready. Just don't leave me all alone out here." She huddled in a snowdrift and tucked her face low, to avoid another gust of icy, stinging wind. "Stay with me, Da. Especially now. I won't be nearly so afraid as long as I know you're here beside me. I'm so weary." She braced against another shuddering wind and burrowed deeper into the snow. "So very, very weary."

Somewhere nearby she heard, above the wind, a sound that froze her blood and had her heart pounding. Had that been the howl of a wolf? She'd heard the stories of wolf packs that roamed these forests. Though they never ventured close to man, they'd been known to snatch the occasional newborn calf and drag it off to the woods to feast.

She lifted her head and strained to hear, but everything was drowned out by the never-ending shriek of the wind. Just as she started to relax she heard it again. Closer now.

She couldn't stay here. She had to move—to flee. If wolves should think her helpless, they would attack.

It was one thing to close her eyes and go to sleep, knowing she would never wake. It was another to sit idly by while wild creatures stalked.

Clamping down on the pain and weariness, she got to her feet and took several plodding steps through the drifts that were nearly waist-high. From close behind her she heard the howl. Turning to face her attacker, she saw the darkened outline of the animal as it lunged. She fell backward into the snow, with the creature on top of her. She flung her hands up to protect her face, but it was too late. A warm, wet tongue lapped at her cheek.

Tongue?

"Chester. Oh, Chester." Laughing and crying, she wrapped her arms around the big dog's neck and held on as her face was licked again and again.

"Fiona. Thank God."

Hearing Gray's voice, she looked up to see him looming over her like some ghostly specter. His dark hair was frosted with snow, as were his clothes.

"Gray. I thought . . ." Her mouth was too frozen to get the words out.

"I know. I know." He reached down and lifted her in his arms, while the hound leaped and danced around them.

In quick strides he waded through the snow and carried her to his wagon. Wrapping her in a thick blanket, he kept hold of her as he flicked the reins.

Chester leapt up beside them and burrowed close.

While the team strained against the drifts, Gray kept his arms firmly around her, as much for himself as for her. He needed, desperately, to assure himself that she was indeed safe.

He'd been so afraid. It was, he realized, the first time in his life that he'd ever experienced such a knot of gut-wrenching fear. A fear so deep, so primal, he'd been driven into the storm like some sort of madman.

"How did you know I was out here?"

He looked down at her face, so pale and frozen. So beautiful. "Your scarf. It was caught on the branch of a tree. I realized that you must have got caught in the thick of the storm and turned in the wrong direction. From the location I found it, I could see that you were headed not toward home, but toward the forest. So I told Chester to find you."

She leaned over to hug the dog. "My hero."

He rewarded her with another swipe of his big tongue.

She snuggled against Gray's chest. "If it hadn't been for you—"

"Shhh. You're safe now."

Safe.

Fiona's eyes closed and the word played through her mind. *Safe.* She'd been prepared to die, but because of this man, she was now safe.

She leaned into his warmth and allowed herself to drift on a cloud of utter, complete relief.

WITH EVERY OBSTACLE, every snowdrift, Gray cursed the delay that was keeping them on the trail. All he wanted was to get Fiona out of this storm and somewhere warm and safe. When at last they reached his barn he lifted Fiona into his arms. With Chester at his heels, he strode through the drifts and shoved open the backdoor of his house.

He didn't stop until he reached the parlor, where coals still gleamed on the grate. Setting her gently down on the sofa he said, "You have to get out of those wet clothes."

He tossed a log and stirred the coals until flames leaped and danced. When he turned back to her she was still bundled in the blanket, her teeth chattering, her body trembling.

"I'll help." He unwrapped the blanket and caught the hem of her gown, none-too-gently peeling it up and over her arms and head. That done he tugged aside her petticoats and reached for the ribbons of her chemise.

"I can do this." Though she was still shaking violently, she managed to remove her most intimate garments before folding the edges of the blanket around her for modesty.

He picked up the pile of sodden clothing and turned away.

"Where are you going?"

Hearing the note of alarm in her voice, he paused. "I'll just hang these to dry and put the kettle on. You need something hot."

"Yes. Of course." She closed her eyes and lay, absorbing the warmth of the blanket and the heat from the fireplace. She'd thought she would never again be warm. And now here she was, snug and safe and warm.

Because of Gray.

If he hadn't come looking for her, she would have surely frozen to death. Most men would have returned to the warmth and comfort of their home, without giving her another thought, but not Gray. He had gone the extra distance, to make certain she was safe.

He returned and noted idly that she hadn't stirred. He sat on the edge of the sofa and held a glass of amber liquid to her lips.

Her eyes fluttered open. "What's this?"

"Whiskey. It'll warm you."

She took a sip and felt the warmth of it burn a path through her veins. "Thank you, Gray."

"More. Drink."

She took another long swallow before pushing aside his hand. The trickle of warmth was now a fire low in her belly. She waited a moment, until she was able to catch her breath. "Do you know what I was thinking, when I was out in the storm?"

He shook his head, watching her eyes.

"I was thinking about your Aunt Gerda, and the fact that she froze in her own barn. And I thought . . ." She shuddered. "I was resigned to the fact that I would never see another day."

"Don't even think such a thing." He set aside the glass and caught her hands in his, wanting to share his warmth, his strength, with her. "You're too good, too fine, to leave this world yet." His voice lowered with feeling. "I couldn't bear it if you did."

Her eyes went wide, staring at him as though seeing him for the first time.

When she could find her voice she whispered, "Do you mean that, Gray?"

He nodded and scrambled to his feet before turning away.

"Where are you going now?"

"To the barn," he called over his shoulder. "I have to unhitch the team and turn them into their stalls."

She listened to the sound of his footsteps as he crossed to the kitchen. Minutes later she heard the backdoor slam.

In the silence that followed, she drifted on a warm cloud of contentment.

COWARD. WHILE HE worked unhitching the team, the word played through Gray's mind. He'd used this as a way to avoid doing what he really wanted.

What he wanted, he thought as he led the horses to their stalls, was to just gather Fiona close and hold her. The way he'd held her on the long, cold journey home. It had been the sweetest of tortures to hold her close to his heart, warming her body with his, and knowing that he would soon have to let her go.

It ought to be enough to know that he'd saved her, but knowing that she was still grieving the loss of Flem ate at his mind, causing him more pain than he would have thought possible.

It wasn't her fault. Flem had always been able to charm women. And he . . . he wiped his hands down his pants and hung the harness before turning away. He was a plain man. Ma had been right about that. Plain and dull and too cowardly to ever risk telling someone as fine and beautiful as Fiona Downey what he really felt. He couldn't bear the thought that she might find his feelings for her laughable. Oh, she was too good to say so. She would be kind, and considerate of him, but her rejection would be no less unbearable. He would die before he would open himself up to that kind of humiliation.

He leaned against the barn door until he managed to get it closed. Then, with his hand on the guide rope he'd strung from house to barn, he began inching his way back toward the porch of his farmhouse.

His, he thought with fierce pride. Even if Fiona Downey couldn't be, at least this was his.

TWENTY-TWO

———◆———

FIONA AWOKE TO the sound of a crackling fire and lay very still, wondering where she was. Then it all came rushing back. The horror of the blizzard. The belief that she was about to die. Her miraculous rescue.

She was safe in Gray's house. Warm and snug and rested.

She shifted and saw Gray asleep in a big, overstuffed chair. He was shirtless; his head back, eyes closed. His bare feet stretched out toward the warmth of the fire.

When she stirred, Chester, asleep in front of the fire, lifted his head for a moment and looked at her, before laying his head on his paws and closing his eyes.

She sat up, keeping the blanket around her. That simple movement had Gray alert and on his feet. "What do you need? Are you all right?"

"I'm fine, Gray. I don't need anything. I just feel so grateful to be alive." She shook her head, at a loss for words. "I can't believe I'm really safe. And all because of you."

His voice was gruff. "I didn't do anything special."

"Only saved my life." She walked over to lay a hand on his arm before brushing a kiss over his cheek. "I'll never forget that."

He stood, obviously ill at ease, staring at her in that strange, intense way he had. "I made supper while you slept. I'll get you some."

"No." She kept her hand on his arm. "I don't want anything just now." She glanced toward the stairs. "Why aren't you in bed?"

The heat from her touch seemed to rush straight to his loins. A pulse was already throbbing in his temple. "I didn't want to leave you alone down here. I figured you might wake through the night and be afraid." It was honest, as far as it went. He didn't bother to add that it had been such a pleasure to watch her while she slept. Before giving in to the need to sleep, he'd allowed himself to indulge in some grand fantasies.

She heard the howling of the wind outside and shivered. "Is it still snowing?"

"Last I looked, it was over the windows." It could pile higher than the roof, for all he cared, as long as he knew she was safe. And as long as she would continue standing this close, touching him just so. It was the most purely sensual pleasure he could ever recall.

"Have you ever seen a storm like this?"

"Not in my lifetime. But I've heard of them." His tone deepened. "It'll be days before we can dig out."

"Days." She spoke the word softly, as though mulling the implications.

He looked down at her hand, then away, struggling to engage his brain, which seemed to have deserted him. "I should . . . go out to the barn."

"In the middle of the night?"

"I need to . . ." *Kiss you,* he thought wildly. *Take you in my arms and kiss you breathless.* It was the fact that his mind was still muddled from sleep. He needed air to clear his head. "I should . . . check on the livestock."

"I see." She lowered her head and felt him turn away.

In the doorway he paused without looking at her. "I'm sorry about Flem. I know how much you still miss him."

"Flem?" For a moment she seemed puzzled. He wasn't making any sense at all, but he had already walked into the kitchen.

Gathering the blanket close, she started to turn toward the fire. Then, without giving herself time to think things through, she started after him.

He was standing by the backdoor, slipping his arms into the sleeves of a warm shirt. He looked up when she crossed to him.

"Why would I miss Flem?"

"Because he . . . and you . . ." He stopped, one sleeve dangling, unable to say the words.

She sucked in a breath as truth dawned. "Is that what you think?"

"It's what he said."

"When?"

His tone hardened. "When I saw him coming out of your room the night before he left."

"Oh, Gray. If only you'd asked me." She huffed out a little breath and took a moment to choose her words carefully. "I've tried so hard not to think about that horrible scene."

Gray's eyes narrowed.

"Flem came to my room unbidden, and he left only because I threatened to go to your father if he ever did so again."

"Did he manage to . . . hurt you?" Gray felt a moment of hot, blinding fury.

"No." She was quick to reassure him. "I made Flem understand that he was repugnant to me, and that I would never again permit him to come near me."

"You . . . ?" He felt the heavy, painful band that had been wrapped around his heart for all these long weeks begin to slip a notch. "You have no feelings for my brother?"

"None."

Without realizing what he was doing, he grasped her hand. "But most women . . ." He caught himself and said on a sigh, "I should have known. You're not like other women." He looked down at their joined hands. "Flem has always been able to lie convincingly. And since he's always had a way with women, I just . . ." His words died abruptly and he took a step back. "You have every right to hate me."

"I don't hate you, Gray."

He couldn't look at her. "I have to go out to the barn now."

As he turned away Fiona lay a hand on his back, and she could feel the warmth of his flesh through the shirt. "Now that you know the truth about Flem, why are you running away?"

He kept his back to her, wondering how much longer he could bear being this close. "Because I don't deserve your forgiveness. I was so jealous when I thought you and Flem—" He clamped his mouth shut, too moved to even speak.

"You were jealous?" She felt the first spark of hope flare in her heart. "That's such a strong emotion."

"All my feelings for you are too strong. And if I don't get out of here right now, I'm afraid of what I might do."

The spark was now a quick, bright light in her heart. "What would you do, Gray?"

He kept his back to her, ashamed to face her. "I wouldn't be able to keep from holding you. Kissing you."

Fiona felt her heart soar. How long had she waited for those words? Her voice was soft, breathy. "What if I told you I wouldn't mind?"

He turned. On his face was a look so fierce, her joy turned to wariness. "I'm not a saint. It wouldn't stop there. If I kissed you, held you, I'd want more."

Though her heart was pounding, she lifted her chin in that way he'd come to recognize. "What if that's what I want, too, Gray?"

Her words were nearly his undoing. Without thinking he touched a hand to her cheek. Just a touch, but she moved against him like a kitten. He lowered his face to hers, aching for the touch of her mouth.

Just in time he came to his senses and caught her roughly by the upper arms, holding her a little away. "I have nothing to lose. But you must think about your reputation. You're a teacher. When the people of this town learn that you spent the night alone with me, there will be talk." He released her and lowered his hands to his sides before turning away. "Think of that while I cool off in the barn."

He picked up his boots. When he straightened, she stepped in front of the door. "Let them talk, Gray. I only know I want you to stay here with me."

"Do you know what you're saying?"

She met his look. "I do. Yes."

He might have smiled at the thickness of her brogue, if it hadn't been for the way his heart was pounding in his chest. Like a runaway team heading straight toward a high, sheer cliff. If he didn't find a way to stop it now, they would both take a fall that might destroy them.

He shook his head. "I'm big and clumsy. And you're . . ." He stared into her eyes. "You're sweet and untouched. I could never be gentle enough for you."

"I'm not asking you to be gentle, Gray." She touched a hand to his face. Just a touch, but she saw his eyes narrow on her with such intensity, it had her breath backing up in her throat. "But if you don't soon kiss me, I think my poor heart might just stop beating."

He managed a grin that was both appealing and dangerous. "We can't have that now, can we?"

He leaned close, intending to merely brush his mouth over hers. But the moment their lips met, everything changed.

His boots dropped from his hands and fell to the floor with a thud, though he wasn't even aware. His arms came around her in a fierce embrace as he dragged her close and covered her mouth with his.

He'd known she would taste this clean and sweet. *Dear God, how sweet.* Like a cool, clear stream on a hot summer day. Had known, too, that there would be this fresh innocence. He'd even tried to anticipate the heat he knew would be generated by her touch. What he hadn't expected was the need. This hard, driving need that had him changing the angle of the kiss and taking it deeper, as he drank her in like a drowning man.

Without realizing what he was doing he drove her back against the door and covered her mouth in a kiss that spoke of all the hunger, all the longing that he'd stored up for so long.

She returned his kisses with a hunger of her own.

Against her mouth he whispered, "I knew." His big hands moved up her arms, creating sparks that had her sighing.

"Knew what?"

"One kiss would never be enough." He pressed himself against the length of her until she could feel the thundering of his heartbeat inside her own chest. "I have to have more."

He nibbled her lips until, on a sigh, they opened for him. His tongue explored hers, then withdrew, inviting her to do the same. Though she was hesitant at first, she grew bolder, following his example.

His kisses were soft one minute, rough the next. His hands, too, moved over her with exquisite tenderness, before gripping her painfully as if pulling himself back from the brink of something dark and dangerous.

He held her a little away, his eyes hot and fierce. "You need to stop and think what it is we're about to do here."

With a sigh she wound her arms around his neck. "I don't want to think, Gray. I want to feel."

"So do I. You don't know how much." Calling on all his willpower he removed her arms from around his neck and stepped back, breaking contact. "But one of us has to be sensible. Papa taught me that love, real love, means caring more about the other than about your own needs."

"Love?" Her eyes, her voice, took on a new softness. "Do you love me, Gray?"

He wanted so badly to gather her into his arms and tell her just how much he loved her. Instead, he kept his hands at his sides, knowing if he dared to touch her again, he'd never be able to stop. "How could I not? You're the finest woman I've ever known."

She caught his arm. "Then love me, Gray. Hold me. Kiss me. Show me how much you love me. Here and now."

He closed his fingers around her wrist. Even that small touch had sparks leaping between them. "Think about this. Just being here with me will ruin your good name in our town."

"I can't deny that I love being a teacher. I don't want anything to spoil that. But I love you more, Gray."

"It isn't love." He was already shaking his head in denial. "You're just grateful because I saved you."

Stung, she stiffened her spine. "You don't think I know the difference between gratitude and love?"

"I think . . ." He needed to end this, and escape to the

barn, before they did something she would deeply regret in the morning. "I think you're confused."

He yanked his coat from a peg by the door, then bent to retrieve his boots. When he straightened, she was smiling. A little cat smile that seemed full of secrets.

"Maybe I was confused, Gray, but I'm not now."

He shrugged into his coat. "What's that supposed to mean?"

"You're a good man. And I love that you're looking out for me. But you said that we might be here for days." While she spoke the blanket began to slip a notch, baring one shoulder. A look came into his eyes that was more feral than human. Seeing it, she felt a quick rush of fear, before forcing herself to say what was in her heart. "I don't believe either of us is strong enough to resist for that long."

With a muttered oath he reached a hand to the edge of the blanket, hoping to cover the expanse of flesh. Too late he realized his mistake. The moment his fingers came in contact with her skin, he could feel the blood roaring in his temples.

Instead of drawing away she stepped closer, until their bodies were brushing. With a finger she traced the outline of his lips. "Do you realize that in all the time I've known you, I've never once heard you speak my name?"

He couldn't seem to drag enough air into his lungs. There was a pressure on his chest threatening to crush him.

In defense he framed her face with his big hands and stared down into her eyes with a look that would frighten most men. "Fiona. There. I've said it. Are you happy?"

She merely smiled. "Again."

"Fiona." Without realizing it, his tone softened, as did his touch. "Fiona. Fiona." He whispered her name like a caress. His fingers curved around to tangle in the softness of her hair, and he buried his lips at her temple. "How

I've wanted to say it out loud. It's like music. Fiona. I love the sound of your name."

She sighed, feeling a welling of love that threatened to swamp her. "And I love hearing you say it."

He brushed his mouth over hers, nibbling the corner of her lips until she opened for him. Inside her mouth he whispered, "You realize we've already gone too far."

"I do. Yes. I'm frightened, Gray, but I won't go back."

"I'm glad of that, because I can't. I'd rather die." He pressed his forehead to hers on a sigh. "God help me, Fiona. I'm scared to death. But I can no more resist loving you than I can refuse to breathe."

TWENTY-THREE

———◆※◆———

"MY SWEET, SWEET Fiona." Gray ran a hand lightly down her back, gathering his forces for the storm he could feel building inside him. "Do you know how long I've wanted you?"

"How long?" She lay a hand on his cheek.

"Since first I saw you. Do you remember?"

"I do, yes." The memory had her smiling.

"I felt as if all the breath had been knocked out of me. I couldn't breathe. I stood there staring at you, and couldn't think of a single thing to say. I thought I was in the presence of an angel."

"And I thought you were the strongest man I'd ever seen. You carried my trunk as if it weighed nothing at all."

"I wasn't even aware of it. Only you." He drew her close and ran his hands down the length of her. "You're so slim. So small." He framed her face and stared down into her eyes with a look that had her heart tripping over itself. "I'm so afraid I'll hurt you."

"Shh." She pressed a finger to his lips and absorbed a rush of heat when he closed his hand over hers, drawing her finger into his mouth. She had never before experienced anything so intimate. "You could never hurt me, Gray."

"I'll try not to." He ran nibbling kisses over her up-turned face, brushing his mouth over her forehead, the corner of her eye, the tip of her nose. "My beautiful, wonderful Fiona. Now that I'm free to say your name, I can't seem to stop."

They were both laughing when he teased her lips until they opened for him. On a sigh he took the kiss deeper.

She thought she couldn't bear it when his mouth left hers. But when his tongue slowly traced the curve of her ear, she trembled from the pure pleasure of it. He nipped at the lobe, before darting his tongue inside, causing her to gasp and clutch at his waist.

"You taste . . ." He ran hot, wet kisses along the smooth column of her throat. "So very sweet."

She was chuckling as she arched her neck to give him easier access, but moments later, when he dipped his mouth lower, her laughter turned to a moan of pleasure mixed with surprise as little fingers of fire and ice trickled down her spine. And when his mouth closed over her breast, the sensations that ripped through her had her gripping his waist, afraid that at any moment her trembling legs might fail her.

The blanket slipped away to pool at their feet. He stepped back, his gaze burning over her.

She had always thought she would be embarrassed to have a man see her like this, but there was no shame in her. Instead, the look in his eyes made her feel beautiful. Desirable. It was a heady feeling, and one that had her smiling as he drew her close and gathered her into his arms.

"You're even more beautiful than I dreamed." He brushed her lips with his before trailing kisses across her jaw to the curve of her neck. "And I've had more than my share of dreams since you came into my world."

"Would you care to share them?"

He chuckled against her throat, sending a flare of heat straight to her heart. "I may. Some day. Right now, this is better than any dream." He savaged her mouth with kisses until she sighed and moved in his arms, growing weak with pleasure. She wondered that she could still stand.

As if reading her mind, he took her hand and lowered her to the blanket at their feet.

She laughed. "How did you know my legs were about to fail me?"

"Because my own are none too steady." He leaned up on one elbow and traced a finger down the length of her, from shoulder to hip, following that with light feathery kisses along her throat to her collar bone. "Your skin is so pale, it looks like spun glass."

"And yours." She reached her hands under the shirt he'd never managed to button, sliding it from his shoulders before timidly touching a palm to the dark hair that curled on his chest. "You've such a beautiful body, Gray."

That had him laughing. "You have a strange sense of beautiful."

"But you are." Growing bolder she trailed a hand down the flat planes of his stomach and saw his eyes narrow, heard his quick intake of breath before he covered her mouth with his.

The press of his body on hers brought new pleasure. They seemed to fit together perfectly, like the pieces of a puzzle, her soft curves molding to his sculpted muscles.

She sat up, trailing a hand across his shoulder and

down his arm, feeling the rope of sinew and muscle just beneath the firm flesh. "I've never known anyone as strong as you."

"Remind me to thank my father for giving me all those farm chores at an early age." He wrapped an arm around her and pulled her close, while his mouth moved over hers.

His kisses were no longer gentle, but possessive, and the arm that encircled her could have easily crushed her. As if remembering his strength, he softened his kiss and his touch.

Outside the wind battered and howled, causing the walls to shudder from the assault. Inside, the farmhouse was quiet, except for the hiss and snap of the fire in the kitchen stove.

Gray studied the woman who lay in his arms. Her hair, black as midnight, spilled in wild tangles around the face of an angel. But it was her eyes that held him. Blue as a summer sky, fixed on him with a look of such trust, they pulled him in to her very soul.

The storm raging outside was nothing to the storm building inside him. The need to take her was becoming an overpowering force. One he fought to bank. She was an innocent, and he was determined to make this as memorable as possible. It was, after all, the only thing he could give her.

And so he brushed soft, whispered kisses over her face, her lips, her throat, while his hands, those big, rough hands, moved over her with a sort of reverence, igniting fires wherever they touched.

He touched her everywhere, with teeth and tongue and fingertips. At times so gently it was like a whispered caress, at other times with a frantic rush that had her heart racing, her breathing harsh and ragged, and her body aching for more.

She could feel the coiled tension within him, and the

valiant effort he made to control it. Knowing that she was the reason for it aroused and excited her in a way that nothing else could. She responded with a freedom she never would have dreamed possible. What was it about this man that she knew instinctively that she could trust him with her heart, her mind, her body?

Their kisses grew more heated as his hands explored more intimately. Gray thought of all the fantasies he'd enjoyed since first seeing her. No fantasy could compare with this flesh and blood woman in his arms. When he brought his mouth to her breast, she gave a gasp of surprise at the shock waves that rippled through her.

She clutched at him, and he saw the look of alarm in her eyes. At once his touch gentled, allowing her to relax in his arms. His kisses, too, gentled, as he traveled down her neck, across her shoulder, before burying his lips in the sensitive hollow of her throat.

Steeped in pleasure, she began to drift on a web of the most amazing sensations.

With quiet patience he led her to a new level of trust. He could see it in her eyes. Sense it in her whispered sighs and quiet, steady heartbeat. Feel it in the way she wrapped her arms around his neck, drawing him ever deeper into her silken web.

He shed the last of his clothes and tossed them aside before gathering her close in an embrace that had her pressed to the length of him. He could feel the change in her—could see it in her eyes. Passion, that had been slumbering, was now ignited into a flame of need that had her returning his kisses with the kind of wild abandon he'd only dreamed of.

His fingers tangled in her hair, and he drew her head back while his lips covered hers in a savage, possessive kiss.

For the space of a moment she hesitated, as though

startled by this change in him. Then, as his passion fueled hers, she leaned into him, inviting more.

Hadn't she always sensed this darker side of him? Wasn't it this mysterious, brooding man who had first captured her heart? Now she found herself drawn into his darkness. The controlled passion in his kisses made her shudder. She felt the same trembling response in him each time she returned his kisses. With a single touch he could take her higher than she'd ever believed possible.

He touched her everywhere. Where his fingers trailed, his mouth followed, until she felt as though her body had become a bright, hot torch, burning only for him.

"Wait, Gray. I need a moment."

"And I need you. This." Beyond hearing, driven by a blinding, desperate desire, he took her on a dizzying, heart-stopping ride, taking her ever higher and higher. With teeth and lips and tongue he drove her. With his fingertips he pleasured her. He found her, hot and wet, and took her up and over the first peak.

Stunned, she clutched at him, unable to do more than cry his name as her body shuddered. Instead of offering her the relief she sought, he took her again, leaving her no time to recover her senses.

Her body had become a mass of nerve endings. Her mind so blinded by need, she could no longer think. Only feel.

She touched him as he was touching her and was amazed at his quivering response. Reveling in her power, she grew bolder, bringing her mouth across his shoulder, down his chest, and lower, to explore and pleasure him as he had pleasured her.

Pleasure became need. Need was close to madness. He could feel it rising up, taking over his will. Still he held back, wanting to take her to the very edge with him.

Like a man too long starved, he feasted on her as though he would never have enough. In turn he fed her with his kisses. Like one who had glimpsed paradise, he was determined to take them both there. Each time his passion threatened to slip out of control, he eased back until it was contained. All the while he drove her higher, until she writhed and moaned beneath him.

The heat from the stove mingled with the heat of their bodies, until they were slick with sheen. Their throats were clogged, their breathing ragged. And still they were lost in the passion they'd unleashed.

Fiona's world had narrowed to this room. This man. The scrape of his big, rough hands over her skin was more erotic than anything she could have imagined. The taste of him, dark and mysterious, filled her lungs. The feel of those muscled arms gave her pleasure beyond belief.

She shuddered and strained as he moved over her, his flesh as hot and wet as hers. She had long thought of lovemaking as a single act. Now she knew that it was so much more—hunger and need and trust.

Gray loved watching her. The way her eyes widened with each new surprise. The way her body arched for him, before going limp with each new spear of white, hot pleasure. The way she focused on him, as though he'd become the center of her universe.

He had thought he was teaching her the ways of love, but at the first touch of that exquisite body, he'd found himself completely lost. His sweet, innocent Fiona had become, with but a single touch, a temptress, taking him on a path he'd never known before. And he delighted in it. And in her.

He knew it was impossible to hold back the needs that were clawing at him, fighting to be free. Though he struggled to resist, the need was too great. The thought of taking her, hard and fast, had him trembling.

He felt her gasp as he brought his mouth down her body. Felt her shudder as she rode another wave of pleasure.

Her eyes opened, and he felt himself drowning in those soft blue depths. He allowed himself to sink deep as he entered her.

She didn't think it possible to absorb any more pleasure, but now she wrapped herself around him, drawing him in. And then she was moving with him. Climbing with him. She felt this incredible strength, as though she could fly to the heavens and beyond.

His eyes were steady on hers as he cried out her name. It was the last coherent thought before they slipped beyond anything of this world.

Together they leaped into space.

And soared.

THEY LAY STILL joined, their breathing ragged, bodies slick with sheen, and waited for their world to settle.

When he found his breath Gray touched a hand to her cheek. "Are you all right?"

"Fine." It was all she could manage.

He withdrew his hand and stared at the drops of moisture on his fingertips. Tears? His heart stopped as he propped himself on one elbow and stared down at her. "I've made you cry."

"No, Gray. It isn't you. It's us. This was so . . ." She struggled to find a word. "Incredible."

He felt his heart begin to beat again. "I didn't hurt you?"

"Hurt me? Oh, Gray. It was the most amazing thing I've ever experienced." She felt suddenly shy. "Is it always like that?"

"It can be. When two people take care with each other." He gave her a long, measuring look. "You're so beautiful, Fiona. I still can't believe you're here with me."

"Believe it." Now it was her turn to touch a hand to his face. Delighted with such freedom, she sat up and gently pressed him back against the blanket.

"What are you doing?"

"What I've long wished I could do." She traced a finger over the curve of his eyebrows. "Such amazing eyes you have, Gray. I swear you can see clear through to my soul."

"A myth. But I'd be happy to let you go on believing that." Oddly content, he folded his arms behind his head.

"Such thick, dark brows. I've watched them knit together in anger, or lift in surprise." She moved her finger over his nose. "And this perfect, noble nose. It suits this noble face."

"Noble?" He grinned. "I've never thought of my face as anything but plain."

"That's because you have no vanity. Hush now, and indulge me." She followed the slope of his cheek to his lips. "Oh, this mouth. I'd never dreamed it could bring such pleasure."

He couldn't help but be drawn into her playful mood. "Just one of my many talents, Miss Downey."

"I can see that. How many more, I wonder, have you been keeping hidden from the world?"

"If the storm keeps up, we may have endless hours to uncover all manner of secrets."

She gave a delighted laugh. "Who would have thought that a blizzard could bring us so much happiness?"

"Who indeed?" Unable to contain himself any longer, he pulled her down on top of him and kissed her long and slow and deep. Against her mouth he muttered, "Would you like to see what else I can do?"

"There's more?"

"So much more, Fiona."

Her eyes widened as she became aware of his arousal. "Again? Can you? Can we? Truly? Now? Oh, I can't wait to learn everything."

He found himself laughing at her innocence, and in the

next instant groaning as she wriggled over him and brought her mouth to his throat.

He rolled her over and gathered her close, covering her mouth with his. "I can't think of anyone I'd rather teach about the mysteries of love and life than you, teacher."

"GRAY." FIONA'S VOICE, soft as a whisper in the midnight shadows, brought him out of his reverie.

He'd been floating. Drifting on a cloud of such contentment. He would have never believed his life could take such a strange turn. Days before he'd been feeling alone, adrift, cut off from all that he'd known and loved, and now he was lying in the arms of an angel, feeling happier than he would have ever thought possible.

He'd carried her to the big sofa in the parlor, where they lay amidst a tangle of arms and legs, warm, content, and pleasantly sated.

On the hearth, the coals gleamed red-hot, sending off an occasional spark.

"Hmmm?" He turned his face to hers, while his fingers played with a strand of her hair.

"I never had a brother or sister, but I always thought it would be nice to have someone I could turn to, in times of trouble." Just thinking about the shocking deaths of her parents had her wishing again that she'd had someone who understood that loss.

He drew her close. "I wish you did, too. I'm afraid my family wasn't much comfort to you."

"I wasn't thinking about me, but about you and Flem. Something has caused a wall between you."

She felt him begin to withdraw and immediately regretted her words. "I'm sorry, Gray. I shouldn't pry."

"You have a right to know." After a lengthy silence he said, "There were so many little things, but I always overlooked them, because it had been drummed into my head that I should take care of my younger brother. Clean up after him. Finish what he started. It was obvious to everyone but Ma that he'd become her pampered darling. I didn't mind until . . ." He paused, and Fiona could see his eyes narrow in thought. "Three years ago Foster Enders . . ." He felt the need to explain. "Foster owned the dry goods store in town, before selling it to the Schneider family and moving away."

Fiona nodded, though she had no idea where this might lead.

"Foster and his wife took in a niece, Amelia. She was sweet. Young—no more than fifteen. She and Flem . . ." He paused, choosing his words. "Apparently fell in love. When she learned that there was a baby coming, she went to Flem. He refused to marry her."

"But why? I thought you said they fell in love."

Gray nodded. "I thought so, too. Whatever the reason, Flem told me that he'd rejected her. I knew what would happen to her if the townspeople should find out, so I went to her uncle and asked for her hand in marriage."

"You? But why?"

"Because it was the right thing to do. I reasoned that if Flem wouldn't step up to his responsibility, I'd do it in his place. But I was too late. I learned that, overcome with shame and remorse, Amelia had gone to a woman in Little Bavaria who had offered to help her get rid of the baby. She was already in bed with an infection. Three days later she was dead."

"Oh, Gray. How horrible. She was so young." In the silence that followed she said softly, "But you can take comfort in the fact that you tried to do the right thing for her. Her family must have been grateful."

"Grateful?" He spoke the word on a sneer. "The Enders family, and most of the others in town who heard, believed it was my baby."

"You never told them the truth?"

"And break my mother's heart?" He sighed. "What was the point? It was too late to do anything for Amelia or the baby."

"But your own mother believes the worst about you."

"It doesn't matter, Fiona."

"But it does. Why should you take the blame for something Flem did?"

He shook his head. "Let it go, Fiona."

"Oh, Gray. You're . . ." *So good,* she thought. *So fine.* But all she said aloud was, "Truly a better brother than Flem deserves."

She wrapped her arms around him and pressed her mouth to his, pouring into that kiss all the love, all the emotions that were overflowing her heart. And then, with soft sighs and whispered words, she showed him, in the only way she could, just how very much he mattered to her.

TWENTY-FOUR

—◆◆◆—

Fiona yawned and stretched.

"It's about time you woke up, sleepyhead."

At the sound of Gray's voice her eyes snapped open. He was lying beside her, propped on one elbow, staring at her with that same intensity that always caused her heart to flutter wildly.

She shoved a tangle of curls from her eyes. "What are you doing?"

"Just looking at you."

Sometime in the early hours of the morning they'd left the cramped confines of the sofa and Gray had carried her upstairs to his bed. A curious Chester had trailed behind and now lay dozing in front of the hearth.

Fiona glanced toward the window. "How high is the snow?"

Gray caught her hand. "Let's look."

Wrapping a blanket around them both, he led her to the window, and they stared out at the most amazing sight.

It was a dazzling world of white. Snow had buried the fences and outbuildings and had drifted to the roof of the porch. The branches of evergreens were mounded with so much snow they were bent nearly double, and several trees had collapsed under the weight of it. And still the snow fell, in a gauzy white curtain that softened the landscape and blurred their view of the sky.

Her voice was hushed. "I've never seen anything like this. It's so beautiful from here."

He nodded. "And so deadly, if you're trapped in it."

"I need no reminder of that." She shivered and glanced across the room. "I see you've already tended the fire."

"And brought you something to eat." He pointed to the tray on a bedside table.

"Oh, Gray. Food." With a laugh of delight she led him toward the bed.

He handed her one of his shirts. "It's going to be awhile before your clothes are dry, so you might want to wear this. Otherwise I might forget about food."

"Which is what you did all night, as I recall." She slipped her arms into the oversize sleeves and drew the fabric around her.

"Are you complaining, Miss Downey?"

Her laughter was warm and rich, wrapping itself around his heart. "Not at all, Mr. Haydn. As I recall, I was most grateful for your kind attentions." She blushed at the thought of their wanton behavior. Like children with a new game, they couldn't seem to get enough of each other. They had loved, slept, only to wake and love again. "But now you've come bearing food." She placed a hand to her heart. "What did you make for breakfast?"

"Last night's supper," he said with a laugh.

She breathed deeply. "I don't care. It smells wonderful."

He picked up the tray and settled himself beside her in the bed.

"Such luxury." She turned to him. "I've never eaten breakfast in bed before. Have you?"

"No. But I'm discovering the joy of having my own home." He winked at her. "I like being free to make my own rules." He leaned over to brush his lips over hers. "Or to break them."

"Just what rules are you thinking of breaking now?"

"I believe we've already broken most of them." He poured her a cup of tea. "I've been meaning to tell you. That shirt looks much better on you than it ever did on me."

He loved the pretty blush that stole over her cheeks. To put her at ease he said, "Tell me what you were like when you were a little girl."

"Why?"

"I want to know everything about you, Fiona." He buttered a biscuit and handed it to her. "Where you lived, and how. What you liked. Your favorite foods."

"All right." She bit into the biscuit and leaned back against the pillows. "And then I'll expect you to do the same."

He glanced at the snow that continued falling outside their window. "I don't see why not. It looks like we have all the time in the world."

ALL THE TIME in the world.

Those words played through Fiona's mind as she settled into a tub of warm water. What a grand and glorious luxury—one they were both determined to use to the best of their ability.

Gray had hauled buckets of snow indoors and placed them on the big kitchen stove before braving the elements to check on the animals in the barn.

She'd watched him dig a path through snow until all she could see was his dark hair blowing in the wind above

the snow line. It would take him the better part of the day
to make it all the way to the barn.

It was hard to believe, soaking in the comfort of a bath,
that just yesterday she'd feared she might not live to see
this day. Yet here she was, snug and warm and deliriously
happy.

And all because of Gray. He'd not only lifted her from
the depths of despair and saved her life, but he'd brought
her more joy than she would have ever believed possible.

She stepped from the tub and dried herself before
dressing quickly. With her wet hair falling in curls to her
waist, she made her way to the kitchen and began mixing
dough.

By the time Gray stomped up the steps and rushed
inside on a swirl of snowflakes, she had a pot of soup
simmering on the stove, and the air was redolent with the
wonderful aroma of baking bread.

"You can cook?"

She laughed at the look of surprise on his face. "Of
course I can cook. My mother was frail, and most of the
household chores fell to me. I've been cooking since I
was a wee lass. I'd have been happy to share the cooking
with your mother, if only she'd have let me."

He hung his coat and crossed the room to wrap his
arms around her waist. Pressing his mouth to the nape of
her neck, he breathed her in. "How can this be? A woman
who looks like an angel, and spent the most amazing night
in my bed, is now cooking something that smells heavenly. Tell me I'm not dreaming."

She set aside the wooden spoon before turning in his
arms. "If it's a dream, it's the best one ever, and we're in
it together."

"Together." He brushed her lips with his and felt the
jolt clear to his toes. *Would it always be like this?* he
wondered. Would she always have this affect on him? The
slightest touch, the simplest kiss, and he couldn't think of

anything except how much he wanted her. "I love the sound of that word."

"I was just thinking the same thing." She lay a hand on his cheek. "You're cold. I have some soup that will warm you."

"The soup will keep. I have something else in mind to warm us both."

Her laugh was quick and lilting. "Is this the same shy man who was going to spend his night in the barn?"

"Now you've found me out." He gathered her close and pressed his mouth to a tangle of hair at her temple. "A word of warning. Beware the bear hibernating in his den. Once awake, he's ravenous."

"I don't mind feeding the bear."

"Ah, but soup isn't the food I have in mind."

She laughed and arched a brow. "Perhaps that wasn't what I had in mind either."

"Like minds. I love that about us." He brushed kisses over her upturned face. "Can you spare an hour upstairs?"

"Just so we don't forget about the bread in the oven."

He scooped her up and started toward the stairs. "After an hour of your loving, I won't complain if the bread is a little burned."

"I LOVE YOUR home, Gray."

"My home." He smiled. "It is mine now, isn't it?"

They were curled up together on the sofa in the parlor, staring quietly into the flames of the fire, after enjoying their supper. Gray lay with his head in Fiona's lap, loving the feel of her fingers playing with his hair.

Outside the snow had finally stopped, and the wind had died down, leaving an eerie silence to settle over the land.

"I've already stopped thinking of it as Herman Vogel's place. It's mine. The fields, the barns, and this house."

"It's a lovely big house. And the furniture." She

sighed. "How could he bear to part with all these lovely things?"

"Herman said his daughter's house was too small for all this. And, he said, they were only things, after all. They weren't important." He threaded his fingers through hers and brought her hand to his mouth, feeling again the pleasant rush of heat. "He said to remember that it's the people who live in it that make a house a home."

"That's lovely." She felt the warmth of his lips against her flesh and shivered. "Do you ever feel lonely here, Gray?"

He was quiet for a long moment before saying, "I've learned that it's possible to feel lonely anywhere. Even with an entire family around."

"Were you lonely often?"

"Not often. But there were times. Ma and Flem have a way of shutting others out."

His admission tugged at her heart. "I was sad when you left. I don't believe I've ever felt so alone. But I understood why you had to go."

"Papa was right. It was time for me to have something of my own." Seeing the look of sadness in her eyes he added, "No tears now. Look at what this has done for Chester. I think he's happy to be able to spend these cold nights in front of a fire, instead of buried in hay in a cold barn."

Hearing his name, the dog walked over to thrust his nose into Gray's palm.

"How do you like your new home, Chester?"

The hound's tail swished like a pendulum.

"There's your answer."

Fiona scratched behind his ears and Chester started to climb into her lap.

"Not on your life." Gray nudged the dog aside. "Right now my woman is busy with me. Go back to your fire."

My woman. Fiona wondered at the way her heart

soared at his words. And then she thought about all the sadness that had been in his life.

As the hound settled down on the rug, Gray sat up and drew Fiona into his arms. Seeing the look of sorrow in her eyes he pulled a little away. "What's wrong?"

She shook her head. "I can't stop thinking about Amelia, and the fact that your attempt to do the right thing brought you so much shame."

He brushed her lips with his. "Don't waste a minute thinking about the past, Fiona. We can't change it."

"I know. Nor should we wish to. If things had been different in our past, we wouldn't be where we are now. If Amelia had lived, you'd now be wed. And if Papa hadn't died so suddenly, I'd have never had the chance to meet you."

"So." He smiled. "Let's look only to the future. Think about all the unknowns that are around the corner."

"Then I'll think about springtime," she said softly.

"It's already come." He welcomed the quick rush of heat as his lips skimmed hers, and his hands began moving over her. "Here in my heart, it's already springtime, Fiona."

There was no more need for words as they took each other, with soft sighs and whispered kisses, to that place where only lovers can go.

TWENTY-FIVE

———◆※◆———

FOR TWO DAYS and nights the countryside lay entombed beneath a frigid white blanket. No birds sang. No farm animals could leave the shelter of their barns. Even the creatures in the wild stayed inside, huddled in dens and caves and tunnels.

On the third morning the sun broke through the clouds and a southern wind blew its warm breath across the land. Melting snow ran in rivers down the side of the roof, starting a symphony of drips that soon turned into a torrent, running from the highest peak of the barn's roof and forming little tributaries across the yard.

Gray came rushing into the kitchen, followed by Chester. While his master removed his boots, the hound gave a series of violent shakes before stretching out on the big hooked rug to groom his long, thick coat.

Gray crossed the room to wrap his arms around Fiona, who stood stirring something on the stove. As always, he was forced to absorb the now-familiar jolt at the simple touch of her.

"The way the snow's melting, it'll be gone in a couple of days."

His words brought her no joy. Instead, she felt her heart hitch.

She turned and touched a hand to his cheek. "I made stew."

"I'm not hungry."

"Well then. Maybe later." She set down the spoon and turned to look out the window. "How soon?"

She didn't have to elaborate. It was the only thing on both their minds now. How much time did they have left, before she would have to return to the home of his parents?

He shrugged and avoided her eyes. "I'll keep an eye out for wagons on the road. If not tonight, tomorrow."

"Tomorrow."

As she sighed and started to turn away he caught her hand and brought it to his lips. "Come up to bed, Fiona."

"Now? In the middle of the day?"

He managed a smile. "My house, remember? We break the rules here."

She laughed as she danced along beside him. "I've begun to like breaking the rules."

SUNLIGHT STABBED FIONA'S eyelids, and she squeezed them shut, determined to blot out the morning. A chorus of birdsong drifted through the open window, and she pressed her face to Gray's chest, hoping the sound of his heartbeat would drown out all else.

All night they'd clung together, knowing their idyll was about to end. Their lovemaking had taken on the desperation of two lovers about to be separated for a lifetime.

He'd been so tender, it had made her weep. But she'd hidden her tears, waiting until he was asleep before allowing herself even that small weakness.

Now, as the sun climbed higher in the sky, there was no denying that the time of reckoning was at hand.

Gray was the first to speak. "Guess I'd better get out to the barn." He brushed a kiss over her mouth. "Are you all right?"

"Fine." She managed a smile. "I'll make you breakfast."

"I'd like that." He kissed her again and slid out of bed. After slipping into his clothes he eased down on the edge of the bed. "We could always pray for another blizzard."

He was relieved to see the hint of a smile that came into her eyes. "Do you think there's a chance?"

He kissed the tip of her nose. "I believe in miracles." Then, because he had to, he gathered her into his arms and kissed her until they were both breathless.

As he eased her back against the pillows she arched a brow.

He grinned. "I figure the cows can wait another hour."

FIONA SET GRAY'S place at the big wooden table, slicing thick slabs of bread still warm from the oven and steeping the tea until it was strong, the way he liked it.

She glanced out the window. Except for the remnants of snow it might have been just another spring day, with birds chirping and squirrels chasing each other around the base of the tree.

She leaned a hip on the sill and surveyed the kitchen. It was obvious that it had been built with a family in mind. The big, intricately carved table and six sturdy chairs. The stove, with an oven big enough to accommodate several loaves of bread and enough burners to cook an entire meal at one time.

For these few precious days she had been able to pretend that this was hers. She had been the lady of the house, and Gray her man.

Because he was still in the barn, she took her time walking around the house, as though trying to store it all away in her mind. The big cozy parlor, with its overstuffed furniture and fireplace made of stone. The upstairs bedroom with a matching stone fireplace, and the big soft bed where she and Gray had so recently slept—and loved. She peered into the other bedrooms and smiled at the thought of curly-haired children asleep in each of the beds.

A lovely fantasy. But now she had to face the reality of this day.

She saw Gray heading toward the house, a bucket of milk in each hand, Chester trotting happily alongside.

She hurried to the kitchen and busied herself at the stove.

That was how Gray saw her. Looking more like a schoolgirl than a teacher. Dressed in her usual prim skirt and shirtwaist, her dark curls tied back with a ribbon.

She turned, and he drank in that sweet smile.

"Your breakfast is ready."

He even managed to return the smile. "Thank you."

He set down the buckets of milk and carefully hung his coat and pried off his boots.

"I bet the cows were glad to see you."

He nodded and bent to the basin to wash. "And even happier to be turned out to pasture. They're not used to being locked up in the barn for so long."

Fiona set a plate of meat scraps in front of Chester and poured herself a cup of tea.

Gray glanced at her empty plate. "You're not eating?"

"I'm not hungry." She filled his plate, then turned away to pour him a cup of tea.

When she joined him at the table, he moved the food

around his plate, all the while avoiding her eyes. Finally he shoved the plate aside. "I guess there's no point in trying to put this off any longer. It's time I got you home."

HE TOOK THE long way. It wasn't, he told himself, because he was a coward. It was simply that he needed to prolong, for a few precious minutes, this special time with her.

She sat beside him on the high, hard seat of the wagon, with Chester sprawled across her lap. When Gray turned the team away from the road, she glanced at him.

"Are we heading toward the falls?"

He nodded. "I want you to see it when the snow melts."

She heard the roar long before they rounded the bend. When Gray brought the team to a halt he helped her down and they walked to the edge of the cliff.

As they stood staring at the sight, Fiona pressed a hand to her heart, at a loss for words.

This was no lazy spill of water over rocks. Now, with the torrent created by the melting snow, it had become a roaring wall of water thundering like a train over the rocks and ledges that formed the barrier to the stream below. Mounds of snow still clung along the sides, and foam bubbled up, creating a mist as the water churned and boiled and tumbled, all wild and primitive and looking for all the world as though it belonged to some other civilization.

Gray turned to her and could see, by the look on her face, that she was as moved as he always was by the sight of it.

He took her hand. "I knew you'd like it."

"Like it? Oh, Gray. It's more than beautiful. It's . . . soul-stirring."

It touched him deeply to know that she shared his feelings for this special place.

"Like you, Fiona." He framed her face and stared deeply into her eyes before lowering his mouth to hers. "You stir my soul the way no one else ever has. I hope I'm not overstepping my bounds. You're an educated woman, and I'm just a farmer. But I love you, Fiona. You'd make me the happiest man in the world if you would agree to be my wife."

Tears welled up in her eyes, and she blinked them away. She wanted no tears to mar this happy moment. The lump in her throat was threatening to choke her.

When she didn't speak he lowered his head. "I'm sorry. I know I have no right."

"No right?" She swallowed hard. "Oh, Gray. I was just remembering back to when I was a little girl, on the boat that brought us to America. My da told me something I've never forgotten." Her brogue thickened, as she repeated the words. "My da told me that I'd know when I met the right man, for it isn't just the way he looks, although that may be what first attracts me. Nor, he said, will it matter what he does. Whether a man works with his hands, or has the greatest mind in the universe, it's what's in his heart that matters. He told me to never waste my love, but rather to give my heart to someone whose own heart is worthy." She lifted shiny eyes to Gray. "I've saved my love for a man who has the grandest heart of all. I love you, Gray. And I'd be so proud to be your wife."

With the roar of the water thundering in their ears, they stood locked in an embrace until at last, aware of the passing of time, they returned to the wagon and headed toward the Haydn farm.

BRODERICK STOOD FRAMED in the door of the barn when Gray's team pulled up. He took one look at Fiona and started forward shouting, "You're alive!"

The sound of his shout had Rose rushing out the backdoor. As it slammed behind her, she hurried to join her husband.

Gray climbed down from the wagon and hugged his father before circling around to help Fiona to the ground.

Rose ignored her son and spoke directly to Fiona. "When you didn't come home, we were afraid you'd been trapped in your school with your students, but no one could get there to find out."

"I would have been. Mr. Rudd came for the children and told me to hurry home, but the storm came in so quickly, I couldn't make it."

Rose glanced at her husband. "Broderick and I worried that you might not have enough firewood to stay warm. I'm glad we were wrong."

"I didn't stay at the schoolhouse, Mrs. Haydn." Rose smiled at Gray who stood beside her. "I foolishly started for home, but I fell and lost my lantern, and then I got hopelessly lost. If Gray hadn't come along and rescued me, I'd have surely frozen to death."

Rose's eyes narrowed slightly. "Are you saying that Grayson found you and didn't bring you home?"

Before Fiona could answer Gray lifted a hand to stop her. "There was no time, Ma. Fiona was nearly frozen when I found her. I had no choice but to take her to my place and see that she was warm and dry."

"And the two of you have been alone there all this time?"

Broderick put a hand on his wife's arm. "Now is not the time, Rose. Let's bring these young people inside—"

She shook off his hand and turned to Fiona. "The good people of Paradise Falls have the right to expect a teacher to live by a higher code than most. That means there must be no hint of scandalous behavior by one entrusted to mold the minds of our young. I already know what my son is capable of doing. If you are a righteous woman I will expect you to stand up at Sunday services and state, in front of the entire congregation, that you did not give in to temptations of the flesh while you were alone with Grayson."

"Ma—" Before Gray could say more Fiona lay a hand on his arm to stop him.

"You ask something I cannot do, Mrs. Haydn."

"Cannot? Or will not?"

"I cannot, for it would be a lie."

At Fiona's admission Rose shot a triumphant look at her husband before turning her back on all of them and stalking into the house.

Seeing his mother's reaction Gray caught Fiona's hand. "We'll go back to my place now."

"No." Broderick drew an arm around his son's shoulders. "This isn't over."

"It is. I won't have Fiona attacked. She deserves better."

"Yes, she does." There was a look in Broderick's eyes that his son hadn't seen before. "Now come inside, both of you."

Though he still walked with a pronounced limp, Broderick needed no help as he led the way up the steps. Inside they found Rose slamming pots and pans around the stove. When she saw Gray and Fiona, she turned her back on them and began setting two places at the table.

"Sit." Broderick took his place at the head of the table and pointed to the chairs on one side.

Gray held a chair for Fiona, then sat beside her and reached for her hand. Though her heart was pounding, she took comfort in his touch.

Rose stared daggers at her husband. "They are not welcome at my table. He is no longer my son. And this woman will no longer be a teacher in this town when I'm finished with her."

His tone was pure ice. "Sit, Rose."

She shot him a startled glance, then took her seat at the other end of the table.

Broderick turned to Fiona. "I haven't had time to tell
you how happy I am that you're unharmed. Rose and I
had feared the worst."

"Thank you, Mr. Haydn. If it hadn't been for Gray, I
would surely be dead. I had already prepared myself for
it when he came along like my guardian angel."

"I hardly think it appropriate to compare him with an
angel," Rose sniffed.

"I love your son, Mrs. Haydn."

Rose's head came up sharply. "Love. What would you
know about such things?"

"I know that I love Gray, and he loves me. He's asked
me to be his wife. And I've agreed."

Broderick smiled at the young couple. "Married. I
couldn't be happier."

Rose got to her feet. "You would make a mockery of
love and marriage?"

"Sit, Rose." Broderick motioned to her chair and had
the satisfaction of seeing his wife do as he ordered.

He steepled his fingers and peered at her. "I've been
giving your edict some thought." He saw Rose's eyes
widen. "It would probably be good for the soul to stand
before the congregation and confess."

Feeling vindicated, she gave a quick nod of her head.
"As I said, a teacher ought to be held to a higher—"

"I wasn't talking about Miss Downey." Broderick met
his wife's eyes. "I think they have the right to know of
any guilt that might be festering in the souls of those who
sit in judgment of them. Would you like to tell them,
Rose? Or will I?"

Speechless, Rose could only stare at her husband.

"Very well. I'll tell them." He turned to Gray and Fiona.
"I was twenty years old when I was persuaded by some
friends to attend a church dance in Little Bavaria. When I
walked into the hall I saw a woman who completely capti-

vated my heart. For the rest of the night, I couldn't even see anyone but her. We danced every dance."

Rose's jaw dropped. "You never told me you were taken with me."

"Why do you think I danced with no other woman?"

She fell silent.

Broderick returned to his narrative. "Before the night was over, we slipped away from the others and took our pleasure in the hay of an empty stall."

Rose stared hard at the table top, refusing to meet her husband's eyes.

He cleared his throat. "I later learned that the beautiful stranger was making plans to pursue a life as a maid to a wealthy relative who traveled to exotic lands. She wanted no part of life as a dull farmer's wife. I resigned myself to the thought that I would never see her again, but one day she came to me and told me that she was expecting a baby. My baby. I was only too happy to marry her. But the happiness was one-sided. As you can see, she has spent a lifetime punishing me for stealing her dreams." He inclined his head toward his son. "And in the process, has punished you, as well, for the part you innocently played in stealing those dreams."

Gray turned to his mother. "I can't say I'm sorry, or that I wish none of it had happened. But I am sorry that you couldn't pursue your dreams."

"You'll never know how many times I've wished the same."

He lowered his head, then came to a sudden thought. "Why didn't you hate Flem, as well?"

"Fleming was different. You belonged to your father. He chose your name. He took you with him everywhere. He lavished all his love on you, leaving none for me. I realized that I wanted something of my own. Fleming was all mine. I conceived him freely. I wanted a daughter, to share my dreams. But when he was born, so perfect, so beautiful, I vowed that he would have all the things I'd been denied. I would allow him his dreams, his pleasures, the future I couldn't have."

Gray shook a head in disbelief. "It never occurred to you that you were teaching him to shun his responsibilities? To be lazy, and devious, and sly?"

Rose slammed a hand down on the table. "Sly? You would call Fleming sly, after all the evil things you have done?" She turned to Fiona. "If you knew about Gray, I doubt you would be so eager to be his wife."

"I know about Gray." Fiona met his look and her own softened. "He has told me everything, and I love him, Mrs. Haydn."

"Love." Rose spat the word. "We'll see how soon love turns to duty. And duty to drudgery."

Broderick's voice had all their heads turning to him. "Are we agreed then, Rose, that you and I will be first to stand before the congregation and confess our past sins?"

Rose's eyes flashed. "You're as sly as your son." She folded her arms over her chest. "Very well. I'll not speak publicly about their weaknesses. But until you can arrange to marry, Miss Downey will continue to live under our roof, for the sake of propriety, and you, Gray, will return to your own farm."

He squeezed Fiona's hand. "For the sake of propriety, for I know how much that means to my mother." Then he lifted it to his lips. "I'll go into town now and speak to Reverend Schmidt. Is tomorrow soon enough to be wed?"

Fiona was smiling. "Not nearly. But I'll abide by whatever day you and he can arrange."

"He must announce your banns from the pulpit three times." Rose seemed to take particular delight in giving them the news.

"Three weeks then." Gray shoved back his chair and touched a hand to Fiona's cheek. "Until then, Chester and I will be miserable."

TWENTY-SIX

THE SNOW HAD disappeared as quickly as it had arrived, but evidence of the blizzard littered the landscape. Giant trees lay toppled, awaiting the farmers who would chop them into logs for next winter's fireplace. Sheds and outbuildings had collapsed under the weight of so much snow and were slowly being rebuilt.

As if to compensate for the fickle weather, the countryside had turned especially green and lovely. The pale, spring green of the willows was complimented by the darker green of the evergreens. The lush meadows were dotted with mayflowers and tiny violets. Fields of rich, black earth had been neatly plowed and planted, and already the first tiny shoots could be seen breaking through the ground.

Twice the reverend had announced the banns of the town's teacher to the son of one of the town's oldest families. Outside of church on Sundays, while the men talked

of calves and foals and piglets and the renewed cycle of
life, the women talked of weddings.

"So, Rose." Greta Gunther nudged Brunhilde Schmidt.
"Didn't you once say you thought the teacher would make
the perfect mate for your Fleming?"

"Did I?" Rose shot daggers at her neighbor for being
so bold. "Actually, now that Fleming is in Chicago working as a musician, I expect he'll marry someone with a
similar background. Someone talented, educated, and successful."

"Have you heard from him?" Brunhilde asked gently.

Rose wasn't certain what galled more. Greta's pointed
sarcasm, or Brunhilde's attempts at comfort. "As you well
know, we haven't heard. But I expect that it's only because he's so busy."

"Are you helping Miss Downey plan her wedding?"

This from Emily Trewe, who was hoping for business
for her millinery shop.

"Of course I'm helping her. We're the only family the
girl has." Though Rose had not softened toward Gray and
Fiona, she was wise enough to avoid tempting her husband's ire, and so she joined the women in bland talk of
the coming wedding.

She lowered her voice and noted with satisfaction that
everyone gathered closer, afraid of missing a single word.
"If you ask me, however, they're much too impetuous. I
would have been happier if they had waited."

"The young are always impetuous." Greta Gunther
sighed as she glanced over at Fiona and Gray, standing
off to one side with Charlotte and Schuyler Gable. "I seem
to recall that you and Broderick were just as impetuous."

Rose had the good sense to spot someone she needed
to speak with at once, and made a quick departure.

*   *   *

FIONA COULD HARDLY keep her mind on each day's lessons. Her students seemed to share her excitement.

Whenever she got too close to Will and Edmer, they would fall silent, until she began to wonder if they might be planning a wedding gift for her new home.

New home. The thought of it always brought a lump to her throat. She couldn't wait to make her home with Gray.

Because she had no family, she had asked Broderick to walk her up the aisle.

Rose had been horrified. "He's none too steady on his feet yet. What if he should stumble?"

Fiona merely smiled. "I suspect, with my nerves, I'll be the one to stumble." She turned to Broderick at the supper table. "We'll hold each other up."

He shook his head. "Rose is right. I don't want to do anything to embarrass you."

She lay a hand over his. "You could never embarrass me, Mr. Haydn. I would consider it an honor if you would take my father's place beside me."

Gray later told her that his father had wept when he'd relayed their conversation to him. "You've made my father a very happy man."

"It's the least I can do, since his son has made me so happy."

He brushed a quick kiss over her lips, then drew away when Rose stepped out onto the porch between them. "You know the rules, Grayson. You're to have no private contact with Miss Downey until the wedding."

He turned away and climbed up to the seat of the wagon. On the way home he mentally counted the days left, and then began counting the hours. If he was a caveman, he thought miserably, he could have simply carried her off to his cave. There was a lot to be said for early civilization.

*   *   *

"THERE'S NO DOUBT about it." Rose tied the ribbons of her bonnet. "Spring is early this year. Why, it's positively balmy."

"Perhaps even Mother Nature is eager for the wedding." Broderick winked at Fiona as he held the door for his wife.

Wedding. The very word had Rose bristling. The closer they drew to the day, the more prickly she became. She paused in the doorway. "We won't be long. I just want to measure the windows in Grayson's parlor."

Fiona bit the inside of her lip to keep from laughing. When she and Gray had learned that his mother intended to make draperies for their parlor as her wedding gift, his first thought had been to refuse to allow her inside his home.

"She's only using that as an excuse to see where I live."

Fiona had placed a finger to his lips. "Hush, Gray. Whatever her reason, it's her first gesture toward some sort of peace."

"Peace." He'd huffed out a breath. "You've lived in her house long enough to know that peace with my mother comes only on her terms."

Fiona merely smiled. "Then do it for me, Gray. Let your mother satisfy her curiosity about your home, and let her make draperies for the windows."

"I hate dark covers that hold out the light."

"As do I. But once the wedding is over, we can use them . . ." She thought a moment. "In one of the upper rooms if we choose. Or maybe in the barn. Do you think the cows would mind them so very much?"

With a roar of laughter he'd dragged her close and kissed her. "What did I do to deserve such a smart, clever woman?"

Rose's parting words broke through Fiona's reverie. "Just remember that if Grayson should come over while I'm gone, I will expect the two of you to behave in an honorable manner."

"You needn't worry, Mrs. Haydn."

"But I do, Miss Downey. You don't know my son as I do. There was an incident in the past—"

"Rose." Broderick caught her by the arm and practically dragged her out the door.

Fiona listened to the sound of the wagon before returning her attention to her dress. She was grateful that today was Saturday, and she could spend some time trying to make over her mother's old wedding gown. It had been in the box with the other things her aunt had sent from Chicago. Almost as if, Fiona thought with a smile, her dear mother had known that she would have need of it. Though she'd spent many an evening sewing, it needed a bit more work before it would fit her like a proper wedding dress.

She could have taken it to the millinery shop in town, but she didn't want anyone else touching this fabric. She lifted it to her face and breathed deeply. It still bore the lingering scent of roses. The scent that would always remind her of her beloved mum.

FIONA WAS SO engrossed in her work she had no notion of the passing of time. She was seated cross-legged on the floor of the parlor, her dark hair spilling like a veil around her face, with the wedding dress spread across her lap.

Hearing the backdoor open she pressed a hand to the small of her back and set aside the needle and thread. When a shadow fell across the threshold, she looked up with a smile.

Her eyes widened when she saw not Rose and Broderick, but Flem.

"You're alive! Oh, Flem, your mother was so sure the man who'd been hit by the train wasn't you." In her eagerness to make him welcome she began to gather up the folds of the gown and set it aside. "Why didn't you send word that you were alive?"

When she turned he was still standing in the doorway, looking at her in a way that had her smile fading. "What's wrong, Flem?"

"Wrong? Nothing's wrong, teacher."

He looked faded and worn. His once golden hair was dull and lifeless, as were his eyes. His clothes were shabby. A stubble of beard darkened his cheeks and chin. It was obvious, by the way his clothes hung on him, that he'd lost weight.

He crossed his arms over his chest and leaned lazily against the wall. "I figured I'd come back and fleece the locals out of a little money before heading back to Chicago."

"You aren't staying?"

"In this godforsaken place?" He snorted.

"But your mother is so lonely without you, Flem. She's been miserable since you left."

"She's been miserable all her life. Why should that change?"

"Flem." To hide her shock she turned away and gathered up her gown, carrying it to her room.

When she turned, she was startled to find that he'd followed her and was standing directly behind her.

"I hear there's going to be a wedding."

She felt the first thread of fear along her spine and knew that she needed to get him out of her room. Lifting her chin she started toward the open doorway, but he stepped in front of it to block her way. "The whole town's talking about the pretty little teacher and my big brother."

"Step aside and let me pass, Flem."

He merely grinned. "What'll you do if I won't?"

"I'll shout for your father."

He threw back his head and laughed. "I'll give you this. You know how to use that brain." His hand snaked out, snagging her wrist. "But I'm smarter." He dragged her close. "No use pretending my folks are around. I saw their wagon at Gray's when I passed. That's why I'm here now. I wanted the house, and you, to myself."

She nearly gagged at the stench of his breath. "You're drunk."

"That's right. What're you going to do about it, teacher?"

She tried to push free, and he gave her a shove backward that had her stumbling against her bed. She scrambled to her feet and stood facing him. "What is this about, Flem?"

"It's about having what I want. I've always known Ma keeps money in the house." He reached into his pocket to display a wad of bills. "The sugar bowl, the flour sack— even the root cellar. She thinks I don't know, but I've always been able to help myself when I needed some. Whenever I won enough, I put it back so she never even knew I'd borrowed it. That's the only reason why I came back. But when I heard the talk about the wedding, I decided to take care of some unfinished business between you and me while I was here."

"There is nothing between us, Flem."

"You don't think so?" He looked her up and down in a way that had her skin crawling. "When I'm through with you, it'll be between us forever. I've just decided on the perfect wedding present for my big brother. Every time he beds his wife, he'll know that I had her, too."

*   *   *

GRAY HAD LEFT a note for his mother on the kitchen table, inviting her to make herself at home, then he'd left for town.

There wasn't anything he really needed, but he hadn't wanted to be there when his mother came calling.

He knew Fiona was right, and that he had to let the anger go, the same way he always had in the past. But before, he was the only one hurt by Rose's out-of-control temper. Now he had a wife to think about.

Wife. The word had him whistling. Chester perked up his ears at the sound and moved closer to lay his head on Gray's lap.

He still found it hard to believe that Fiona was willing to spend the rest of her life with him. He knew he didn't deserve her. She was the finest, sweetest woman he'd ever known. On top of that, she was so beautiful she took his breath away.

He knew one thing. He would never settle for a marriage like that of his parents. He marveled that his father could have endured for so long. As for himself, he'd have rather lived alone for a lifetime than submit to that sort of quiet desperation.

Now, with Fiona, his entire life had changed.

He scratched behind his dog's ears. "We're the luckiest ones in the world, Chester."

He pulled up at the train station and called a greeting to Gerhardt Shultz.

The stationmaster walked up to Gray's wagon and lifted a hand to shield the sun from his eyes. "Sorry, Grayson. You're too late."

Gray arched a brow. "Too late for what?"

"To pick up your brother."

"Flem?"

Gerhardt nodded. "Came in this morning on the train. I told him about the sad news I'd delivered to your folks, but he just laughed and said he sure wasn't any ghost."

Gerhardt shook his head. "Same old Fleming. Still able to make a joke out of everything."

"Yeah, that's Flem. Where was he headed?"

"Why, home of course. He was going to go into town first and sober up a bit—"

"Sober up?" Gray was suddenly alert. "He's drunk?"

Gerhardt shrugged. "Don't know about drunk, but I could tell he'd had a bit of whiskey. Anyway, after I told him about your wedding, he said he wanted to get right out there and offer his personal congratulations to your bride."

Gray was already leaping down from the wagon where he proceeded to unhitch the team. As he pulled himself onto the back of one of the horses he called, "I'll be back for the rest later."

With Chester running alongside, he took off in a cloud of dust, leaving the stationmaster to stare after him in confusion.

FIONA GLANCED AROUND wildly, looking for something with which to defend herself.

Flem merely laughed as he advanced toward her. "Don't think a pitcher and basin will stop me this time. If you try it, I'll use them to slash that pretty face of yours." His smile turned into a snarl as he caught a handful of her hair and dragged her close. "And I think you know me well enough by now to know I mean it. With the mood I'm in, I don't care if my brother marries a beauty or a beast."

Fiona felt tears sting her eyes and blinked them away. This was no time to show him any weakness. "Let me go. This is evil." She shoved roughly at his chest, but that only added fuel to his anger.

"Oh, teacher, you have no idea what evil is." He

slapped her hard enough to snap her head to one side. "But I'm about to show you."

For a moment she saw a shower of stars dancing before her eyes. When her vision cleared, she felt his mouth on hers and tasted his fetid breath. His rough hands tugged at the neckline of her gown and she felt the buttons pop as he tore at it.

"No." She pushed hard enough to have him staggering back a step before he steadied himself with a hand to the wall.

"Oh, yes, teacher. You don't have a chance in hell of stopping me."

Knowing she needed to keep him talking, she searched her mind for something, anything that might distract him. "What has made you this way, Flem?"

He tugged his shirt over his head, baring his chest, and began fumbling with the fasteners at his waist. "What way?"

"So angry with all those who love you. Is it the fact that you feel you failed someone who needed you?" Even as she said the words, she remembered. "It was Amelia, wasn't it?"

His head came up sharply. "You know about Amelia?"

"I do. Yes." She was aware that he'd gone very still, though whether it was a good sign or not, she had no idea. She knew only that she had to keep him distracted. "Gray said that you and Amelia had fallen in love, but when she came to you with the news that she was expecting a baby, you refused to marry her."

"Did my noble brother also boast that he offered to marry her in my place?"

"He did. But he was too late."

"Oh, no. Not too late. His timing was perfect, as always. And so was mine."

"I don't unders—"

"You're as dense as he is, teacher." He gave a hollow

laugh. "The two of you deserve each other." When she merely stared at him he said, "I didn't love Amelia. I didn't even like her. But I saw her making eyes at my brother after church one Sunday and decided to prove to him that I could take her away from him. The same way I always took everything I wanted. And do you know why?"

Without waiting for Fiona's response he sneered, "Do you know what it's like to have to live up to a big brother who is always so damnably perfect? In school, the earnest student. In the fields, the one who worked harder than the mules. To the people in town, to the congregation in church, he was considered a model citizen."

"Surely you know that you're your mother's favorite."

Her words had him peeling back his lips in a snarl. "That wasn't enough. Ma was too easy. I learned how to play her before I could walk, but I always knew that Gray could see through my little games. He didn't have to tell me. I could see that look of disapproval in that quiet manner of his, and I hated him for it. Hated that everyone admired my big brother instead of me. But that all changed after Amelia." Flem's tone lifted in triumph. "Amelia was so easy. All I had to do was smile at her and she thought she'd died and gone to heaven. Of course, getting her out to her uncle's barn wasn't as easy. She kept whimpering like a stuck pig. I warned her that if she ever told him, I'd make her out to be the town whore. Afterward, when she told me she was having a baby, I told her the truth. That I didn't love her. Didn't even like her. That it had all been my plan just to prove something to my brother. Of course, Gray didn't know any of that. So when he went to her uncle and offered to marry her out of some sense of nobility, it got even better. Now it looked like Gray's mess."

Fiona couldn't hide her horror and revulsion. "You allowed the whole town, and your own parents, to believe that the baby was Gray's?"

"Why not? I thought it was the perfect touch." He laughed when he saw her eyes fill with tears, and his fingers clutched the front of her dress, dragging her close. "Now it's time for my ultimate revenge on my big brother. Maybe, if I'm really lucky, you'll present him with my baby nine months from now."

"No! Oh, no!" The sound of Rose's voice, high-pitched with shock and fury, had him turning toward the doorway, where she was standing beside her husband, clutching his arm. "God help me, I can't believe what I've just heard."

Her face was twisted with pain, and her words were wrenched from a heart shattered beyond repair. "I wish to heaven that had been your body on the tracks, Fleming. At least then I could have mourned your death. But now, to learn of such hideous deceit from your own lips . . ." She turned to her husband and buried her face against his chest, sobbing pitifully.

Gray was standing just behind his parents, and it was plain, from the look of black, blinding fury in his eyes, that he'd heard everything. The sight of his brother naked to the waist, and the bodice of Fiona's gown hanging in tatters, sent him over the edge.

As he pushed his way past his parents and into the room he paused to touch a hand to Fiona's cheek. "Are you all right?"

She nodded. Before she could speak he lunged across the distance that separated him from his brother and locked his arms around Flem's waist, driving him into the wall. The two of them fell to the floor and Gray rose up, landing a fist in Flem's face. He had the satisfaction of feeling bone crunch as a fountain of blood spurted from a broken nose.

With a howl of pain Flem doubled over and pressed his hands to his face.

"Get up," Gray shouted. "Get up and fight me, you miserable coward."

He picked Flem up and stood him against the wall before landing a second blow to his midsection that had Flem dropping to his knees on the floor, where he curled into a ball and lay sobbing.

"Enough, son." Broderick stepped in front of Gray and placed a hand on his arm.

"No." Gray shook it off. "It will never be enough for what he's done."

"I know." Broderick's tone was rough with pain.

"You don't know the half of it." Gray brushed past his father and yanked Flem roughly to his feet.

Blood spilled down his face and stained a chest heaving with sobs. When Gray lifted a fist, Flem flinched and covered his face with his hands.

"I understand your need for vengeance," Rose called from the doorway. "If I were a man, I'd do the same. But there's no need, Grayson. My revenge will be enough for all of you."

Gray turned in time to see his mother cross to the bed and sink down on the edge. Her eyes revealed the depth of her shock.

"I've been blind to so many things." She shook her head. "But no longer. I see clearly now." She pinned her younger son with a look he had never seen before. "You have brought shame to our family, Fleming. You took the innocence of a young girl. That was evil enough, but you then allowed your brother to publicly bear the blame. All these years I've believed the worst about Grayson. And now, you would despoil the woman he loves." She shuddered at the very thought of what had almost happened. "You will leave my home and never return."

"Ma . . ." Flem snatched up his shirt and mopped at the blood that spilled from his nose before kneeling in front of her.

She forced herself to look directly at him. Even the sight of him bleeding and broken failed to soften her heart. "I am no longer your mother. You are no longer my son. You are dead to me, Fleming. Dead. Go now."

"You don't mean that, Ma."

Repulsed, she got to her feet and crossed to her husband, who wrapped his arms around her.

Gray drew Fiona close and wondered if the anger pulsing inside him would ever subside.

No one spoke as Flem's footsteps echoed across the parlor, through the kitchen, and down the porch steps. They heard the door slam behind him, and watched through the window as he pulled on his shirt and stumbled down the lane.

The warmth of the sunlight and the happy chorus of birdsong seemed to mock the somber cloud that had settled over their day.

TWENTY-SEVEN

GRAY FINISHED MILKING the cows and scraped dung from his boots before stepping into the steamy kitchen, with Chester close on his heels. He lifted the buckets of hot water from the stove and slowly climbed the stairs to his bedroom. Once there he filled the round wooden tub and bathed, then shaved, before dressing in his new black suit and stiff shoes.

He'd learned from his father that his mother had kept to her room for days. There was no reason to believe today would be any different. He was resigned to the fact that his mother wouldn't be attending his wedding.

Not that it mattered, he told himself as he turned away and started down the stairs. The only thing that mattered to him was Fiona. She was his sun and moon and stars. She'd become his reason for living.

He climbed up to the wagon and grinned when Chester leaped up beside him. "Going to a wedding, are you?" He chuckled as the hound's tail wagged furiously. "And why not? You love her too, don't you?"

He flicked the reins and struggled to calm the hive of bees that were flying around in his stomach.

When he reached the church, he could see that the entire town of Paradise Falls had turned out for the wedding. The road was lined with horses and carts. The men had set up long wooden planks in the churchyard, which were already groaning under the weight of every kind of food imaginable. The women stood guard over their treasures, to assure that no one gave in to the temptation to sample the wares before the brief service. The children were dressed in their best Sunday clothes. Instead of chasing each other in games of tag, they were standing about eagerly awaiting their first glimpse of the bride, since their teacher had invited all of them to not only attend, but to participate in the ceremony.

"Gray." Schuyler Gable offered a handshake and led him around to the back of the church, where Doctor Eberhardt was passing out cigars, and Christian Rudd was pouring glasses of foaming dark beer from a jug.

"How're your nerves, Gray?" Dolph VanderSleet picked up one of the glasses and downed it in one long swallow.

"They've been better." Gray accepted a glass and noted that his hand was none too steady.

The others shared knowing smiles.

They looked up when his father approached.

Gray arched a brow. "You brought Fiona?"

His father winked at the men standing around. "You'd better hope so, son. What's a wedding without a bride?"

"Is she all right?"

"And why wouldn't she be?" Seeing the look in his son's eyes he lay a hand on his sleeve and steered him a little away from the others. "You look good, Grayson."

"I look like Doc Eberhardt about to go off to a surgery."

Broderick grinned. "Come to think of it, you do. All you need is a black bag."

"Why couldn't we just go off to Little Bavaria and let the minister there say the words?"

Broderick handed him one of the two glasses of beer he'd snagged before walking away. "Because, son, from the beginning of time women have wanted to make their wedding day special."

"I don't mind special." Gray looked over at a snort of laughter from the men, regaling one another with tales of their misspent youth. "But I don't see why we should have to stay here and eat with the whole town, when all I really want to do is . . ." He stopped and flushed when he realized what he'd been about to say. "Besides, all they'll be talking about is the fact that Ma didn't come to the wedding."

"Your mother is here."

Gray's head came up. "She agreed to come? How did you get her to do that?"

"It wasn't my doing. It was Fiona who persuaded her."

"How?"

"She told Rose that it was never too late to put the past behind again. And then she hinted that, in order to be a proper wife to you, she might be needing some help with all Rose's fine, German recipes."

"And, just like that, Ma decided to come today?"

"Well, it might have also been the thought that in a few years she could become a doting grandmother. At any rate, you can see for yourself in a few minutes. The last I saw your mother, she was in the church with your blushing bride, fussing over her gown." Broderick lifted his glass. "Before you go inside and say your vows, I'd like to offer a toast to my father, your namesake. He'd have been so proud." His voice faltered a moment before he added, "Just the way I am, Grayson."

"Thanks, Papa." Gray touched his glass to his father's before taking a drink.

"And now we'll drink to your mama." Broderick sipped his beer. "She's suffered a terrible shock, but Rose is tough. She'll get through it."

"But will I?"

Broderick chuckled. "You will. Every man does. You're marrying an amazing woman, Grayson. She's smart and pretty, and best of all, wise enough to know how to forgive. That ought to prove to be quite a blessing in the years to come."

"You think I'll need forgiving?"

"Don't we all?"

The two men smiled and drank.

Gray took another sip of beer before tossing the rest aside and handing the empty glass to his father.

Broderick looked at his son in surprise as he turned away. "Where are you going?"

"I need to see Fiona."

"Now? Before the wedding? Those women will never let you near her."

Gray never even heard him as he stalked away.

"I DON'T BELIEVE I've ever seen a prettier bride." Greta Gunther stood in the back of the church, watching as the crowds surged up the aisle toward their pews. "Have you, Rose?"

Rose adjusted the wildflowers in Fiona's hair. "She is, indeed. Why don't you join your family now, Greta? I think Fiona and I can handle this."

"But I—"

"Go, Greta. We'll be fine."

When the old woman walked away Rose gave a sigh of relief. "Old fool would have walked up the aisle with you if I'd let her."

"She just wanted to be helpful."

"About as helpful as a millstone around my—" Rose caught herself and stopped. "There I go, running my mouth, and on your wedding day. Old habits, I suppose . . ."

The two looked up when Gray approached.

Rose put out a hand to stop him. "You know you can't see your bride before—"

"Step away, Ma." At the fierceness of his whispered words, several heads turned.

Rose squared her shoulders. "Grayson, it isn't proper—"

Fiona caught her hand. "Give us a moment, Mrs. Haydn."

"I told you. From now on, I'd like to be called Mother Haydn."

Fiona smiled. "Give us a moment, Mother Haydn."

Rose stepped away, but not before giving her son a warning look.

The moment he turned his full gaze on Fiona, Gray wasn't sure he could remember how to breathe. Slowly it came to him and his chest rose with each measured breath.

"You look . . ." He couldn't find the words. Beautiful seemed inadequate. "Amazing." Still not enough, but he was too dazzled to think.

The dress was a simple column of white lace, with a high, modest neckline and long, tapered sleeves that perfectly suited her slender body. Her dark hair fell in a spill of curls to her waist. It was adorned only by a few sprigs of wildflowers. In his eyes she looked more like an angel than a bride.

"Thank you." She dimpled. "And you look very handsome."

Just seeing her, his nerves were forgotten. "Papa told me what you said to Ma."

"She's going to be fine now, Gray. And so will we."

"I know." He drew her close and pressed his forehead to hers. "But I needed to see you. And touch you. Just for a moment."

She sighed. "It's the same for me. Now I feel better."

He drew back with a little moan of disgust. "I almost forgot." He ran out of the church, and returned minutes later with an armload of roses. "I went by the woods behind the schoolhouse and picked these this morning."

"Oh, Gray. Roses." She buried her face in them to hide the quick rush of tears.

Brunhilde Schmidt began playing the music that would summon the bridal party to the altar.

"You have to go now." Rose shot her son a warning look.

"I will." He brushed a kiss over Fiona's cheek. "I can't wait until this is over."

"Soon," she whispered.

He turned away and stiffly offered his arm to Rose. "Come on, Ma."

Just as awkwardly Rose walked by his side to her seat at the very front of the church.

Gray took his place beside Reverend Schmidt, and at the urging of Fiona, the boys from her school joined him. Will and Edmer, taller than the bride, looked every bit as uncomfortable as the groom as they watched his father step up to offer his arm to the bride.

The little girls in their bright dresses and shiny hair walked up the aisle, some waving shyly to their parents until they reached the front of church and turned to watch as Fiona and Broderick walked slowly up the aisle.

Fiona paused to press a kiss to Broderick's cheek as she whispered, "Neither of us stumbled."

Touched, he gathered her close. "Nor will we. Be

happy, Fiona." He brushed a kiss to her cheek before walking away to sit beside his wife.

With a smile Fiona linked her fingers with Gray's.

Facing each other they spoke their vows for the entire church to hear. And then, when the service was over, they sailed down the aisle and out into the bright sunshine, to accept the congratulations of all in attendance.

The first to approach them was Christian Rudd, followed by his wife and son.

"I wish to offer my sincere congratulations to the happy bride and groom."

After offering his hand to Gray, he stood back, allowing his wife and son to offer their best wishes as well. Then, before they could turn away, he startled Fiona by bending to brush his lips over her cheek. "I wish also to offer my apology to you, teacher." Seeing the look of surprise in her eyes he added quickly, "This time, it is a sincere apology, not given because of any threat, but because I realize I was wrong. I consider you a fine addition to our community, and I hope you will overlook the things I said earlier in anger."

Fiona was as touched by the relieved smiles on the faces of his wife and son as she was by his words. "Thank you, Mr. Rudd."

As they walked away, she felt Gray's big hand close around hers and turned to give him a smile that dazzled the sun. Before they could speak, they were caught up in the crowd as they accepted hugs and kisses. While the guests ate and drank, Fiona and Gray refused all offers of food, too excited to think about eating.

Finally, as the lager flowed and desserts were passed around, the couple found themselves alone for a moment.

Just then Rose approached. "I have something to say."

Gray put an arm around his bride's shoulders, as though to protect her. Seeing it, Rose flushed. "I'm not here to attack you or your wife, though I can't say I blame you for thinking such a thing." She clasped her hands together tightly and cleared her throat. "These last few days have given me much to ponder, and I can't say that I like facing the truth. But face it I must. A better mother would have seen through Flem's lies. Looking back, I realize that I didn't want to. Revealing his shortcomings would have revealed my own, as well, and I have too many to mention. I'm truly sorry, Grayson, for the way I've treated you. I believed Flem's lies and allowed you to stand alone against an entire town. I will always regret that I refused to stand by you when you most needed me. I hope that in time you will find it in your heart to forgive me."

As she started to turn away Gray placed a hand on her shoulder. "Thank you."

She spun around with a look of surprise. "For what?"

"The words you just spoke are the only gift I wanted on this day. Better than gold." There was just the merest hint of humor in his eyes. "Surely better than draperies."

She forced herself to meet his look. "Are you saying that you can forgive me?"

"I already have, Ma."

"Oh, Grayson. I don't deserve you." Her eyes filled as she felt his big arms come around her. And though she felt stiff and awkward in this son's embrace, she managed to close her arms around his neck and hug him before stepping back.

Because her eyes were blinded by tears, she was grateful to find Broderick standing there with his hand outstretched to steady her. She caught it and held on tightly as Gray led his new bride toward the wagon, which was now abloom with bright ribbon streamers.

Gray paused. "What's this?"

Fiona laughed. "I heard the children whispering. Now I see why. Apparently they've been planning it for some time."

She was still laughing as he helped her up to the hard wooden seat, where Chester was waiting, a ribbon around his neck.

As the crowd gathered around them, Gray flicked the reins, and they started away, waving to those who called and cheered.

Fiona nodded toward Rose, who stood to one side, clinging tightly to her husband's hand. "She loves you, you know, Gray."

"In her fashion."

"It took courage for her to admit her mistakes."

"The Haydn family is a brave lot." He drew her close. "That's why I figured you'd fit right in."

When he veered off the path Fiona put a hand to his arm. "This isn't the way."

"I know." He smiled. "There's someplace I have to go first."

She knew at once.

When they'd left the lane behind he brought the horse and cart to a halt and helped her down. As they approached, the roar of the water grew louder. And then they were standing in Gray's favorite spot, watching the spill of water over rocks and seeing the mist rise up to catch the rays of sunlight.

"Look." She caught his hand. "A rainbow."

He nodded. All his nerves had settled. With the celebration behind them, all his fears had fled. "I knew there'd be one today. It's good luck, you know."

She merely turned to him with a smile. "I do love you, Gray."

"And I love you, Fiona. More than life itself."

As he drew her close and brushed his lips over hers, she felt again the familiar rush of heat, and the way her bones seemed to go all soft and fluid at his touch.

Oh Da. Mum. Be happy for me. For I've truly found a man worthy of my heart.

Gray took her hands in his. "Are you ready to go home?"

Home. Was ever there a word so fine? Her heart was nearly overflowing with love for this man. "I am. Yes."

As they turned toward the wagon Fiona couldn't contain the lilt of laughter that bubbled up. On the train here she'd promised to make this journey an adventure, and what an adventure it had become.

Paradise Falls had lived up to its name after all. For here in this strange place, in this good man's arms, she truly had found paradise—and a love that would last for a lifetime and beyond.